MAKE YOUR SHOT

ASTON ARCHERS
BOOK FIVE

CALI MELLE

Edited by Amy Pritt
Proofread by Emma Cook | Booktastic Blonde LLC
Cover Art by Essasketch
Cover Design by Cali Melle

PLAYLIST

STATE LINES - NOVO AMOR
BLAME THE MOON - HAZLETT
BEACH BABY - BON IVER
ARE YOU EVEN REAL - TEADDY SWIMS, GIVEON
FROM GOLD - NOVO AMOR
DRESS - TAYLOR SWIFT
DAISIES - JUSTIN BEIBER
WHEN THE PARTY'S OVER - BILLIE EILISH
IN MY VEINS - ANDREW BELLE, ERIN MCCARLEY
FALSE GOD - TAYLOR SWIFT

To the ones with welded iron around their scarred hearts;

don't be afraid to let your heart be soft
find the joy in life and let love in

CHAPTER ONE
CALEB

My lungs constrict, emotion spilling into my veins as a heavy sorrow settles inside my chest. Standing outside of the arena, I stare at the building before my eyes look past it. Our preseason games are in a few weeks and this will be the sixth season without her here with me.

I stare at the moon until it becomes blurry. My eyelids fall shut and I inhale deeply, breathing in the scent of the wet, rain laden pavement beneath my feet. I imagine the warmth of her hand, sliding into mine, fingers weaving through the empty spaces. The scent of the floral perfume she used to wear, lacing with the smell of rain.

"What are you doing?"

I pinch my eyelids shut, hanging on to the fading memory of her, hoping that if I ignore him long enough, Rowan will disappear. He's silent and I let my mind drift back to her. Back to my late wife.

The last five years have felt like a time warp without

Amelia. At times, it feels like it's been an eternity since I lost her and others, it feels like I blinked at her funeral and now it's years later.

"Caleb." Rowan's voice is a bit softer. "Are you okay?"

The thought of her hand in mine begins to dissipate and I slowly peel my eyes open, turning my head slightly to the side as I stare at our goalie. "I'm fine," I tell him, clearing my throat.

I think she would be proud of me. Proud of Estella. It's been challenging without her—raising our daughter alone—but I know I wouldn't have been able to do it without the support system I have in place.

And Rowan Taylor just so happens to be part of that support system.

"Your brother said that Estella is staying at his house tonight." He tilts his head to the side, his hair falling across his forehead. "Do you have any plans tonight?"

Biting on the inside of my cheek, I shake my head from side to side. "I just planned on going home."

I'm a widower. A professional hockey player. A single dad. My time is either spent on the ice or with Tella. I don't have time to reacquaint myself with the world outside of the safe little bubble I live in. I wouldn't even know where to start, if that were something I wanted to do.

"Why don't you come over?" he offers, an eager smile on his lips.

"I don't know, man," I start, my voice dropping as I shake my head and run my fingers through my locks.

"Come on," Rowan persists, urging me. "Just come hang out for a little bit."

I stare at him for a moment, pursing my lips. It's a tempting offer. I've become comfortable with my own company and just settling into the silence, but there are times where it's lonely. Sometimes, I'll go out to the bar by myself, but I usually never stay for more than one drink.

"Okay, fine."

Rowan's eyes widen. "Really? That was easier than I thought it would be." He pulls out his phone, tapping on the screen. "Carson owes me fifty bucks now."

I roll my eyes at him and snort. I'm not surprised, My brother Carson and him are always betting on stupid shit. "I'll meet you at your place," I tell him, nodding my head before turning my back on the arena and Rowan.

I head over to the car, slipping behind the driver's wheel as I look back at the arena once more. Emotion wells inside my throat and I swallow hard over the lump. The image of the last time I was here with her— Amelia sitting in the passenger's side floods my mind.

Midnight colored hair falling down her back as she tipped her head back. Her lips spread wide open, the sound of her laughter filling the car.

"What are you laughing at?" I questioned, my voice light as I tilted my head to the side, absolutely mesmerized by her.

"I'm sorry, baby," she said, reaching for my hand as she regained herself. Her warmth wrapped around me, seeping through my pores as she gave me a gentle squeeze. "Sometimes you are just too serious."

My eyebrows pulled together. "No I'm not," I argued.

"Caleb Ford, yes you are," she half scolded me before her words turned to laughter again. "You almost backed your car into Lincoln and you didn't even laugh about it."

I stared at her with a look that questioned her sanity. "What part of hitting someone with my car is funny?"

"You didn't hit him," she pointed out, shaking her head at me. "It's just the chain of events and the way you didn't even crack a smile. You just apologized and waved it off like nothing happened."

The corners of my mouth twitched. Not from the situation, but from the amused look on Amelia's face. "Should I have done something differently?"

"Nope," she said, shaking her head at me. "You're just you and that's what I love about you." She paused, the corners of her eyes crinkling. "I just think there's a benefit in relaxing sometimes. In letting yourself feel the silly, goofy parts of life. It's too short to be so serious all the time, you know?"

A chuckle rumbled in my chest. "Am I not silly enough for you, Amelia?" I reached for her seatbelt, unbuckling it before reaching over to her. I grabbed her hips, hauling her across the center console and onto my lap. Her lips parted but her words were drowned out by her laughter as soon as I began to dig my fingers against her ribs.

"Ohmygod, Caleb, stop!" Amelia exclaimed, her breathing labored as she fought against my hard tickles. "Okay, you win. You're silly and goofy and not serious at all."

My own laughter mixed with hers as I slowly removed my fingers from her ribs. Amelia cupped the sides of my head, her chest heaving with shallow breaths, lips parted and cheeks tinted pink. She leaned forward and pressed her lips to my forehead.

"I love you just the way you are, Caleb." She pulled away, her blue eyes settling on mine. "Just remember to always find the joy in life. Laugh and love, always."

My hands slid up her arms, along her collarbones and neck before resting on her face. Her eyelids fluttered shut as she leaned into me, the smell of orange blossoms invading my senses. "Always."

Amelia begins to fade from my mind, the entire memory vanishing into thin air as I find myself sitting in my car alone once more. There's a conflicting contentment that ripples through me. Grief is such a weird fucking thing. One moment you're feeling guilty for being here while they're gone and then next, you're wanting to keep moving on, knowing they would hate to see you upset.

Amelia wouldn't want me sitting here alone. She would want me surrounded by love and light.

But how do I achieve that when the only love and the brightest light I've ever known ceased to exist?

———

When I pull up to Rowan's house, I park in the driveway behind a dark colored sedan and head to the front door. The front porch light shines bright overhead and I lift my hand to knock on the screen door when Rowan's voice comes from somewhere inside.

"Come in!"

With one final deep breath, I reach for the handle, pulling it open to let myself inside. Muffled voices come from the kitchen. I kick my shoes off in the entryway and follow the sounds.

As I step into the threshold, I find Rowan standing on one side of the counter talking to a woman whose back is to me. My eyebrows pull together in confusion. I immediately know it's not Hadley. Her hair isn't dirty blonde and she's a little taller, a little fuller.

She glances over her shoulder, her long hair swaying as her brown eyes meet mine. Recognition shimmers in her irises, her soft pink lips lifting as she takes me in. She looks away and tucks her hair behind her ears. *Is she nervous?* "Hey, Caleb."

I clear my throat awkwardly. "Hey, Mia."

Mia Landry. Coach Landry's daughter.

I don't know her well, but enough to know that she's been helping some of the families with any babysitting needs. Mia interned with the Aston Archers marketing department last season. I'm not sure what happened, but it doesn't look like she's pursuing it as a career, currently.

To be in my early twenties again, without a single care in the world. I'm a bit envious.

"Thanks again for watching Lucy on such short notice," Rowan says to her, nodding his head. He moves over to the fridge, pulling open the doors. "You're a lifesaver."

"Lucy is so sweet and always so good," she tells him, her soft voice soothing. "I'm just glad I was free and able to help you guys out." Mia lifts her bag from the floor, slinging it over her shoulder. "Have a good night." She turns, and her gaze collides with mine. Her lips part, as if she's going to say something, but instead she dips her chin at me and walks past.

"Goodnight, Mia!" Rowan calls after her with two beers in his hand as he pushes the fridge doors shut. He walks across the kitchen to me and hands me one of the bottles. The front door softly closes behind me. "Do you wanna sit or should we just stand here awkwardly?"

I lift my hand, giving him the middle finger before stepping farther into the kitchen. I set my beer down, pulling out a stool at the island and plop onto it. "Better?"

Rowan smiles. "Much."

"So," I start as I twist off the top of my beer. "Where's Hadley?"

"She had to go visit her grandmother. She should be back tomorrow." He pauses, taking a swig of his drink. "Have you figured out what you're going to be doing this season?"

My forehead creases. "What do you mean?"

"Have you found a replacement for Gloria?"

Oh, yes, that.

My nanny, Gloria, broke the news to me at the end of last season. She's friends with my parents and kindly stepped in to help me after my parents decided to go traveling. But Gloria is getting older and decided it's time for her to retire. Her arthritis has been bad with the humidity here and her doctor recommended she move somewhere drier.

She's leaving next week for her new chapter in New Mexico.

And I still haven't found someone else to watch Tella for me.

"Umm—" I pause, chewing on the inside of my cheek again. "No, not yet."

Rowan stares at me. "We're traveling in two weeks. What are you planning on doing with Tella?"

My hand rakes through my hair, and I clutch the back of my head. "I don't know." I pause, letting out a ragged breath. "The off-season flew by and I haven't really thought much about it."

Emotion passes through Rowan's eyes. "I can't pretend to know what it's like to be you, but you have to figure something out." He pauses, rolling his lips between his teeth. "Have you asked Mia? She's great with kids, man. I would recommend her to anyone."

I shake my head. "I didn't really think about her."

"You should ask her, I'm sure she'll help if she can."

"I don't know, Rowan." My voice is low, heavy with defeat. The thought of having to find another nanny is overwhelming. Mia would be the easiest solution. She's familiar and if the guys all trust her, then there's no reason why I can't.

"Just think about it, okay?" He insists with a shrug.

There's a soft knock on the front door and it slowly opens. I watch Rowan turn around, confusion passing over his expression. "Mia. Is everything okay?"

"Oh, yes." She smiles brightly, nodding before looking at me. My breath catches in my throat and I immediately push whatever the fuck that was away. "You're parked behind me, Caleb."

"Oh."

Why the hell is my brain short-circuiting?

She stares at me, her smile fading when I don't hop up and shifts her weight on her feet. "Um. Are you able to move your car?"

Rowan half glares at me. "Ford."

Him saying my name knocks me from my stupor. I shake my head, blowing out a breath as I climb to my feet. "Yes, of course."

"What the fuck was that?" Rowan mutters under his breath, raising an eyebrow. I lift my eyebrows and shoulders simultaneously before following Mia out through the front door.

She's well over a foot shorter than me and her dirty blonde hair is pulled back in a clip now. My eyes travel down her petite frame, to her waist and ass before moving back to her shoulders.

I may have lost my wife, but I didn't lose my vision. Mia Landry is beautiful. And off-limits. And luckily for both of us, I have no plans on ever getting involved with anyone else again.

"I'm so sorry to bother you," Mia says softly, as she slows her stride to fall in step beside me. A hint of vanilla and lavender infiltrates my senses. "I tried to see if I could get around you somehow, but I couldn't."

"It's okay," I tell her, my voice low. "I didn't realize it was your car that I parked behind."

"Well, either way," she says, a smile lifting her lips

as she glances at me. "I appreciate you coming out to move it."

"No problem," I reply in a gruff voice as I stop beside my car. Mia walks to hers, turning to look at me once more over her shoulder before lowering herself into the driver's seat. I follow suit, getting into mine to back out of the driveway. I move my car in front of the house, parking it along the side of the street.

As I get out and shut my door, Mia pauses beside me and her window slides down. "Thanks again, Caleb," she says, leaning forward to see me. There's just enough of a glow from the porch light to make out her brown eyes, a lighter shade almost like dark honey.

"Of course," I tell her, my voice barely audible. My throat bobs with a rough swallow.

I could ask her right now. I should ask her before she leaves, but the thought of burdening her stops me. Mia might help all the guys out, but that is just for a night here and there. I don't need a babysitter for me to go out to dinner. I need someone I can depend on for the entire season.

Someone who can stay at my house with Tella when I'm not there.

And I know I can't ask that of her.

"Have a good night, Mia," I finally say, bobbing my head at her.

A gentle smile caresses her lips. "You too, Caleb."

I stay beside my car and watch as she pulls away. I don't move until her tail lights fade in the distance and I'm left wondering what the hell I'm actually going to do.

The season is about to start and I need to figure my shit out.

I need to find a nanny—and fast.

CHAPTER TWO
MIA

Frustration rolls over me as my shoulders sag in defeat and I shut my laptop in a rush. My chest deflates, the air exiting my lungs in a rush as my stomach knots with a familiar anxiety.

Suddenly, the coffee shop is too loud. Too busy. Too small. Panic tangles with the knots and my throat tightens. Blocking it all out, I let my eyes shut, counting to four as I inhale and exhale for a beat longer. I repeat it three times, until my heart rate slows to a steadier beat beneath my ribcage.

I pick up the receipt beside my plate, double and triple checking the line items to make sure my order is gluten free.

"It was from their gluten free case."

My eyelids lift, and my surroundings come back into focus as I lock my gaze on my friend Willow sitting across the table from me. Her blonde hair is pulled back away from her face and her sage eyes are locked on mine.

There's no judgment in her expression at all. She knows my compulsions that are driven by the fear of accidentally eating gluten.

"We can go if you want," she offers, her voice gentle as she lifts her iced coffee, sucking down a sip through a reusable silicone straw she carries in her purse.

My throat bobs as I swallow hard. "I'm okay," I tell her, my voice quiet as I tuck my hair behind my ears. "I'm good now."

"You seem pretty anxious today," she states, flipping to a new page in her notebook. "Want to talk about it?"

Willow and I met during our freshman year at Aston University and the rest was history after that.

"I don't know what to do," I admit, a frown tugging the corners of my lips down. "I didn't expect it to be this difficult to find a job in marketing."

Willow chews the inside of her cheek before releasing it. "What about the Archers? Could you still work for their marketing team?"

Reaching back, I pull the hair tie from the bottom of my braid, threading my fingers through my long locks as I shake out the waves. "I don't know," I tell her with a sigh. "I'm not even sure that's what I want to do."

My father is the head coach for the Aston Archers hockey team and I did an internship with their marketing department during my final semester of college, but I didn't love it.

Sure, it was an easy job and one that was practically handed to me, but it just didn't feel like the right fit for me. When I first decided on my major in college, it was because of my father's voice in the back of my head reminding me that I needed to get a job that would provide financial stability.

In a perfect world, I would have found my dream job working with horses, riding and training them. In a perfect world, I wouldn't be sitting here with no idea of what I'm going to do with my life.

When I was a child, I was obsessed with horses and I was a persistent little girl. My father put me in riding lessons and supported my hobby until I was in high school. He bought me my first horse when I was in middle school. Hank is retired, fat, and happy, grazing in the meadow at Willow's family's farm.

It was an expensive hobby that I loved with every ounce of my being and my father wasn't hesitant to support it, but he just didn't see how it could provide a viable career path.

"You're twenty-three, Mia," Willow reminds me, her eyes twinkling beneath the lights above. "I don't think you're supposed to have it all figured out."

"Says the girl who actually does have it all figured out," I retort, raising my eyebrows at her.

Willow's spending a few weeks here with me in Aston before she heads back home for the weekend. Both of her older brothers run their family's maple farm in Sugar Hill Hollow, which is only about forty-five minutes west of Aston. She's visiting them before heading off to Portland for her internship before grad school.

Sugar Hill Hollow isn't far away, but it feels like a completely different world. It's a small, quaint town nestled at the base of the mountain, surrounded by the

Sweetwater River that runs along the perimeter of the town and spills into Sugar Hill Lake.

"Hardly," she says with a laugh, shaking her head at me.

My father moved to Aston a few years ago, but he didn't sell my childhood home at the lake. Instead, it's become more of a vacation home, with memories etched in the wood and stone exterior. Personally, I miss it there. Time just has a way of moving slower there. Like the world outside of the small lake town ceases to exist.

Right now, lake life sounds like a nice distraction from trying to figure out what the heck I'm going to do with my life. I should have gone back when I had the option to, before my father decided to list it as a vacation rental.

"I'm leaving at the end of the week. Pack your bags and come to Portland with me."

I stare at her for a moment, picking at the gluten free blueberry muffin in front of me. "That actually doesn't sound like a bad idea," I admit, popping a piece into my mouth before chewing.

"Think about it," she says with a shrug. "You can come for a change in scenery and maybe it will help you figure out what you want to do." She pauses, a sheepish grin drifting across her lips. "It would be just like it was when we were in college living together."

A chuckle escapes me. It is weird to think about Willow not being here. We've grown so close over the years and I'm not used to going long without seeing her.

"Okay, okay," I agree, smiling at my best friend. "I'll think about it."

————

"Mia." My father's voice is muffled by my door as he knocks on it. "Are you and Willow still planning on coming to the game tonight?"

I tilt my head back, gathering my hair to secure it in a high ponytail. Willow is sprawled out on my bed reading on her kindle. She doesn't bother looking up as I walk over and open my bedroom door. My father adjusts his tie and his eyes meet mine from behind his designer glasses.

"I was just finishing getting dressed."

Some times my father comes home in between meetings and practice on game days, and other days, I don't see him until he comes back late at night. He tries to balance his work and home life, but now that I'm grown, it's a little easier for him to pour himself into his work completely.

It's always been just the two of us.

My parents were both barely twenty when my mother got pregnant. They weren't married, but my dad told me he planned on making her his wife after I was born. At the time, they didn't realize my mother had a weakened uterine wall from a congenital anomaly.

When she went into labor, her uterus ruptured. They immediately rushed her into the OR for an emergency c-section because both of our lives were in danger.

Unfortunately, she didn't survive.

"I have to leave a little earlier than I planned so I can meet with the owner. Are you able to drive yourself or do you want me to order you guys a car?"

"I planned on driving," I assure him as I turn back around to grab a pair of sneakers from my closet.

When I first left for college, I felt immense guilt for leaving him, but he was too busy with his job as the head coach of a professional hockey team to seem bothered by it.

My father shrugs on his suit jacket, securing the buttons as he nods at me with tired eyes. "Okay, just drive safely and if I don't see you at the arena, I'll see you in the morning most likely."

"I'll text you when we get there." I offer him a small smile. "Love you."

"Love you too, Meep." He smiles and this time it reaches his eyes. I see him glance at Willow, shifting his weight on his feet. "See ya, Willow."

Willow glances up from her kindle, a moment of confusion washing over her face. "Later, Mr. Landry."

My father gives us a wave and I watch him as he disappears into the hall and listen to his footsteps as he trudges down the stairs. When the front door closes, I head into the bathroom to put on my makeup. I don't normally wear a lot, so I just put on a light base layer, subtle blush, and some mascara. I was blessed with perfectly shaped eyebrows and long, naturally curling eyelashes from my mother's side.

I tighten my ponytail and give myself a once over before heading into my bedroom again. Willow hasn't made a single attempt to get up from my bed. She's made it quite known that she's not exactly the biggest fan of hockey.

"Are you coming along?" I question her as I grab my sneakers and a light jacket from my closet. The arena will undoubtedly be cold, so I need something more than just the T-shirt I'm wearing.

"I think I might just hang out here tonight," she says, looking up from her book, a smirk working its way across her lips. "The shadow daddy just killed the fae who looked at her wrong and I'm not ready to put it down yet."

Laughter bubbles in my throat and my hair shifts as I shake my head back and forth at her. "You're going to pass up watching hot men play an aggressive sport to read about fictional men instead?"

Mischief dances in her green eyes and she brushes a stray strand of hair from her face, rolling over onto her stomach to look at me.

"You know I'm not into boys like that," she says with a wink before wagging her eyebrows at me. "Although, some fun might not be a bad idea." She rolls onto her side, propping her kindle up on a pillow. "I think I've been single for too long and this book has my ovaries ready to burst."

"I think we need to find you someone for a quick hook-up," I tell her, shaking my head and giggling with her. "That way you stop trying to flirt with my dad."

She snaps her fingers, moving her arm in a sweeping motion. "Ah, shucks," she grumbles, biting back her grin. "For the record, I'm just joking around. He's too old."

Rolling my eyes, I shake my head at her, snorting. "Maybe we can hook you up with one of the players. I'll do some recon."

Willow nods at me, giving me a thumbs up. "You know how I feel about athletes, but maybe I'll make an exception. You'd better hurry, though. I'm leaving soon, remember?"

According to Willow, men who are athletes are nothing but trouble.

"Consider it my top priority." I salute her back, spinning on my heel to head out of my room.

"Don't forget to find someone for you too!" Willow calls out after me, her voice following me down the hall and as I make my way down the stairs.

As I slip my feet into my sneakers, I shake my head and blow out a breath. I'm not like Willow. I've never really been a no-strings kind of girl. I don't know how to separate my emotions and not get attached. After having my heart broken by my long-term boyfriend in college, I've found it's better if I don't get involved with anyone.

No involvement means I won't fall in love.

And if I don't fall in love, I don't get hurt.

CHAPTER THREE
CALEB

"Cale."

I slowly lift my head, turning to the side to look at my brother Carson as he walks up beside me, a bouquet of pink roses clutched in his fist. His lips lift into a tender smile and he tips his chin.

"Where are Andi and Matteo?" I ask him, glancing around for any sign of his fiancée or their son. The sun shines brightly above, poking through the fluffy white clouds, its warmth seeping into the grass beneath our feet.

"I left them at home," he says quietly, looking in the direction I'm facing. I follow his gaze. My daughter Estella is crouched in front of the gravestone, rambling away to the piece of marble as she twirls a flower stem between her fingertips.

Amelia Renee Ford

Loving mother and wife

Forever in our hearts, until we meet again

It's been five years since I lost my wife. Five short

years that I've watched Tella grow without her mother. Five long years that I've been doing it all without her.

What a strange thing, how time can feel so short, yet so long at the same time.

"I can't believe it's been five years already," Carson says softly, lifting his hand to adjust the sunglasses shielding his eyes. It's an unusually warm day for the start of October. It's almost as if summer is trying to poke through one last time before we shift into "flannel shirts and falling leaves" season.

"I know." I'm silent for a moment, staring down at Tella as she talks to Amelia through the gravestone. Guilt engulfs me like tendrils wrapped around my chest, clenching tighter until I can't breath and tears blur my vision. "When I close my eyes and think of her, it feels like the memories are fading away. The images of her aren't as clear as they once were."

Carson lets out a soft breath. "I think that's normal," he says gently.

I swallow roughly over the lump lodged inside my throat. "I know," I say again. It's completely normal, according to my therapist and the grief counselor I saw. It's something they told me would happen, but every time I close my eyes and the images of her grow blurrier, it's even more startling.

Carson steps toward Amelia's grave, crouching down beside Tella. "Hey, T," he greets her with a warm smile. "Can you find somewhere to put these?" he asks her as he hands her the bouquet.

"Yep!" Tella moves over to the headstone, rearranging two other vases to find the perfect spot for Carson's.

Carson stands upright and takes a step back to me. "Have you been to see your therapist?"

"Yeah," I tell him, nodding as I lift my hand to run it through my hair. After the first few years of going weekly, I cut back to once a month. Now it's more on an "as needed" basis. The time around her birthday always hits me harder than the anniversary of her death. "I went and saw her yesterday morning."

Carson's throat bobs, his head moving up and down as he looks at the headstone. "She'd be really proud of you, you know."

I blow a quick breath through my nostrils. "I don't know about all that."

The first few months after her death are not something I'll ever be proud of. I lost myself for a little while after I lost her.

"Sure she would," Carson argues, turning to look at me. "Look at the life you've given Tella. Look at how well you are doing."

I stare at my brother for a moment. Is he forgetting the shell of a human I became after she died? Is he forgetting the fact that I couldn't take care of my daughter's basic needs for the first two months because I was crippled. Paralyzed by grief.

Unable to do anything for myself or my daughter.

I glance down at Tella as she slowly rises to her feet, brushing the dirt from the fronts of her tan riding pants. She turns back to look at me, a smile lifting her lips and the sun making her eyes sparkle. She looks like her mother in so many ways. The way her nose curves up at the end, just the slightest bit.

She has my dark hair, but her eyes are a mixture of blue grey, the green she undoubtedly got from Amelia. My nostrils flare, my throat thick with emotion as I struggle to swallow down.

Even after the way I struggled after Amelia passed, I did get it together eventually. I got my life back on track and made sure that I would never let myself slip like that again. Tella is my priority in life and I will do whatever it takes to keep her safe. To make sure her needs are met—emotionally, mentally, and physically.

Tella turns back to the gravestone and leans down to place a soft kiss on the marble. I slowly turn my head, looking back at my brother, and note how the corners of his eyes soften as he watches my daughter. My brother has been by my side since we were kids. When I lost Amelia, he refused to leave me at first.

He's been there every step of the way, his support a constant, unwavering anchor in my life.

"I wouldn't be where I am now without you."

Carson turns to look at me, his eyes slowly searching mine. "It was nothing," he tells me, his voice low as he tries to dismiss it. "You're my brother and my best friend. I know you'd do the same."

I swallow roughly over the lump lodged in my throat, nodding at him as Tella turns around to face us. "You ready to head to the barn, kiddo?"

Tella's face lights up. "Yep!" She walks over, stepping between Carson and me as we turn away from Amelia's grave, stepping onto the walkway that winds around the cemetery. "Are you coming too, Uncle Cars?"

My footsteps slow, the two of them walking past me as they fall into conversation about Tella's pony Sodapop, her riding lessons, and the upcoming horse show. A soft breeze blows past, whipping up my hair as I turn back around to look at Amelia's grave. My eyes drift back over the words etched in the stone.

Forever in our hearts.

"I love you," I murmur, the words barely audible as my lips tug down in a frown. God, I miss her. "Until we meet again."

The grief isn't as suffocating as it used to be. It isn't as hard to get out of bed anymore. I still love and miss her so much, but life continues on. I have a daughter to raise—a fiery little girl who deserves to have her only parent completely present and involved.

I'll never love again, but that's okay. I'm perfectly fine with being alone, as long as Tella knows she has a father she can always lean on.

"Daddy, are you coming?" Tella's voice breaks through my thoughts, pulling me back into the present. I let my gaze linger for a second longer, a breath leaving my lips as a sigh. My chest feels a bit lighter, although my heart constricts in contrast.

I turn back around, finding Tella and Carson patiently waiting. I can't help but smile at my little girl. "I'm coming." My legs begin to move, and before I know it, I've sped up into a jog. "Race you to the car."

A giggle escapes Tella as she spins around, breaking into a sprint. Her boots meet the ground in light steps as she races through the cemetery. Carson laughs, jogging along as I run past him. I inch closer to Tella, but I slow down, letting her get a steady pace ahead of me.

The three of us are out of breath as we reach the gravel parking lot, kicking up stone and dust on the way to the SUV. Tella reaches out, her fingers stretching toward the side of the car, but just as she's about to touch it, I snake my arm around her waist and lift her into the air.

She lets out a gasp, the sound of her laughter filling the air as she wiggles against me, kicking her legs. "No fair!" she yells out, giggling harder as I dig my fingers into her ribs. Carson breezes past us, his eyes meeting Tella's as he stops by the SUV and touches the side in a dramatically slow fashion. "Come on!" Tella lets out a frustrated sigh.

I release her, letting her back onto the ground as she pins her gaze on Carson. "That doesn't count. You cheated."

"Did not," Carson argues back, sticking his tongue out at her. "Blame your dad, not me. I won fair and square."

"No, you didn't!" She sticks her tongue out at him, scrunching her nose. "It wasn't even a real race, anyways."

"She's just like you, man," Carson laughs, clasping my shoulder with his hand. "Such a sore loser."

I glance at Tella, a smile tugging on my lips as she climbs into the SUV, sticking her tongue out at Carson once more before shutting the door. My shoulders rise and fall in a shrug, a chuckle rumbling in my chest as I look back at my brother. "I mean, you were just arguing with an almost six year old, so are you really any better?"

Carson huffs out a laugh and shakes his head at me. "You're ridiculous," he blows out a breath. "I'll see you later at the game."

I roll my lips, nodding my head at my brother. My breath quickens, dread rolling in the pit of my stomach, but I don't bring it up to my brother before we part ways. I don't bother telling him that I'm going to have to beg his fiancée to watch Tella when I show up at the game with her later.

I still haven't found a nanny like I was supposed to before the season started.

And I've officially run out of time.

CHAPTER FOUR
MIA

"Miss Mia!"

A smile pulls across my lips at the sound of Posey's voice as I step into the family room at the arena. Her step-dad, Lincoln Matthews, plays for the Aston Archers and I see her mom sitting on one of the couches, waving from across the room.

Posey climbs off the couch, leaving Nova there with another one of the wives. "Miss Mia, look!" She runs over to me, almost barreling into me as she holds up a piece of paper for me to look at. I immediately crouch down to her level, taking it from her.

"Oh my goodness, I love it!" My smile spreads across my face as I hand it back to her. "You're so talented, Poe!"

"Miss Mia," another voice calls from my other side. I slowly spin on my heels, turning to see Matteo, Carson Ford's son, holding out a piece of paper. "Look at mine."

Posey scoffs, but doesn't say anything as I take the picture from Matteo, inspecting his drawing like I did Posey's.

"These are both really good, you guys," I tell them, nodding as I take in the colorful swirls of crayon across the page. "We should have a competition. A draw off."

Matteo's face lights up. "I know I'll win."

"Will not," Posey snorts, moving over to Matteo to stand in my line of sight. "My drawings are better than yours."

"Wrong," another child's voice cuts in.

A little girl who could pass as Matteo's sister walks up behind them. Estella Ford. Caleb Ford's daughter.

She's a sassy, fierce little thing. Truly, she's a force to be reckoned with.

"Hey, Tella," I say softly, smiling at her as she moves to stand between Posey and Matteo, crossing her arms over her chest. "Did you draw something too?"

She rolls her lips between her teeth, shaking her head. "Not yet."

"Would you like to enter the drawing competition?"

Tella levels her gaze on mine, lifting a dark brow above her blue grey eyes, as if to challenge me. "What do I win?"

"You're not gonna win, Tella," Matteo mumbles, rolling his eyes at his cousin.

Tella doesn't respond. She doesn't even bother to look at him. Instead, she looks at me, waiting for a response. But my attention is pulled to the opposite side of the room. Caleb is there talking quietly to Andi, his brother Carson's fiancée. He drags a frustrated hand down his tense face, gripping his chin as his gaze collides with mine.

My breath catches in my throat as his stare lingers for a second, before his hand falls away from his face. Andi's lips move, pulling his attention once more.

"Miss Mia?" Tella questions me, her head tilting to the side. I immediately clear my throat, glancing back at her. *What did she ask? Oh right, a prize.*

"Well, I don't know. What do you guys think the winner should get?"

Matteo and Posey immediately start talking over one another as Tella looks past me, her eyes squinting as if she's trying to come up with an answer.

"Poe, can you come here for a second?" Nova, her mother, calls out to her from where she's sitting next to Hadley, Rowan Taylor's fiancé. Rowan's the star goalie for the Aston Archers and his daughter Lucy is the cutest little baby girl.

Hadley bounces Lucy on her lap as Lucy's little face crumbles. She's about to start crying. Posey trots over, immediately going to Lucy to try to make her smile. I watch the two of them for a moment, a smile tugging on my lips as Lucy giggles and reaches for Posey.

Matteo is the next to go and I slowly stand upright as he walks away, heading over to where Riley's standing, bouncing her baby on her hip. Andi turns away from the door, where Caleb no longer lingers. It's like a big family tree here.

I look down at Tella for a moment, who lingers by my leg, slowly surveying the room. I know bits of Tella's story. Her mother passed away just before her first birthday and her father Caleb has been raising her as a single dad since.

My eyes follow after Tella's, my eyebrows pulling together as I realize there isn't an unfamiliar face here. Caleb's previous nanny, Gloria, is nowhere to be seen. I overheard Riley and Andi talking recently about how she was retiring, so I'm not surprised she isn't here.

However, I can't help but wonder who's responsible for Tella right now.

The little girl abandons her spot next to me and heads over to the opposite side of the couch, looking up at the TV as the pregame talk show comes on. I watch her for a moment before walking around the room, saying hi to all the ladies as I find a seat on one of the opposing couches with a view of the big screen TV.

"Hey, Mia," Andi says as she plops down onto the couch beside me. Matteo slides in next to her and Tella takes the seat at the end of the couch. They settle in, both of them balancing a container of French fries on their laps.

"Hey," I smile back at her. "How are you?"

"Oh, I'm good," she says, nodding at me. "Just staying busy with work and Matteo and Carson. And now trying to figure out how I can help Caleb with Tella."

My eyebrows pull together. "What do you mean?"

Andi lets out a sigh. "Well, Gloria retired and she's leaving for Florida in two days. Caleb has had plenty of time to find a nanny but hasn't yet."

"Are you watching her for him?"

Andi nods again. "He failed to mention it to anyone and showed up tonight with her and no plan."

A frown tugs at my lips and her words tug at my heart.

"He stopped by the family room with her, half panicked, but I assured him she's fine with me." She pauses, her throat bobbing as she swallows. "She's always fine with me and never a bother, I just think he needs a better solution for the whole season, you know?" She lets out another sigh. "Matteo has an early appointment in the morning so I didn't plan on staying here late tonight, but I don't know what Caleb's plans are, so I don't want to just assume and take Tella with me."

I get distracted for a moment by Matteo and Tella behind her in some kind of a discussion. Then I shift my attention back to Andi, my mind already made up. "I can watch her."

Andi's eyebrows lift. "Wait, really?"

"Of course," I say, smiling brightly. "Tella's great. It's really no problem at all."

"Oh, you are an absolute lifesaver," Andi laughs, pulling me in for a side hug. "I swear I owe you for everything. Whenever we need someone to watch the kids, you're always there to help."

"I like hanging out with all the kids," I laugh, hugging her back before we separate. "They're all very well behaved and it gives me something to do with my time right now."

Andi settles back in her seat, her eyes meeting mine

as she tilts her head to the side. "Still haven't found a job?"

I shake my head at her. "No. I'm not really sure a marketing career is for me . . . which is unfortunate, considering the fact that I have a bachelor's degree in it."

"Hmm," Andi muses, lifting her drink to take a sip. "I'm sure there's something out there for you. Maybe something unconventional. Something you could use your degree for, but not fully in the corporate marketing world, you know?"

I stare at her for a moment before my face cracks and laughter spills from my lips. "That sounds made up."

Andi chuckles, shrugging her shoulders. "I mean, maybe." Her shoulders shake with laughter. "Although, it might be a real thing, you just haven't found it yet." She pauses, a smile breaking out across her face. "And you don't know what it is exactly yet."

"I don't even know where I would start searching for a job with that criteria."

"You still have plenty of time to figure it out," she offers, her smile like a warm embrace.

She's not wrong. I am fortunate enough that living with my father allows me the freedom and time to figure out what I want to do with my life. Although, at twenty-three, I thought I would have had things more figured out by now. I thought I would have been starting my career and living on my own.

Andi grabs one of Matteo's fries, popping it into her mouth before turning back to look at me. "Have you ever considered being a nanny? You're such a natural with kids and they love being around you."

My lips purse, eyebrows pulling together as I mull over her words. "No, I've honestly never even thought about it."

"That's definitely an option for you." She pauses, chasing her French fry with a sip of her drink. "If you would decide to, I'm sure Caleb would be interested. He's going to need someone to help him when he's on the road. Someone who can provide some stability for Tella, instead of her going back and forth between our house and his, you know?"

My heart ticks a little harder inside my chest. "I didn't even think about that," I admit, my voice soft as I tuck my hair behind my ears. "I don't know if he would want to hire me, though. He knows who I am, but our interactions have been fairly limited."

Andi nods in understanding. "That makes sense," she agrees, glancing out at the ice and back at me. "It's worth a shot, though, if it's something you'd want to do. He has some trust issues, but I will totally vouch for you, and so will everyone else he knows."

Screwing my lips to the left, I chew on the inside of my cheek for a moment, my gaze drifting past Andi to study Tella. Her lips move as she says something to Matteo, a mischievous look in her eye, almost like she's plotting something. I release my cheek, biting back a grin. "You know, that might not be such a bad idea for right now," I tell Andi as my eyes find hers once more. "I'll mention something to him when I see him later."

"If he's smart, he'll take you up on the offer," she

says, rolling her eyes. "Caleb Ford is not the type of man to ever ask for help and Lord knows he needs it."

"We'll see what he says," I tell her, both of our gazes traveling back up to the TV lights as they begin to change colors, the announcer's voice bouncing through the speakers.

I don't know if Caleb will want my help, but it's worth a shot. Best case, he takes me up on the offer and it buys me some more time from having to find a job. Worst case, he says no and then I have no choice but to finally decide what I'm going to do with my life.

Even if it means completely changing my career and potentially disappointing my father.

CHAPTER FIVE
CALEB

Pulling my shirt over my head, I run a tired hand through my damp hair to push it away from my forehead. The last remaining guys are finishing up in the dressing room. Most have left already and when I catch sight of Rowan leaving the room, the coast is clear.

And then I see Carson waiting for me by the door.

"Did you see Andi's text in the group chat?"

I tilt my head to the side, reaching into the side pocket of my duffle bag to retrieve my phone and unlock the screen. Normally, I have it completely charged with the volume turned on, just in case there's something emergent with Tella that I need to be available for.

My eyebrows pull together in a furrow. It somehow ended up on "Do Not Disturb" mode. My heart immediately speeds up and my stomach rolls as anxiety grips my insides. "Is everything okay?"

"Yeah, everyone's good," he assures me, rather than

scolding me for jumping directly to the worst case scenario. He's always been able to read me like an open book. "Mia offered to watch Tella so Andi could get Matteo home and in bed at a decent time."

My heart stops in my chest, my eyes flashing to my brother's. "What?"

Carson shrugs, feigning a look of innocence. "Mia's great. If I trust my kid with her, you can trust her with yours too."

There is a prick of annoyance inside my chest that Andi just left like that. I don't have a problem with Mia Landry. Hell, everyone loves her. But she hasn't been properly vetted. I'm not sure I completely trust her with my daughter.

My phone vibrates. I turn it over and find a text from an unfamiliar number on the screen.

UNKNOWN

Hey, this is Mia. Tella and I are waiting for you outside of my father's office.

"Was that her?"

I nod at my brother, not bothering to look at him as I type my response and send it.

CALEB

Thanks. I'll be there in a few.

"They're waiting outside of Coach's office."

"I'll walk with you," Carson offers, shifting the strap of his bag on his shoulder as we walk out into the hallway together.

"That's okay," I tell him, running my tongue across

my teeth. "I'll catch up with you tomorrow. Tell Andi thanks for keeping an eye on Tella."

Carson nods, his lips falling into a flat line. "You need to figure out a better situation for Tella's sake," he says, his voice low. "She's always more than welcome at our house, but she needs some stability. Someone to stay at your house with her."

"I know," I sigh, guilt settling deep as his words strike me in the chest. He's telling me everything I already know—everything we've already talked about.

"Just talk to Mia, Cale. Even if it's just a temporary thing, it will buy you some time to find someone permanent."

I suck in a deep breath, my lungs expanding, chest rising, before I blow it out. "Okay."

My brother and I head separate ways, him toward the exit of the building and me down the hall toward Coach Landry's office. I pass a few of the staff members, nodding as I keep moving and slip into the smaller hallway to the left. As I round the corner, I see them sitting on a bench out front of Coach's office.

Mia sits against the wall, her head tilted back and eyes closed. My gaze travels down along her side, where Tella is tucked in against her, her head resting on the side of her chest as Mia holds her upright with her arm extended around her.

My expression softens and my shoulders relax, the constricting feeling dissipating inside my chest knowing my little girl is safe and sound. My footsteps are light and I'm not sure either of them hear me as I walk to the bench, stopping a few feet away.

"Hey," I say, my voice soft in an effort to not scare either of them. Tella doesn't move, soft snores escaping her lips. Mia's eyelids peel open, her head tilting away from the wall as she whips it to the side to look at me.

Her honey brown eyes meet mine instantly. "Hey." She lets out a breath, her lips lifting into a soft smile. "You scared me."

"Sorry," I say, my own voice quiet. "I didn't mean to."

"No, no, it's okay," she assures me. She moves into more of an upright position rather than slouching, and dips her head down to Tella as she squeezes her arm. "Hey, Tell, your daddy's here."

Tella stirs awake, lifting her head from Mia's side as she rubs her eyes. She turns on the bench out of Mia's arm as she glances over at me. "Hi, daddy."

"Hey, T. Are you ready to get home?"

Tella climbs off the bench and stumbles over to me, her body colliding with mine as I crouch down to scoop her up. "Mhm," she murmurs, wrapping her little arms around my neck and resting her head on my shoulder.

Guilt washes over me. It's well past her bedtime, yet here she is, falling asleep in the hallway of the arena, waiting for me to take her home. I glance over at Mia as she rises to her feet, closing the distance between us. "I'll walk you to your car," I tell her, waiting for her to fall in step with me.

"That's okay," she says, giving me a small smile. "I'll be fine."

I stare at her for a moment as we both begin to walk down the hallway. "It's late, we'll walk you out."

She turns to look at me, her lips parting like she's about to argue, but instead she shuts them, turning her attention back in front of her as we continue to walk side by side.

"Thanks for staying with her tonight," I tell Mia as we reach the exit. I step in front of her to push the door open and hold it as she steps out into the darkness. The lights above the parking lot hum, dampened by the blanket of fog descending toward the ground.

"It wasn't a problem at all," she says, her tone light as she smiles. "She's a great kid."

"What happened with Andi and Matteo?"

"Andi said Matteo had an early appointment tomorrow and she was worried about him getting to bed too late, so I offered to watch Tella." She pauses, her throat bobbing on a swallow. "This is me," she says as we reach a small silver sedan. She pulls out her key fob, unlocking the door as she stops by the driver's side. "Thanks for walking me out."

"Anytime," I nod. Our gazes are locked and I adjust a sleeping Tella in my arms. Mia reaches up and brushes her hair away from her face, tucking it behind her ear. There's a small freckle to the left of her eye, right along her temple. "I um—I actually have a favor to ask you."

Mia cocks her head to the side. "Sure. What's up?"

"Well," I pause, shifting my weight on my feet. My nostrils flare, sweat beads on my forehead, my stomach twists in knots as Mia stares back at me. Her eyes shimmer beneath the lights, the darkness almost making them look gold. There's no judgment on her face, only patience. "I'm not sure if you know, but my nanny retired after last season and I've been meaning to find someone to watch Tella when I have games and practices and whatnot."

"Andi had mentioned you were in need of some help and I was going to offer, but you beat me to it." Mia straightens her head, a smile pulling on her lips. "I'd be more than happy to help."

My breath catches. "Really?"

"Absolutely," she says, nodding while pulling open the driver's side door. She bends down, her jeans tightening around her backside as she puts her bag over onto the other side of the center console. I tear my gaze away from where it drifted, heat rising up my neck as I clear my throat. "I've actually been having a difficult time job hunting, so this would be perfect."

I wet my bottom lip as she turns back to face me. "It can just be a temporary thing, if that works better for you. You know, until you find a different job."

"We can just play that by ear," she offers, biting back a grin.

"That works too." My own lips curving to smile at her. "We have practice tomorrow morning, but perhaps we can get coffee afterwards and iron out the details?"

"That sounds perfect. Who's watching Tella during practice?"

I inhale deeply, releasing the air slowly. I may not have figured out a nanny situation, but I do have Nova and Riley both on standby to help during practices if Andi can't. "I planned on dropping her with Nova."

"Why don't I just come before practice? I can watch Tella and we can just talk afterwards?"

I stare at her for a moment. "Are you sure?"

"I'm positive, Caleb," she smiles, her bright white teeth peeking out from behind her full lips. "If I didn't want to, I wouldn't offer."

"Okay. I'll text you my address."

Mia nods, her gaze lingering on mine. "I'll see you in the morning."

I swallow, watching her carefully as she turns around and climbs into her car. "Goodnight. Drive safe."

Mia's eyes meet mine once more. "You too," she says, pulling the door shut behind her.

Adjusting Tella in my arms, I walk across the lot to where I'm parked. She snores lightly, stirring in her sleep as I open the back door and slide her into her booster seat. As I stand upright, I glance back across the lot, catching sight of Mia's taillights as she heads toward the exit.

I don't know how this situation is going to pan out, but at this point, I don't have any other options. It's weird to imagine someone other than Gloria being in my home, taking care of my daughter while I'm not there. I'm going to be putting my daughter's life in the hands of a woman I barely know—a woman everyone swears I can trust to take care of Estella.

Shaking my head, I push away the thoughts and slide into the driver's seat. Mia's actively looking for another job, so I can't expect her to drop everything to become my full-time nanny, unless that's something she wants to do.

Regardless of what happens in the future, I desperately need this to work out right now.

I need Mia to be someone I can count on. Someone I can depend on.

Someone I can trust.

CHAPTER SIX
MIA

"I thought I smelled coffee," Willow says, lifting her arms above her head to stretch. Her tank top creeps up her torso and she doesn't bother to fix it as she slides into the seat next to my dad at the counter. Willow pins her gaze on me, tilting her head to the side. "Where are you going this early?"

My father lifts his gaze from his laptop, eyes also gluing to my face as I duck my head, pouring myself and Willow a cup of coffee. I glance at him and then at Willow as I stir in the creamer.

"I'm going to go watch Caleb's daughter while he's at practice."

My father doesn't say anything and Willow raises an eyebrow. "Caleb. He's the hot, older one, right? You said he plays middle or something."

My father snorts. "Center," he corrects her, his voice low as he shakes his head. "How did this come about?"

I explain the situation to both of them, telling them what happened last night and how I ended up watching Tella. "His old nanny retired, so he needs someone to help watch his daughter until he finds a permanent one."

"You're not coming to Sugar Hill with me then, are you?"

I swallow roughly, shaking my head at her. "I don't think so."

"What happened to getting a job?" my father interjects.

"Technically, it is a job."

"She doesn't want to work in marketing, Dean," Willow adds at the same exact moment, the words flowing from her mouth before she realizes what she's saying. Her eyes flash to mine, widening as she holds her breath. "Shit, sorry," she mumbles, closing her eyes as she blows out a breath.

My father's eyebrows tug together. "What?"

My stomach plummets. I planned on having this conversation with him at some point . . . just not right now.

"Um, yeah. I wanted to talk to you about that," I admit, shifting my weight and ignoring my coffee that's cooling on the counter in front of me. "I'm not sure marketing is what I want to do, but I'm thinking about exploring some other career opportunities that would hire me with a marketing degree."

He stares at me for a moment, gaze fixed and unwavering. He abruptly stands up, moving away from his seat as he closes his laptop. "You're an adult, Mia. You can make your own decisions." He pauses, sighing deeply. "This is news and a little unexpected. I'm not mad. I support whatever you ultimately decide to do, although I do think it's important to find a good paying job."

I swallow hard over the lump lodged in my throat. "I know."

"Caleb Ford has had a rough go at things, after losing his wife and juggling his career and daughter." My father takes another sip of his coffee before he walks over to the sink and dumps it out. "I'm sure your help is greatly needed. I just don't want you to throw away a degree you worked so hard for to be someone's babysitter."

"It's just a temporary thing."

My father purses his lips, slowly nodding his head. "Okay. I have to head out, so I'm sure I will see you later." He glances at Willow quickly before looking back at me. "Love you. Bye, Willow."

Willow bats her eyelashes at him, even though he's turning in the opposite direction, heading toward the door that leads into the garage. "Bye, Mr Landry," she calls out, her tone changing as she says his name.

I stare at her, raising my eyebrows. "Willow."

"Sorry," she giggles, shaking her head. "My boredom is getting to me."

My eyebrows relax, dropping lower as I narrow my eyes. "I swear to God, if you make a move on my dad, I might go jump off the nearest, tallest building."

Willow waves her hand at me, lifting her mug with her other hand to take a sip. She hides her smirk behind the ceramic cup. "You're dramatic," she rolls her eyes, setting her coffee back down. "Daddy Dean looks good in those glasses, but he's unfortunately not my type at all."

My eyes widen, again. "Daddy Dean? What the hell is this?"

Willow breaks out into laughter, her head falling backward, then turns to smile at me. "I'm kidding, I'm kidding!" She pushes her strawberry blonde hair over her shoulder before placing her hand on her chest. "You're so easy to get a rise out of."

"I'm going to be late," I mutter, letting out a sigh as I shake my head at my best friend. I know she's joking, but I also know her taste in men. I close my eyes, pinching the bridge of my nose. "I don't even want to think about this."

"So, don't," Willow says with a shrug. "I promise I will never do that. You know who I still think about?" She pauses and immediately waves it off. "Nevermind, it doesn't even matter."

I cock my head to the side. "No, who?"

Willow climbs off the stool and walks over to me. Her hands find my shoulders and she spins me around. "It's not important. You'd better go before you're late." She gives me a gentle push. "Have a good first day, honey."

I look at her over my shoulder. "I'm not your child."

"Not yet!" She smirks and winks before her laughter fills the space again. I let out another exasperated sigh, turning away from her as I head out to my car. Willow Alder is my very best friend and a goddamn menace.

———

I double check the address on my dash as I pull up along the curb in front of a big white house with black trim and white pillars. I don't know what I was expecting his house to look like, but I didn't think he'd need one this big for just him and his daughter.

I shift my car into park, kill the engine, and grab my bag from the front seat before getting out. The cool breeze drifts past, pushing a few stray hairs in front of my face as I step onto the sidewalk. The lawn is perfectly manicured and there are a few different potted plants on the porch, along with two wooden rocking chairs.

Just as I reach the front door, it's yanked open, revealing Caleb standing on the other side. My eyes meet his, noticing the black-rimmed glasses sitting on his face. His gray eyes almost look like molten steel.

"Good morning," he says, his voice gruff as he reaches up to scratch at the stubble along his chiseled jaw line.

"I'm not used to seeing you with glasses," I blurt out, feeling heat creep up my neck. "I'm sorry, that was rude. What I meant to say was good morning."

Can I be any more embarrassing?

Caleb chuckles, then in a low voice, he says, "I normally wear contacts and honestly rarely wear these unless I absolutely need to." He lifts his hand higher, the bottom hem of his sweatshirt lifting as he runs his hand through his wavy locks. "I have to go pick up my new ones on my way to practice."

My head bobs and I adjust the strap of my purse on my shoulder. "They look good."

"Thanks," he says after a beat passes between us. "Please, come in," he offers after clearing his throat. He steps out of the way, holding the massive black door open for me. I step into his space, and am struck by how clean and pristine the foyer is as I kick off my shoes.

"I woke T up about an hour ago, but she isn't exactly a morning person," he explains as he steps deeper into the house. I follow after him, my eyes scanning the walls in the foyer as we head to the kitchen. There are professional photos of Estella and Caleb hanging on display. "She wanted to play with her dolls before eating breakfast."

A chill seeps through my socks from the wood floor as we step into the open concept kitchen. I stop by the island in the center, my hands caressing the edge of the marble countertop as Caleb walks over to the stove. "I used to hate mornings."

"No?" Caleb questions me, turning around with an eyebrow raised as he sets a plate of pancakes in the center of the island. "I wouldn't have guessed that."

His comment catches me off guard. My head tilts to the side. "Why's that?"

"Oh, I don't know," he says in a rush, his tone dismissive as he shrugs his shoulders. "You just have a morning personality."

I'm not sure what he means, but I don't question him on it any further. The way he ducks his head and skirts around the kitchen makes his discomfort noticeable.

Caleb and I aren't strangers. We've spoken numerous times and have been around each other enough to know one another, but an assessment like that feels a little deeper than all the short lived conversations we've had.

"I made breakfast, so please feel free to help yourself," Caleb offers, grabbing a water bottle from the fridge. "There are also snacks in the pantry and food in the fridge. Just make yourself at home." He pauses, the corners of his lips twitching. "I wrote down what Tella's day typically looks like, although I should be home in a few hours."

He grabs a notepad from the side of the fridge and walks over, handing it to me. My fingers accidentally brush his as I grab the pad of paper. My breath catches in my throat, and his hand lingers for a passing second before he removes it.

Heat creeps up my neck once more and I immediately distract myself by looking at the helpful list he's created. He has everything listed on three sheets of paper, covering any question I might possibly have about taking care of Tella.

"Come on," he says softly from the kitchen door. He motions for me to follow him. "I'll show you around, then I need to head out."

Caleb gives me the official tour of his massive home and by the time we head up the stairs to the second floor, I'm fairly certain I could get lost here. As we head down the hallway, he points out the bathroom at the end before we reach Tella's room.

The door is ajar, but he still lightly knocks on the door instead of pushing it open. "Hey, T," Caleb says as he pokes his head through the gap. "Are you ready to come eat breakfast? Miss Mia is here."

There's commotion in her room, the sound of toys hitting the floor before Caleb steps out of the way. Tella comes barreling through the door, coming to a halt in front of me. Her hair is pulled back in a messy braid and her jammies are pink with white polka dots.

"Hi, Miss Mia."

"Good morning, Tella!" I smile down at her.

"Come on, T," Caleb says, reaching to usher her downstairs. "The pancakes are going to get cold if you don't eat them now and you know how much you dislike cold pancakes."

She scrunches her nose in disgust. "Yuck."

I try to suppress a small laugh with the back of my hand as I follow the two of them back down to the kitchen. Tella climbs up onto one of the stools and Caleb quickly gets her situated with a plate of pancakes, butter, and syrup.

He takes a step away as I sit down next to her. "You have my number in case you need anything." He pauses, his throat bobbing as he swallows. "You have Andi and Riley and—"

"Caleb," I interject, raising my eyebrows at him. "We'll be fine and I'm fairly certain I have everyone's phone number that you're about to list."

He huffs a chuckle. "Okay, sorry." He clears his

throat and turns to Tella. "You be good for Miss Mia." He leans forward, kissing the top of her head. "I love you."

"Love you too, daddy," she says around a mouthful of pancakes.

"I'll be back after practice," he says, directed at me now. "Eat some of the pancakes. They aren't as good when they're reheated."

"We'll be here." I smile at him, tipping my chin, not commenting on the pancakes. I'm not ashamed of my body's inability to tolerate gluten, it just feels like a bit of a burden at times. Sometimes it just feels rude or awkward to turn down food because of the ingredients.

Caleb's movements are slow as he makes his way toward the garage. I watch him for a moment—the way he pauses as he turns the knob and glances back over his shoulder. He looks at Estella first, his eyes lingering before bouncing to mine.

He gives me a small nod before finally slipping through the door, closing it behind him. I know this has to be hard for him. He's not leaving his daughter with a stranger, but it's clear he's leaving her with someone he doesn't fully trust.

I need him to trust me. I need him to feel comfortable so he's not worrying about Tella when he needs to be focused on his career.

"Miss Mia, eat before they get cold," Tella reminds me, half scolding me as she pushes an empty plate in my direction. I look at the pile of pancakes, back to the plate, then at the little girl next to me.

"You can just call me Mia," I say, as she takes

another bite of her food. "I already ate breakfast, but don't tell your daddy, okay?"

Tella swallows down her food, a grin breaking out across her lips. "So, it's a secret?"

I nod, biting back my own grin. "I don't want to hurt his feelings by not eating the pancakes."

Tella bobs her head in understanding. "I won't tell him. Cross my heart," she promises, drawing an X across her chest. She directs her attention back to her food, shoveling another forkful past her lips. "Do you say bad words?"

My eyebrows pull together, confusion washing over me. "Sometimes, but I try not to."

"Well, if you do, you have to pay," she informs me, giving me a very serious look. "Daddy has a swear jar, but you can just put your dollars in there too."

My lips press into a straight line. "I don't think I brought any money with me."

Tella gives me a mischievous look, a twinkle in her eye. "You better not say any bad words then."

"I will try very hard not to," I assure her, stifling a laugh. Tella's quite mature for her age. Her vocabulary is advanced and the way her mind works just seems a bit different than other children.

"Good," she tells me, her chin dipping again. She finishes up her food and I take the plate to wash it. Tella follows me to the sink, pressing up on her tiptoes to watch what I'm doing. "Do you want to play with my dolls?

"I would love to," I say, turning to face her as I dry the plate and find the cabinet it belongs in.

"We can only play with the girl dolls," Tella says, grabbing my hand to pull me along with her.

"Why's that?"

"Because boys are gross," she scoffs. "Everyone knows that."

A laugh escapes me as she heads up the stairs first. "They are, aren't they?"

"Mhm," Tella nods, leading me up to her room. "Except Daddy, but he isn't a boy. He showers and smells good."

"Well, that's good to know."

When we reach her room, I have to step around some toys to get to her dollhouse. Just as I'm about to crouch down, I step on something sharp that digs right into the center of my foot.

"Dammit!" I cry out, dropping down onto the ground to remove the toy heel from my foot. "Ouch, that hurt."

Tella stands beside me, her eyes narrowing at me. "You said a bad word."

My eyes widen as I look up at her. "Oh no."

Tella stares at me for a second before a mischievous grin lifts the corners of her lips. "It's okay." She waves her hand dismissively as she moves to sit on the floor next to me. "I won't tell my Daddy you don't have any money."

"I didn't say I don't have any money."

Tella shakes her head at me. "It's our secret." My lips part and I'm about to argue with her when she grabs a doll and hands it to me. "This is Penelope. You can be her."

I stare at the little bossy girl for a moment before a smile cracks my face. Tella starts to tell me the whole backstory for her dolls and what I can and can't do with them. She's a sassy little thing, but I like her.

There isn't a single doubt in my mind that she won't grow up to be a strong woman.

And I know it has everything to do with the way Caleb Ford is raising her.

CHAPTER SEVEN
CALEB

Carson skates over to me, his blades cutting through the ice as he comes to a stop and taps my shin guards with his stick. "How did it go last night?"

I look over at my brother, my eyebrows pulling together as I tilt my head to the side. "What do you mean?"

Carson looks past me, over to the guys as they battle for the puck in the corner. "With Mia."

My eyebrows are still cinched close to one another as I try to figure out what he's getting at. "You mean with her watching Tella?"

He gives me a perplexed look, like he doesn't under-stand why I don't know what he's getting at. "Yes, Cale. The woman who watched your daughter. How did she do with Tella and did you finally get your head out of your ass and ask her for her help?"

My face relaxes. "Oh, yeah." I let out a breath, ignoring the prickle of irritation inside my chest from the way he spelled things out. "It was fine. Tella likes her and there were no issues last night. She's agreed to help me out temporarily."

I look out at the ice, watching Lincoln score a goal against Rowan as I try to tap into my memory. I could have sworn I texted Andi earlier this morning about the situation. *Why is he asking me about the Mia situation?* Unless she already told Carson and he's just making conversation.

"All right boys, you three," Coach Landry says, pointing at Carson, Hayes, and me. "And you three." He points at three other players standing in a line. "You're up."

My brother and I nod our heads at one another, both of us heading to the half of the ice we're currently using. He has us practicing 3v3 in close quarters. I head over to the face-off dot, bend my knees and tap my stick on the ice to show I'm ready to go. Trent, our third line center takes his position in front of me and we wait for the puck to drop.

One of the assistant coaches, Connor, waits before dropping the piece of frozen rubber between Trent and me. He tries to gain possession of it, but I win the face-off, passing the puck to Hayes. He skates around the two of us as Trent and I break apart.

Every outside noise, every outside problem—it all melts away as soon as I dig deep and lock in. The only thing that ever matters when I'm on the ice is winning every damn battle. And the men on the ice are my brothers—my teammates. The ones who will be there to fight for me and with me, on and off the ice.

At the end of the day, I know I can always count on them.

I just hope the same stands for Mia too . . .

————

CALEB

I'm going to stop by The Daily Brew. What do you like?

MIA

Iced vanilla latte with two pumps of vanilla and vanilla cold foam.

If that's too much, I don't need a drink, but thank you!

I stare at my phone for a second, rereading her message as my forehead creases. I don't know why she would be concerned about it being too much. I wouldn't have asked her what exactly she wanted if I didn't plan on getting whatever it is.

CALEB

It's not too much. I'll be home in about thirty minutes.

MIA

See you soon!

I lock my screen and tuck my phone into the cupholder before I start the engine and pull out of the parking lot. The coffee shop is only a few minutes away from the practice facility, so I make my way through the drive thru, double checking Mia's order from her text as

I read it off to the woman working. It doesn't take long for both of our drinks and a kids smoothie for Tella, then I'm pulling back onto the road.

When I pull up to the house about fifteen minutes later, Tella and Mia are sitting in the driveway, an array of colors on the blacktop around them. A smile tugs the corners of my lips, a warm, softening feeling in my chest as I park at the end of the driveway in the street.

Tella comes running over when she notices me parking, and waits for me on the sidewalk. I grab all three drinks, juggling them in my hands as I get out of the car and greet Tella. Her pink dress is covered in chalk and there's a smudge above her eyebrow.

"Daddy! How was practice?"

"It was good," I say and hand her the smoothie. "I got you strawberry-banana."

"Yummy!" She licks her lips before taking a long sip of her drink. Her eyelids flutter shut and she lets out an "ah" sound as she gives me a smile of satisfaction. "Thanks, daddy," she says, spinning on her heel as she trots back over to Mia.

My gaze follows her and I find Mia rising to her feet, dusting her hands off on the fronts of her jeans. Her eyes meet mine, a smile stretching across her lips as I approach, my arm extending to hand her the coffee.

"My savior," she laughs softly, taking it from me. "Thank you so much."

She looks at the cup for a second, spinning it around as she reads the drink ticket that lists everything she asked for.

She pinches the straw between her forefinger and

thumb, her perfect pink plump lips wrapping around the end of it. Something stirs in the pit of my stomach, something that mimics excitement. Arousal? *Where the fuck did that thought come from?* She releases the straw, her tongue darting out to lick her lips. I immediately divert my gaze from her mouth, ignoring the blood rushing between my legs.

"Oh man, that's a good one," she murmurs, lowering her cup. "They seriously have the best drinks in Aston."

I wasn't sure if she'd like the drinks there or not, but it's good to know that she does.

My eyebrows pull together as I store the information in my brain. For what reason, I don't know. It shouldn't be something of importance, but at least I'll know what she likes in case I get her coffee again. *As a nice gesture . . . nothing more.*

"What are you guys working on out here?" I glance down at the chalk mural sprawling across the driveway. "I hope Tella was good for you," I add, tipping my head as I look down at Tella. She glances up at me, her expression giving nothing away but I don't miss that familiar glimmer of mischief in her irises.

Mia laughs softly again, and it's smooth like molasses. "She was good," she tells me. "I think she's probably always good."

A chuckle rumbles in my chest. Tella frowns and I pat the top of her head as she takes another sip of her smoothie. Tella moves away from me, dropping back down onto the ground as she picks up a piece of pastel purple chalk and starts to color in a unicorn that Mia must have drawn. There's no way Tella did that herself.

I stare at the drawing for a moment, really looking at the outlines of rainbows, unicorns, and butterflies that Mia drew on the blacktop. It's clear she's incredibly talented. I lift my head and study the side of her face as she stares down at my daughter.

Her features are delicate, her skin like silk, nose straight and rounded at the end. My eyes trace her soft jawline, up and over her subtly lifted cheekbones. A tender smile lifts her plump, pouty lips and she lets out a sigh as she tucks some of her dirty blonde hair behind her ear and turns to look at me.

My breath catches in my throat, our gazes colliding as she catches me staring at her. Heat creeps up my neck and I adjust my weight on my feet, looking away and clearing my throat to try to play it off.

What the hell is my problem?

I don't know what has gotten into my body. Maybe it's the mercury in the microwave or whatever the hell I see people posting on social media about the planets when life gets weird.

"Did you want to sit on the porch so we can talk about things?" I gesture toward the house with my coffee in hand .

Mia's head slowly bobs up and down. She tips her head back down toward Tella. "Hey, Tell. Finish this up while your daddy and I talk about things."

"Okay!" Tella complies, not bothering to look at her as she grinds the chalk faster and faster until there's a pile of dust on the ground.

Laughter bubbles in my chest again as Mia and I turn away from her, walking along the concrete walkway to the front porch. I step up first, Mia directly behind me as I move toward the white wooden rocking chairs. Something tugs at my heart, a lump lodging in my throat as I pause. Those damn chairs have been around for forever.

Amelia and I bought them for the front porch of our old home. The house we bought together. After she passed, I had to sell the property. I couldn't stand to be there, expecting to see her around every corner I turned. All of her belongings were just painful reminders of what I had lost. I got rid of almost everything except for a few keepsakes and these two chairs.

For whatever reason, I couldn't bring myself to get rid of them.

I extend my arm for Mia to move around me and sit. She takes the left one. And I take the one on the right, the wood creaking beneath my weight as I settle against the back slats. Mia begins to slowly rock in hers, her lips wrapping around the straw once more as she takes a sip of her iced drink.

"How was practice?" she asks, as she turns her head to look at me.

"It was good." Mimicking her actions, I start to rock in my own chair. I turn to look at her, her eyes slowly searching mine.

"What were you thinking in terms of me watching her?" Mia questions me, cutting right to the chase.

"Since kindergarten has already started and just to have the normalcy for T, I think it would be better if you stayed here with her while I'm away." I pause, my throat bobbing as I swallow hard. "I have two guest rooms, so you're more than welcome to make one your room."

"That makes complete sense," she agrees without any hesitation. "I can just stay while you're gone, that way I'm not encroaching on your space when you're home."

I let out a breath. "If you would rather move in, I'm open to whatever you'd like to do. I just would mainly need you here during practices, games, while I'm out of town and for any other events that may pop up."

Mia lets out a soft chuckle. "Maybe moving in would make more sense."

The corners of my mouth twitch. "We can play it by ear, see how things go."

Mia rolls her lips between her teeth, biting down as she bobs her head. "That works for me," she says, her voice softening. "If you need me to watch her for more than work stuff, I can do that too. You know, if you have a date or just anything."

Her words catch me off guard and I inhale sharply, immediately shaking my head. "I don't go on dates, Mia," I tell her, my voice dropping. "That's not something I'll ever need you for."

Her lips part, eyebrows drawing together as she lets out a breath and closes them. She pulls her bottom lip between her teeth, dragging them over it as her brows relax. "Okay," she says softly. "Sorry, I just thought I would offer, at least."

I rake my hand through my hair, letting out a sigh.

"No, I'm sorry," I say, pursing my lips. "I appreciate it. I don't normally do much outside of work but take care of T. I will keep your offer in mind, in case I do need you for something random."

"I get it," she tells me, saving me from the awkwardness of this conversation. She gives me a gentle smile, her eyes warm and inviting. "Do you have your schedule for the season?"

"I have our game schedule. Practice is normally the same, but can vary on a rare occasion. I can send you everything scheduled so far. Can I give you event details and any practice changes as I know about them?"

"Of course," she says, nodding eagerly. "I'm at your disposal, so whenever you need me, I can be available. I do plan on going to Sugar Hill Hollow to visit my friend at some point, but I can work that around your schedule."

"If you need any time off or a date doesn't work for you, I can figure something out," I assure her as my mind drifts to a previous conversation with her. The one about her wanting to look for a job. "I don't want this to affect you finding another job or anything like that."

Mia's silent, slowly scanning my face. "Yeah, I'll let you know if anything changes." There's something off about the way she says it, but she immediately moves past it. "Do you want to just email me your schedule?"

"Absolutely," I say, nodding as I pull out my phone. "What's your email address?"

She reads it off to me and I forward her all the

emails sent from the coaching staff with information, when we leave for each away game, return dates and times. There's also a tentative practice schedule and anticipated events email that I send her. "That should be everything," I say, locking the screen. "I wanted to discuss pay with you as well and if you have a contract."

Mia's eyebrows tug together and she lets out a breath. "I don't have a contract, but I can have my father's lawyer draw something together."

"Perfect. It's important to have, especially in a case like this with my schedule being insane." I scratch the back of my neck while trying to figure out how to broach the next subject. "I was paying Gloria $50 an hour. Is that a rate you would be comfortable with? All other expenses would be paid for and I would give you a credit card to use for any purchases for T and the house."

Mia's eyes widen. "Um." She pauses, wetting her lips. "I—um—isn't that a bit much?"

I shake my head at her. "No, not in my opinion. You are taking care of Tella in place of me when I'm not able to. I pay enough to ensure she's receiving the best possible care. It is also a demanding job. You're responsible for and taking care of a child for extended periods of time."

"Okay," she says, her chin tipping with understanding. "Yes, I accept. Do you need to see any of the training I've done or certifications, like CPR?"

"No, I believe you." I roll my arm, glancing at my wrist. "Shit. I forgot we're supposed to go see Gloria before she leaves." I look back at Mia. "Are you able to officially start tomorrow? I will obviously pay you for today, I just want to make sure you're able to start immediately?"

"Yes, of course," she says, rising to her feet as I do. "I'll get in touch with my father's lawyer and have a contract for you then, as well."

"That's great. If you have time after practice again tomorrow, I would like to sit down and go over every-thing for Tella's schedule and what not."

"Absolutely." Mia smiles at me, dipping her chin as we're about to fall in step together, but she abruptly stops. "I need to grab my bag from inside."

"Sure, no problem." She heads back into the house and I walk over to Tella on the driveway. "Hey, T. We have to get ready to go see Miss Gloria."

"Okay." She climbs to her feet, dusting her hands off on her dress, covering it even more with chalk.

"Can you go inside and get changed please?"

"Yeppers," T says, as she skips past me toward the house. "Bye, Mia!"

"Bye, Tella!" Mia calls out to her as they pass one another on the porch, her voice light on the gentle breeze. When Mia reaches me, there's a brief pause in her movement as her gaze meets mine. "I'll see you tomorrow around nine," she says softly, her eyes shim-mering in the sunlight.

I swallow roughly, the smell of lavender and vanilla invading my senses. "See you then."

Mia gives me one last lingering look and I don't miss the way the corners of her lips twitch as she makes her way past me. I can't take my eyes off her as she walks toward her car, the way her legs shift in her tight jeans.

My throat constricts, nostrils flaring as I blow out a frustrated breath. I glance at the house, waiting for Tella, but instead my eyes drift toward the white rocking chairs. I rake my hand through my hair, tugging lightly on the strands as I run them through the gaps between my fingers.

The effects of being alone for so long must finally be getting to me. I've grown accustomed to being alone. I'm no stranger to lying in the dark by myself night after night. Regardless of the deep seeded loneliness, I have no intention of ever finding someone to take Amelia's place.

There isn't a single person on this planet that could ever replace Amelia, that could ever fill the hole she left inside my chest.

But fuck me—sometimes I wish I didn't have to be so alone.

CHAPTER EIGHT

MIA

Lifting up a pair of pants, I fold them over two separate times before tucking them away in my bag. Caleb is leaving later this afternoon to head to the west coast for a week of away games. I'll be staying at his house with Tella while he's gone, so I'm making sure I pack enough clothing that I don't need to come home for anything.

"I wish you were coming with me," Willow says as she comes in with her toiletry bag and drops down onto the bed, her shoulders sagging in disappointment. She's packing to head to Sugar Hill Hollow today.

"I know," I tell her, tucking another change of clothes into my bag. "I wish I were too, but I can always come visit."

She looks up at me and gives a little nod. "Yeah, I know." She lets out a sigh. "Will you let me know when you think you'll have some free time?"

"Of course," I assure her, giving her a small smile.

"Caleb said he will only need me for when he's working and when he's away."

Willow arches a brow. "Girl, you know damned well how insane those hockey schedules are." She snorts, shaking her head. "You might as well just move in with him for how much time you'll be spending there." She pauses, both eyebrows shooting up to her hairline. "Then again, he's pretty hot, so that might not be such a bad thing."

I blow a breath out through my nose, rolling my eyes as I walk over to my best friend. Stopping directly in front of her, I clasp both sides of her face in my hands and tilt her head back to look up at me. "I love you but please do us all a favor and get laid when you get back home. Your sexual frustration is spilling into every part of your life." I chuckle, patting her cheek as I release her and walk back to my bag.

"Is it that obvious?" she questions, tilting her head to the side.

"Yes," I laugh, shaking my head as I finish packing my bag. "It's blatantly obvious."

"Well, shit," she mutters, then chuckles. "Okay. I'll find someone, but I don't want anything more than a casual hookup."

"I'll be sending you all the good dick vibes."

Willow lets out a breath and presses her palms and fingers together, holding them to her nose as she closes her eyes. "Dear Lord, she has spoken. Please send all the good dick."

"Big ones too!" I giggle while zipping shut my bag.

"*Only* big ones. Amen."

"Amen," I concur. My shoulders shake with laughter as Willow opens her eyes and drops her hands. "You're insane and I'm going to miss you."

Willow climbs off the bed, walking over as she wraps her arms around me, pulling me in for a hug. "Okay, well I am only like an hour away, so we are still going to see each other."

"I promise I will come visit as soon as I get my schedule coordinated with Caleb's."

Willow gives me a squeeze then releases me, taking a step back. "I can come visit too, ya know."

"If you don't text me as soon as you get there, we're fighting."

Willow's head tips back, blonde hair falling down along her spine. "Girl, please," she laughs, shaking her head as she looks back at me. "As if we ever go a day without talking.

"Okay, true." I grab my bag and throw it over my shoulder as we both turn toward the door. Willow heads out first with me right behind her. After we drop our bags by the front door, we head into the kitchen where we find my father sitting at the counter.

He adjusts his glasses, tearing his gaze away from his notepad in front of him to look up at me. "Are you heading to Ford's house?"

I clench my jaw and nod my head. I told my father about the arrangement after I came home from Caleb's the other day and had to ask for his lawyer to draw up the contract. He was extremely supportive. While I expected nothing less knowing my dad, I do think his supportiveness has everything to do with the soft spot he has for Caleb Ford.

"Yep. Willow is getting ready to head to Sugar Hill and then I'll be on my way."

My father looks between Willow and me, then he glances at his watch. "I'll walk you both out."

My father clears his throat as he closes the distance across the kitchen, his stride long. He pauses in front of the two of us, towering above. He's well over a foot taller than both Willow and me. He's fit and always has been. He played hockey in his younger years and with the help of a village, he played professional hockey through his twenties before retiring at thirty.

"I'm planning on leaving within the next hour," my father chimes in, his voice gruff. He looks at Willow. "Can you do me a favor and stop by our lake house and check to make sure it hasn't burned down or something? Maybe bring in the mail? Mia can give you the code to get into the house."

"Yeah, sure," she says with a nod and a smile. "And I already have the code."

"Okay, great." My father steps over to me, pulling me in for a hug. "Thank you for doing this for Caleb. I'll text you when we land."

"Okay," I say, hugging him back. "Safe travels."

"Love you," he says, kissing the top of my head before releasing me. "Thanks again, Willow," he says to her, dipping his chin and looking down his nose at her. "Mia can give you my number so you can let me know if there are any issues while I'm gone."

Willow's lips pull into a grin. "Yes, Mr. Landry."

The muscle in my father's jaw twitches and he rolls his eyes. "Drive safe, both of you." Without another word, he turns on his heel and heads up the stairs to the second floor.

I cut my eyes at Willow, and wait until my father's footsteps are out of earshot.

"What?" she asks with a shrug, a coy look on her face.

"I have nothing to say," I huff, rolling my eyes as I turn around and head through the foyer. "I'll text you his number."

"Hey, wait," she calls out after me, grabbing her own suitcase as she follows me through the foyer and out the front door. The wheels of her suitcase clatter as it plunks down each step off the porch. "I'm just messing around, okay? I'm sorry."

I let out a breath. "Yes, I know." I stop at the side of my car and Willow walks over to hers. "Love you. Let me know when you get to the Hollow," I say as I throw my bag across into the passenger seat.

"Love you too," she says as she lifts her suitcase into her trunk.

Willow climbs into her car the same time I enter mine. I unlock my phone, entering in Caleb's address before putting my car in reverse. Willow gives me a wave and blows a kiss in my direction before pulling out of the driveway first. I back out into the street, sliding the gear shifter into drive and head in the opposite direction of my best friend.

Caleb's house is only a short drive from my father's. A little over fifteen minutes. My stomach twists, knotting with anxiety as I get closer to Caleb's house. *I don't know why I'm so nervous. I babysit all the time. But this feels different.*

He gave me the run down and printed out sheets the other day of Tella's activities, school hours, and typical schedule. She has riding lessons twice a week, but she likes to go as often as possible to feed Sodapop carrots and apples. She attends kindergarten in the mornings only, so she has to be picked up around lunchtime.

There isn't anything unusual or out of the ordinary in her schedule. I feel prepared, like I know what to expect. I know Tella well enough and have babysat her a few times now. I've been in Caleb's house enough to know the way he likes things.

None of that is what has the anxiety building in the pit of my stomach.

It's the fact that Caleb Ford is trusting me to be the one to care for his daughter. He's leaving her in my hands while he's hundreds of miles away. I'm the one who's responsible for her—the one he picked to keep her safe and out of harm's way.

And coming from a man who lost the woman he loved and the mother of his child, I can't imagine how hard it must be to put that level of trust in another person.

It's a trust I know I can't break.

CHAPTER NINE
MIA

Tella's pony blows a breath through his nose, his long neck stretching as he drops his head, tucking his muzzle closer to his chest. Tella rises up and down in the saddle, her heels pressing lower than her stirrups as her pony trots past.

"Good job, Estella!" her riding instructor, Magnolia, calls out from where she's standing in the center of the arena. "Do you see the way he tucked his head from just a small amount of pressure on the reins?"

She bobs her head, her black velvet helmet moving as she tucks her bent elbows closer to her ribs. Reaching into the back pocket of my jeans, I pull out my phone. I lift it into the air and swipe open my camera, pressing record.

"All right, Estella, sit in your seat and urge him into a canter."

I watch Tella as she stops posting, tucking her tailbone to sit deeper in her seat.

"Squeeze your legs against his sides and roll your

right wrist while lifting your reins. We want him to pick up the correct lead."

Tella follows Magnolia's instruction, the movements of her body fluid, as if she does this everyday. She's a talented rider for being a little under six years old, but it's obvious that it's just natural for her. A smile tugs at my lips as I remember my days like this as a child. Hours upon hours spent at the stables and on the back of a horse.

I wonder if Caleb would mind if I took Tella to see Hank. He carried me through my showing days in middle and high school, but after he started to have issues with his knees, I decided it was time to retire him, so he could grow old in the pastures. He's twenty now and his health is better than it was, but he's content and happy in one of the meadows by the lake.

He's still technically my horse, but Willow convinced her brother to let me keep him at the farm instead of boarding him at the stable I had him at. Noah takes care of him for me now and I visit when I get the chance.

Tella's pony picks up the correct lead, his inside front leg leading with each stride. Tella holds perfect form, her body rocking with him as they circle around the arena. I keep my phone in front of me, recording and taking pictures of her as she canters past.

"Good, Estella, keep him moving!"

My phone vibrates and Caleb's name flashes at the top of the screen with a message.

CALEB

How are things?

I slowly turn around, flipping the camera to my front one and take a selfie, smiling at the screen with Tella in the background. I send it to Caleb, turning back around to watch her as she slows Sodapop to a trot then back down to a walk.

Just finishing up her lesson.

Good. How is she doing?

She's a natural. How long has she been riding?

I look up, watching Tella ride to the center of the arena to meet with her instructor.

She started taking lessons when she was three.

She looks like she belongs on a horse.

She's happy there, that's for sure.

I was the same way as a kid.

Did you ride?

Tella slides down the left side of her pony, her toes touching the ground before she stands on flat feet next to the gelding. He cranes his neck, turning to her as he nuzzles his nose against her hair. Tella giggles, reaching over to pet his forehead and down his nose. A smile drifts across my mouth.

> I did until college. My horse is an old man now, so he's retired.

> Maybe you can take T to see him. I'm sure she'd love that.

> Heading onto the ice, talk later.

I stare down at my phone, not surprised by his abrupt exit of the conversation, but feeling unsure as to whether or not I'm supposed to respond. Locking my screen, I slide my phone back into my pocket and head over to the gate to meet Tella as she leads Sodapop back toward the stable.

"Did you have fun?" I ask her as I fall into step next to her and her pony. Magnolia closes the gate behind us and follows behind as we pad through the dusty stone path that leads to the back of the barn.

"Yep!" Tella looks over at me with a grin. "Cantering is my favorite."

"It's mine too." I give her a wink. "You looked great out there."

Tella tilts her head to the side. "Do you have a horse?"

"I do," I say, nodding eagerly. "His name is Hank, but he's retired so I don't ride him anymore. I was telling your daddy about him and he said you might want to go see him sometime."

"Oh, yes! Please. I would love that!"

I chuckle, pausing to slide open the barn door for

Tella and Sodapop to slip inside. "Maybe we can go some afternoon after school. He loves apples, so we can stop and get some to take to him."

"Sodapop loves apples too." She walks past the tack room, leading him into the wash stall. He spins on his hindquarters as she turns him around and stops in the center of the cross-ties. "Maybe we can get him some too."

"We sure can," I tell her, smiling brightly. "Do you want some help untacking him?"

Tella nods eagerly. "Yep! I can't do his girth by myself yet."

I walk over to Tella, handing her Sodapop's halter and lead rope as she takes off his bridle. He bends his head down so she can slip the halter over his ears and Tella holds onto the lead rope as I undo the girth and remove the saddle from his back. Tella tells me where it goes in the tack room, so I carry everything for her, before coming back to the wash stall.

"Are the two of you okay in here?" Magnolia calls out as she walks down the aisle. "Great job today, Estella."

"Thank you, Miss Magnolia," Tella smiles at her. "Did you know Mia has a horse too?"

"Oh really?" Magnolia says softly, tilting her head to the side as her gaze meets mine. She looks to be in her early thirties and it's impossible to miss her pregnant stomach as she absentmindedly runs her hand over it. "Well, I think you're probably in great hands then. Let me know if you need anything."

"Can you hold him for me?" Tella asks as Magnolia walks away.

"Of course," I say, taking the lead rope as she hands it to me. Tella grabs a brush and gets to work smoothing out his coat. She has to get a step stool so she can reach his back. Sodapop presses his nose against my stomach and I laugh, lifting my hand to scratch the whorl marking in the center of his forehead. He lets out a sigh, his head sinking as he lifts one back foot onto the toe of his hoof and relaxes.

"Good boy, Sody," Tella coos, patting the side of his neck before kissing his cheek. She reaches for the lead rope. "We can put him in his stall now and then we have to feed him."

"Lead the way!" I step out of the way, motioning for her to go ahead of me. Tella leads Sodapop down the aisle to the last stall on the left, where she takes him inside, removes his halter and comes back through the door.

Tella shows me the feed room and we mix his food before pouring it into his feed bin together and dropping a flake of hay in the rack in his stall. "That's it," she tells me before turning back to her pony. "See you in two days, Sodapop. Love you!"

He lifts his head and blows out a breath, almost as if he's responding to her. There's a softness, a tenderness in his eyes as he stares at her, dropping his nose back into his feed bin.

I turn to Tella and say, "All right, T, let's head home."

Tella walks beside me as we slip out of the barn. She

moves closer to me and her warm hand slides into mine, curling her little fingers around my hand. I glance down at her, watching as she gets a little bob in her step, half skipping. I bite back a smile, my footsteps matching hers as we head to my car together.

———

Later that night, just as I'm getting Tella tucked away in bed, my phone starts to ring in the front pocket of my sweatshirt. I pull it out and glance at the screen. It's Caleb.

"Hello?"

"Hey," he says, sounding slightly breathless. "Sorry about earlier. We're heading in to get ready for the game, but I wanted to say goodnight to T."

A warmth floods my chest. "Yes, of course." I pull the phone away from my ear, holding it out to Tella. "It's your dad. I'm going to go brush my teeth while you talk to him."

"Okay," Tella says, taking the phone from me as I walk toward the door. "Hi, Daddy!"

I make my way down the hall to the bathroom and get myself ready for bed. I thought it would feel weird, staying at his house like this, but it really doesn't. I think it helps that Caleb is not here. He doesn't make me uncomfortable, not in a bad way at least.

I'm not blind, nor am I immune to the man. His eyes are a striking grey, his jaw bone perfectly chiseled with a straight nose that leads to his perfect, subtly plump lips. I'm allowed to think my boss is attractive, even if it's not reciprocated. Based on Caleb's comment about not dating, I can't help but wonder if he's dated anyone since his wife has passed.

I've never been in his situation. I can't imagine what it must be like to try and move on, but then again, maybe he doesn't want to. Maybe he wants to live with the ghost of her for the rest of his life.

And who am I to really judge?

I finish up in the bathroom and head into Tella's room, just as she's finishing up her conversation with Caleb. She says goodnight to him, a sleepy smile on her lips as she hands the phone to me.

"He wants to talk to you," she says around a yawn as she stretches in her bed before nestling against her pillows. "Goodnight, Mia."

"Night, T."

I pat the top of her head, then put the phone up to my ear as I walk back out of her room, leaving the door ajar behind me. "Hey again."

"Hey," Caleb says, his voice soft, yet gruff. "Sorry about earlier."

"It's okay," I tell him, my footsteps light as I head down the hallway and into my room. I gently push the door behind me, leaving it ajar like Tella's as I slip into bed. "You're supposed to be worrying about work, not what's going on here."

Caleb is silent for a moment. "I know," he says quietly followed by another beat of silence. "It's just hard for me sometimes."

"I understand." I swallow roughly over the lump in my throat. "I can't pretend to know how it feels for you, but just know I understand to a degree. My father hated leaving me too."

"Was it just the two of you?"

"Yeah," I admit, letting out a soft breath as I pull the covers up over my body and settle in against the pillows. "My mother died when I was born. They were young so he had a lot of growing up to do, on top of being terrified of losing me too."

"I'm sorry," he says, his voice barely audible. "For your loss."

"It's okay," I tell him with a half shrug even though he can't see me. "I never got to meet her so it wasn't as bad for me as it was for him."

"Similar to Tella," he murmurs. "Amelia died before T's first birthday. She'll never remember her."

My chest constricts, my throat tightening as the sadness seeps through the phone. "I'm sorry," I say, my voice cracking around the words. I swallow hard, closing my eyes. There's nothing else I can really say. Nothing is going to change the truth behind his words. "She might not remember her, but that doesn't mean you can't keep her memory alive."

Caleb doesn't respond at first and I let the silence stretch, knowing there isn't much else I can say to comfort him. He lost her five years ago and I'm sure he's heard it all from everyone else.

He clears his throat and finally says, "I should probably go. Your father is going to be looking for me soon."

"Don't want that," I laugh quietly, opening my eyes to stare at the wall across from the bed. "Good luck tonight."

"Thanks," he says, his voice hoarse. "Goodnight, Mia."

"Goodnight."

I end the call, but just as I'm rolling over to put my phone on the nightstand, it dings as a message comes through.

CALEB

Thank you, Mia.

The corners of my mouth twitch.

You're welcome.

Night.

Goodnight, Caleb.

I read over his messages once more, feeling a tug on my heart as I lock the screen and set it down on the nightstand. He's a broken man who lost himself when he lost his wife. There's no doubt in my mind that a piece of him died the day she did.

But that doesn't mean his life isn't still worth living. He just needs to find himself—to find that spark that breathes life back into his heart.

He just needs someone to show him.

CHAPTER TEN
CALEB

It's a little after dinner time when I'm pulling into the driveway after getting back to Aston from almost a week of being away. I used to love going out of town. Traveling to different cities to play in different arenas was always one of my favorite things to do, until Estella was born. Now, it's my least favorite thing.

Honestly, I love the sport and the money makes it worth it, but some days I consider retiring early. I'm not sure what I would do without hockey, but I know I would figure it out. Just like every other season of life, I would settle into it.

Not bothering to pull into the garage, I park the car in the driveway, then grab my duffle bag from the passenger's seat and climb out. The house is lit up inside and a smile pulls on my lips. Tella normally goes to bed around eight or eight thirty and I'm getting home just about an hour before she should be settling in for the night.

I unlock the front door, turn the knob, and push it open. The aroma of brownies immediately infiltrates my senses, permeating from the kitchen. Laughter and singing mingles with the soft sound of music playing. My curiosity is piqued, I'm drawn to it. I kick off my shoes, drop my bag on the floor at the bottom of the stairs, and follow the sound of Mia and Tella.

My footsteps are quiet and light as I walk over the threshold into the kitchen, and I immediately pause. Neither of them notice me and my heart constricts in my chest, my throat tightens with a lump. Warmth spreads, seeping beneath my ribcage.

Mia's back is turned toward me and she holds her arm out, bending it slightly as she holds Tella's hand above her head. Tella lets out a string of laughter, her hair swinging around her as she spins on her sock-clad toes on the floor. Her apron reaches down toward her knees, fanning out as she spins once more.

Mia's hair is pulled back in a messy bun on top of her head. I allow a moment for my gaze to wander. It travels down the length of her body, over her yoga pants, to her feet before trailing up to the side of her face as she turns slightly.

Her cheeks are tinted pink, her head dipping as she sings the next line of the song, belting it to Tella. Tella laughs, releasing Mia's hand as the two of them start to shake their hips to the beat. She's so carefree, so pure. I watch her in wonderment, leaning against the doorframe as I continue to go unnoticed.

She's beautiful.

Mia moves away from Tella, moving her entire body

as she lifts her arms above her head, and slowly turns in my direction. Her eyes are half closed and as they drift across the room, they flash to meet mine. She stops in place, her eyes widening as her mouth falls agape.

A chuckle rumbles in my chest and I push away from the doorjamb, fully entering the kitchen. "Hi, ladies."

Mia's face brightens and a nice shade of pink breaks out across her cheeks. "Hi," she half croaks out, pushing stray hairs away from her face. There must have been some flour on the back of her hand because now it's a white streak across her forehead.

"Daddy!" Tella calls out, breezing past Mia as she rushes right toward me. I squat down so I can slide my hands under her arms and lift her into the air, spinning her around. She giggles, her feet flying around before I stop. I pull her close to me, burying my face in the crook of her neck, reveling in the familiar smell of her. "I missed you."

"I missed you too, Tella," I murmur, kissing the side of her face before squeezing her against me. I shift her to my hip and she wraps her arms around my neck, laying her head against my shoulder. I glance at Mia and find her watching us with puppy dog eyes—round and soft, filled with emotion. I swallow hard over the lump lodged in my own throat. "What are you guys making?"

"Mia loves to bake, so we made brownies!" Tella exclaims, lifting her head as she wiggles in my arms. I release her, carefully letting her slide down until her feet hit the ground. She grabs my hand and tugs, pulling me over toward the stove. "Look!" She points at the glass door.

Mia comes beside us as I half bend down. As she reaches past, her shirt lifts up her side and her hip brushes against my shoulder. My breath catches and I immediately look at the stove as the light flickers on.

On the middle rack is a pan of brownies that look like they're about ready to come out. "They look delicious," I say, slowly standing back upright as my gaze collides with Mia's.

"Can I have one before bed, Daddy?" Tella questions me, tugging on my hand again.

"Of course," I smile at her, patting the top of her head.

"Can I watch TV?"

"Yep," I say, nodding at her. "Take off your apron first, though."

Tella pulls the string, whips it off over her head, and tosses it onto the chair at the counter before disappearing into the living room.

I slowly spin on my heel to face Mia. "I hope she was good for you."

"Oh, yes," she says, a smile stretching across her lips as she nods eagerly. "She's a little spitfire, but she's fun. She really is a great kid and I enjoy hanging out with her."

I stare at Mia, my eyes slowly bouncing back and forth between hers before trailing up to the flour on her forehead. "You have a bit of flour on your face," I tell her, wiping my own forehead to show her.

She rolls her lips between her teeth, lifting her hand

to wipe it away. "Did I get it?" she asks me as she brushes half of it away.

"There's still a little bit there."

Mia wipes at it again, missing once more, leaving the tail end of the streak just above her eyebrow. "How about now?"

I shake my head, closing the distance between us. The room shrinks as I enter her space, my toes nearing closer to hers. She tilts her head back to look at me. My heart stumbles over itself, my breath quickening as I lift my hand to the side of her face. She draws her bottom lip between her teeth, her nostrils flaring as I run the pad of my thumb just above her eyebrow. Her eyes fall closed at my touch.

A shiver trails down my spine as I brush away the flour, her skin warm and soft beneath my fingertip. Mia releases her lip as my touch moves down her cheek to her jaw and lingers there, her lips parting slightly as a ragged breath escapes her. My throat bobs as I swallow hard, the muscle in my jaw tightening.

"There," I murmur, my voice low and hoarse as my hand lingers along the side of her face. Her eyes slowly search mine and I pick out the three flecks of amber in her left eye, peppered around her dilating pupil. I could get lost in her gaze.

The timer on the stove begins to beep, ripping me away from the moment. I drop my hand in a rush, and take two large steps away from her in a rush. Confusion and conflict engulf me. Mia's eyes are wide and she spins on her heel, grabbing an oven mitt from the counter. I turn away from her, my cheeks puffing out as I blow out a slow breath.

Mia is six years younger than me.

She is my nanny and her father is my coach.

There are so many things that are wrong about this moment, but most importantly . . .

She's not Amelia.

I swore I'd never replace her.

Tella comes sprinting into the kitchen, sliding across the floor in her fuzzy socks and stops beside Mia. "They smell so good. Can I have mine now?"

"Not yet," Mia tells her, her voice barely audible over the sound of the blood rushing through my veins. "I have to go, but your daddy can cut them after they cool a bit."

I haven't slept with anyone since Amelia. I tried dating last year and it was an absolute disaster. It's only human and natural to feel lonely, to feel the deprivation of the comfort of another, but what the fuck is wrong with me?

I slowly turn back around to face Mia and Tella, guilt flooding me as I catch the look on Mia's face. There's embarrassment etched in her features, but there's something else lingering beneath it. The inside corners of her eyebrows are turned downwards and she gives me that stare again, with her eyes round and soft.

"Mia." My voice is strained as I speak her name. I clench my teeth together as a myriad of emotions rush through me. I'm so goddamn conflicted, but this can't happen. I will *not* let this happen. "Thank you for watching T. I've got it from here."

Her throat bobs and she gives me a curt nod. "I just need to grab my bag."

"Okay. We will see you tomorrow."

She stares back at me, her expression void of any emotion as she straightens her spine. "Have a good night."

She drops her gaze from mine, skirting past me as she heads toward the hallway. Just as she's about to step through the doorway, I find myself glancing over my shoulder at her, calling out after her.

"Mia."

She pauses, looking back at me. "Yeah?"

I swallow over the lump in my throat. "Drive safe."

Her eyes linger once more as she gives me another nod before disappearing down the hallway. I let out a breath, my lungs deflating as I turn back toward the stove, my eyes traveling over the counter. Tella sits down on the floor, rubbing her eyes as she yawns. The sound of Mia's footsteps are quiet as she comes back down the stairs and I close my eyes as I hear the front door open and close.

A part of me regrets the way I just iced her out, but it's for her own good.

She'll thank me one day.

I reach for the knife block on the counter when I see a bag of flour she forgot to put away. Instinctively, I pick it up, carrying it over to the pantry, when I realize it isn't a bag of flour from my house. My eyebrows pull together and I read the front—certified gluten free version. I pull open the pantry door, my eyes scanning the snacks that I told her to help herself to and it doesn't look like she's touched any.

My eyebrows pull together and I find a spot on the shelf for the almond flour before heading back to the stove. I grab a knife, cutting the brownie to hand a piece to Tella. "How does it taste?"

"Good," Tella says, nodding as she chews and swallows a piece. "Mia said they're different from regular brownies because she can't eat gruben but she promised they wouldn't taste bad."

"Gruben?" I question her, chuckling softly. "You mean gluten."

Tella nods again. "Yeah, that's what she said."

I grab one of the brownies, popping it into my mouth as I glance back at the pantry, making a mental note. Whether it's an allergy or not, it's clear she can't eat it and I need to make sure she has options here for when she stays.

Mia might not be my responsibility, but while she's here taking care of my daughter, the least I can do is make sure she's taken care of too.

CHAPTER ELEVEN
MIA

Tella stares at me, eyebrows lowering in judgement as she scrunches her nose. "Aren't you going to wear a jersey too?"

I stare back at her, my eyebrows mimicking hers. I grab the bottom hem of my crewneck sweatshirt, pulling it away from my body to double check that I did in fact grab an Aston Archers one. "I didn't bring any of my jerseys with me."

Tella clicks her tongue at me, shaking her head as her eyes scan my sweatshirt. She glances down at her kid's sized jersey with her last name and her father's number on her back. "You should have brought one."

"I'll grab one next time I go home, how about that?"

She chews on her tongue, giving me a satisfied nod. "Can we get ice cream on the way?"

"No," I tell her, cocking a perfectly arched brow. I push open the front door, holding it for Tella as she walks through the doorway. "But you can after you eat dinner at the game."

Tella lets out a long, exasperated and exaggerated sigh before heading down the front steps off the porch. I pull the door shut behind me, making sure to lock it before meeting Tella in the driveway beside my car. I open the backdoor for her and she climbs onto her booster seat, pulling her seatbelt across her body.

I double check, making sure she's strapped in securely before heading to the front of the car and sliding in behind the steering wheel. "All right, let's hit the road, Tells."

She smiles at me through the rearview mirror, giving her feet a little kick and claps her hands together. I smile back at her as I turn on the car and slowly back out of the driveway. I ease my car onto the street, glancing back at Caleb's house as I move the gear shifter into drive.

The two white rocking chairs on the front porch catch my eye and I pause, focusing in on the one to the left. It rocks slightly, almost as if someone just got up from it. I stare at it for a moment, screwing my lips to the side. I don't remember touching it as I walked past and I didn't see Tella either. It must just be from the wind.

I blink twice, my eyes adjusting once more and now it's still. I clear my throat, shaking my head as I look back into the rearview mirror at Tella. She's staring out the window, not paying attention to me and she giggles softly as she waves goodbye to the house.

I look back at it once more, an unexplainable warmth washing over me before I press on the gas, easing the car away from their house. Tella starts to hum along to the song that plays quietly through the speakers, so I turn it up, letting the sound of the music and her little voice signing along carry us to the arena.

———

"Come on, Mia!" Tella says, tugging on my hand as we make our way down to the area where the players' families can gather to watch warmups. Nova, Riley, Hadley, and Andi are already standing along the glass, all of their kids watching the guys as they come out onto the ice.

I pick up the pace, letting Tella pull me off to the left, where there's an open spot along the glass. She releases my hand, glancing around as she looks for something. "What are you looking for?"

"I can't see," she explains. Her little fingers grip the edge of the boards as she presses up on her tip toes in an attempt to look out at the ice. Her head barely reaches over.

"Come here," I say, reaching for her as she spins back around to face me. She instinctively lifts her arms and I scoop her up, holding her on my hip as she wraps her legs around my waist. She turns her body in my arms, pointing out at the ice as Caleb steps on.

"Look, Mia!" She waggles her finger out to Caleb as he grabs a water bottle, tilting his head back to squirt some in his mouth. My gaze is transfixed on his elongated neck. His throat bobs as he swallows back the liquid and pushes his hair up and out of his face. "There's my daddy!"

"I see him, Tells." She waves as soon as he looks in our direction. It's obvious when he finds her in the family crowd behind the glass because his expression softens. The corners of his eyes crinkle and the apples of his cheeks lift as a small grin crests his lips.

He leaves the bench, his blades digging into the ice as he skates around in a circle, looping over to us while pausing along the glass. He comes up to it and lifts his gloved hand to the glass. Tella lifts her delicate hand and presses it against this side of the glass, as if their hands are touching. He pulls away, pointing at his eye, then at his chest and then at her as he mouths "I love you."

Tella does it back to him, finishing up with swinging her arms wide as she yells more.

Caleb laughs, his soft eyes lingering on hers before he turns them to me. The air vanishes from my lungs in an instant. His stare penetrates my soul, his eyelids lowering slightly as his lips part. My heart stumbles over itself in my chest as he watches me for a moment, the muscle in his jaw tightening as he closes his mouth.

He rolls his lips between his teeth, his tongue darting out to wet them as he gives me a gentle nod. He looks back at Tella, winking at her before he skates back to the center of the ice where the other guys are.

"Did you know he's the best player?"

I stifle back a grin and a laugh. "Is he, really? I had no idea."

It's no surprise that he is the star center and captain for the Aston Archers. I've spent years listening to my father talk about the potential in Caleb Ford and I've had the pleasure of hearing all about how he's been living up to expectations, just as they had hoped.

I've been watching Caleb's career from the sidelines without him even knowing.

Warm-ups finish and we head back down the tunnel to the family room to grab another snack. Tella grabs a bag of chips and turns to look at me. "Can we go back to the glass to watch?"

"I don't know if we're allowed," I tell her, glancing around the room to see if there's anyone to ask, but it's fairly empty already. Everyone has already headed up to the suite to watch the game. There's only two minutes left until the first period starts, so we either need to head upstairs or try to sneak back down the tunnel.

I purse my lips, looking at Tella and back at the clock above the massive TV screen. *It's better to ask for forgiveness than to ask for permission.* A smile pulls my lips and I shrug. "Come on," I say, holding my hand out for Tella's. "We'll go find out."

Tella slides her small hand in mine, giggling as we head out of the room and back down the tunnel together. We slip through a crowd of people and I'm not sure if they notice us or not. I find a spot along the glass, tucking in close to the side of the tunnel as I lift Tella up to my side once more so she can see.

She holds onto her bag of chips, her eyes glued on the center of the ice as we watch her father line up for the face off. He gets into position and the ref stands beside both the centers, time suspended before he drops the puck. He releases it and it falls to the ice, Caleb and the other center battling for it. Caleb wins the face off and sends it back to Lincoln.

The game moves quickly and we watch play as it moves down the ice toward their offensive zone, before the puck gets overturned in the zone. The other team takes possession and one of their guys manages to break away. He heads down the ice while Caleb and Hayes put their heads down, skating furiously after him.

He's a good three strides ahead of them and my heart stalls in my chest as Caleb tries to poke the puck away from him. There's another offensive player waiting by the net and he gets the puck, tucking it right in the corner, flipping it right over Rowan's leg pad.

The light behind the net lights up and the horn sounds through the arena. Rowan doesn't look at anyone as he scoops the puck and tosses it to the ref. Caleb and the rest of the guys look tense as the other team celebrates, the one who scored skating past the glass.

Tella leans forward, lifting her arm as she raises her middle finger and shows it to the other guys while sticking out her tongue. "Losers!"

"Tella!" I scold her, attempting to push her hand down, but I miss and she raises it higher. "Put your hand down."

She whips her head to the side and scrunches up her face. "Why? They scored."

"We can't just give people the middle finger. Do you even know what that means?"

She purses her lips. "Duh. It means 'you suck'."

"Not exactly," I chuckle, shaking my head at her. "It's not a nice thing to do."

"Does it mean I have to put a dollar in the swear jar?"

A smile breaks out across my lips and I bite back my grin, shaking my head at her. "I won't tell anyone about it."

Her face lights up. "Pinky promise?" She narrows her eyes as she holds out her pinky to me.

I curl mine around hers, sealing the deal of our little secret. "Pinky promise."

"Cross your heart?"

"Cross my heart," I tell her, nodding as I squeeze her little finger tighter. "But let's not do it again, okay?"

She lets out a sigh in resignation. "Okay, fine."

CHAPTER TWELVE
CALEB

"Who taught your daughter to give people the middle finger?"

I lift my head from looking down at my plate and pull my fork from my mouth. I lock eyes with Mia through my phone screen, tilting my head to the side as I chew a piece of fish. "I'm sorry, what?"

Mia and I hopped on FaceTime thirty minutes ago so I could talk to Tella before she went to bed . . . and well, that was at least fifteen minutes prior to this very moment. I like to check in with the two of them while I'm on the road and it's been three days since I left. I didn't plan on staying on the phone with Mia, but we just fell into a comfortable conversation that didn't feel right to end so abruptly.

"I meant to tell you before you left, but I forgot to," Mia explains as she crawls into the bed in my guest room. "Your last home game—Tella was giving the middle finger to players on the other team."

I snort, half choking on a mouthful of food before I

swallow it down. Laughter spills from my lips and I catch a questioning look from some of the other guys as they sit down with their plates. I know it's an unusual sight for them to see—me sitting down to eat with my phone propped in front of me and my headphones on.

"Did you teach her that?" Mia questions me, cocking a perfectly arched brow. "I promised her I wouldn't tell you, so you have to promise me that you won't say anything."

"Seems like a lot of secrets," I muse aloud, a playful note in my tone. "And no, it wasn't me who taught her. It was Carson."

Mia's face softens and she lets out a soft laugh, shaking her head at me. "Honestly, I'm not so sure I'm that surprised to hear that. It seems like something he would do."

I nod, chewing another bite of food before swallowing it. I drop my fork onto my empty plate, running a hand through my hair as I let my eyes roam over Mia's features. "It was before he knew about Matteo and he was the cool uncle. He's definitely changed, now that he's a parent."

"I would hope so," she says, her voice quiet. "So, for the record, I should be telling Tella that she shouldn't be giving them the middle finger, right?"

I bite on the inside of my cheek. "I mean, as her father, yes, absolutely. As a competitive professional athlete," I pause and shrug, a sheepish grin lifting my lips. "She's not hurting anyone or anything."

Mia's eyes widen at me. "Caleb!"

"What?" I feign innocence. "It's true. She's not doing

anything *that* bad." I give her a look before my expression softens and I give in. "Okay, yes, please stop her from doing that. I know she already has a bit of an attitude and I don't want her to be that kid."

Mia gives me a look of satisfaction as she dips her chin. "Thank you."

I stare at her for a moment. She drops her gaze from me. She's staring off to the side, looking for something as a frown tugs her lips downward. "What's wrong?"

"I forgot my water downstairs," she says as she climbs out of bed. "I meant to grab it when I came up here but it must have slipped my mind."

She exits the bedroom, slipping into the hall and heading downstairs. She's quiet as she makes her way into the kitchen and as she flicks on the overhead light, it illuminates her face, her focus is past me.

"Why can't I remember where I put it?"

"Try and retrace your steps, maybe?" I suggest, adjusting in my chair as Carson, Lincoln, and Nash come into the room. I came to eat a little earlier than them tonight. I catch Carson's gaze from across the room as he raises an eyebrow. "Hold on a second."

I grab my phone, holding it up to show him as I point at it and rise to my feet. I'm not paying attention to what Mia is doing as I exit the dining room and step out into the hallway, ducking into a corner where no one else is. There's a small bench and as I'm sitting down, I hear Mia's voice come through the speakers again.

"Caleb, what is all this?"

I'm silent for a moment, looking back at the screen

to find her standing in the pantry. A warmth blossoms in my chest and my stomach does a flip. I know exactly what she's talking about. I just don't know how it took her this long to notice. "You left a bag of gluten free flour there." I pause, my throat bobbing as I swallow roughly. "T told me that gluten makes you sick."

Her eyes flash back to mine. "Your pantry is full of gluten free snacks."

I suck in a breath. "I told you that all food and stuff would be provided for you. You couldn't eat the snacks I had in the house, so now you can."

Her eyes start to get glassy with tears as they slowly search mine. "This is too much."

"It's really nothing." I pause, letting out another shallow breath. I'm not sure why there's anxiety lingering in the pit of my stomach, but I immediately shove it away. "If there are certain ones you would prefer, please let me know. Honestly, from all I've read about gluten, I think T and I could benefit from not eating it too."

"You didn't have to do all this," she tells me, her voice soft, dropping even lower. "I don't mind bringing my own snacks. Honestly, I'm used to it."

I screw my lips to the side, absentmindedly chewing on the inside of my cheek as I shake my head once. "It's the least I can do."

A soft smile lifts the corners of her lips. "Well thank you. I really do appreciate it."

"Do you have an allergy?"

"I have celiac disease," she explains, pursing her lips. "Gluten basically destroys my body. It damages my intestines and makes me feel like crap for at least a week." She pauses, giving me a shrug. "I won't bore you with all the symptoms, but I have to avoid it completely, along with any possibilities of cross-contamination."

"How can cross-contamination happen?"

"I have to have my food cooked separately from anything that could contain gluten. No shared fryers and essentially no touching of gluten products. Like if someone makes a sandwich with a knife and then uses the same knife on a gluten free meal, that's cross-contaminating."

Damn. I did a little bit of research, but I didn't know she had celiac disease at the time, so I didn't read all of that. I store the information in my brain, knowing I need to do some more research to make sure she's as safe as she can be while in my home.

"I'm sorry you've had to deal with that," I tell her, my voice low as I frown. "That sounds like it could be quite challenging to live with and to comfortably eat in public spaces."

She lets out a soft laugh, shrugging her shoulders. "Yeah, it is what it is. I'm used to it now and I feel so much better not eating it." She lets out a sigh. "It creates a lot of trust issues with eating at restaurants. I've been accidentally glutened before and it's horrible."

"Well, if I can prevent that from happening at my house, I will."

She gives me a tender smile. "Thank you, Caleb. I appreciate that kindness more than you'll ever understand. A lot of people don't understand the actual damage it does inside your intestines and sometimes think I'm just dramatic by being so particular about food."

"Absolutely not," I say, a sharpness in my tone as irritation pricks my nerves. "You have to take care of yourself and advocate for yourself too."

"You're so right," she says, her chin dipping as her eyes meet mine. "No one else is going to look out for me, except for me."

Something about that statement jabs at my chest. Mia is an adult and can take care of herself. She seems to have a good relationship with her father, so it's not like she doesn't have anyone. I just can't help but wonder where that comment comes from.

Who or what makes her feel like she has no one but herself?

My throat constricts as I let my mind wander further. Mia comes from a single parent household, with a father who has a demanding job and has since she was a child. Even though they're close, is there some wedge between them? Does she feel like he's unavailable to her, even though he's in her life?

Will Tella feel the same way when she gets older?

"I think I'm going to try and get some sleep," Mia says, breaking through my spiraling thoughts. "I plan on staying up later tomorrow night so I can catch your game."

"I'll call tomorrow before dinner."

"Okay," she says softly, her eyes searching mine through the screen as the kitchen light flickers off. Her delicate features glow with the illumination from her phone. "Goodnight, Caleb."

"Goodnight, Mia."

Her gaze lingers a second longer before she ends the call. I don't move for a few moments as I stare at my phone screen, now void of her beautiful face. Mia is nothing more than my nanny, but I feel a weird need to protect her, to make sure she's safe. I'm sure it just has to do with her being like an extension of Tella.

If she's safe, so is my daughter.

Surely, there's nothing more behind it than that . . .

CHAPTER THIRTEEN
MIA

Tella runs around the perimeter of the pool, holding a big beach ball above her head. She lets out a giggle when her foot slips as she leans around the corner. She catches herself, then her little legs continue to move as her feet keep shuffling.

"Be careful, T!" I yell at her from where I'm wading in the shallow end, pushing a raft in front of me. Caleb's pool is heated and since it's a warm afternoon for the fall, Tella insisted we get in because her dad will be closing it soon.

She wasn't sure what that meant or when it would be, but she knew that Caleb tends to do it before Halloween.

Tella slows down to a walk, although her strides are elongated and there's a small bounce to her step, as if it's taking everything she has to not break out into a jog again. She makes her way back to the shallow end and tosses the ball to me. I let go of my raft, catching the ball as she jumps directly into the shallow end.

Somehow, her tiny body creates quite the wave that sends my raft floating farther away from me. I turn my body against the water, although some ends up splashing me in the face anyways. I wipe the water away, turning back to her to make sure she comes up for air like she's supposed to.

Tella swims underwater across the pool, coming directly to me before she stops and pops to the surface. "Want me to go get your raft? I'm a really good swimmer. Daddy had me take lessons so I can swim in the deep end."

A laugh spills from my lips and I feel my expression softening. "Sure. Let's see your skills."

Tella takes a deep breath before plunging back beneath the surface. She doesn't get very deep and her legs kick against the water, splashing all over the place as she swims. Her torso wiggles as her legs kick, her arms moving in a sweeping motion as she heads over to the raft. I watch her as she bobs up, reaching for the raft and half climbs onto it.

"How did I do, Mia? Did I do good?"

"You did a great job, T!" I clap my hands and smile brightly at her. The sun shines down upon us with not a single cloud in sight. "You really are a strong swimmer."

"Thanks," she says. Huffing and puffing, she kicks her feet to head back over to me. She gives the raft a one-handed shove toward me before releasing it. "Here you go."

"Thank you, T." The rustling of the gate lock on the side of the house pulls my attention. It opens up and

Matteo comes running through the backyard, letting out a holler as he jumps right into the pool.

"Matteo Vincent Ford!" Andi calls after him, juggling her drink, their bag, and the gate. She ends up kicking it closed with her foot, shaking her head in disapproval as she walks over to the pool deck. She drops their things onto the table and kicks her shoes off. "You get out right now so I can put sunscreen on you."

Climbing onto my raft, I bite back a grin as Matteo climbs out of the pool. "Hey, Andi."

She looks at me, puffing up her cheeks to blow out a breath while rolling her eyes. "Hey, Mia."

When Tella decided she wanted to swim, the second question from her was whether or not Matteo could come swim too. I texted Andi and thankfully they had nothing going on this afternoon, so they headed over after having lunch.

I texted Caleb to let him know, not that I think he would actually care, but it felt like the right thing to do since this is his house. They're traveling today, so he didn't answer, but I didn't want him to come home to a pool full of people.

Andi quickly helps Matteo dry off, smears him with sunscreen, and sends him back into the pool with Tella. Then she pulls off her coverup and slides her sunshades over her eyes before stepping into the water. "Oh, this feels nice," she says, smiling as she nods her head in approval. "I know Caleb tends to keep it warm, but with it being later in the season I wasn't sure if the temperature would hold up or not."

"I honestly didn't expect it to be this warm," I say as

she grabs another raft floating in the pool. "Then again, I didn't expect it to feel like this in the fall either."

"What a weird day," she agrees. "I'll take the weather though."

"Same."

"So, how are things going here? Is Caleb being nice to you?"

I stare at her for a moment, tilting my head to the side. "It's been going really well. Is he normally not nice?"

Andi chuckles and waves her hand dismissively. "That's not what I meant. Cale can just be a bit . . . abrasive sometimes. Actually, I don't know if that's the right word. He's just a bit closed off at times and can come across as standoff-ish."

I slowly nod my head in understanding. I know what she's talking about, although my interactions with Caleb haven't really been like that. "He's been fine. He's been very kind and nice to me."

"Well, that's good," Andi tells me. "If he's ever not nice, you let me know and I'll beat his ass."

"I don't think that will be necessary," I say, laughing. Her stern face cracks and she laughs with me. "The Caleb I knew before working for him was different. I wouldn't say he was cold before, but he was never very friendly."

"Oh yeah, that's typical Caleb Ford. It's like he's allergic to forming any kinds of bonds or relationships with people," she says, half muttering in disapproval. "I mean, then again, I guess anyone who lost their significant other would probably act like that."

Sadness pricks at my chest and I tilt my head back, closing my eyes against the sun. "Yeah, I think that's a normal reaction, although you would think at some point that would change."

Andi's silent for a moment. "Maybe it's changing now. I haven't been around him much lately, but perhaps he's lightening up." She stares at me through her sunglasses. "Maybe you're changing him."

"Maybe he's changing," I agree, my voice trailing off as I run my fingers through the water, feeling it sliding along my fingertips. "But I doubt it's from me."

"Oh, please, Mia. He's a broken man, but he's not dumb nor is he blind." Andi tilts her head to the side. "You're hot, living in his guest room, and taking care of his daughter while he's away. The Caleb I know wouldn't give two shits about another woman. Gloria was safe for him because she was old enough to be his mother, but you on the other hand . . ."

"He's my boss, Andi."

She raises a brow. "So, what? What is he going to do? Report you to HR?" She lets out a chuckle. "Honey, he *is* HR."

I laugh with her, shaking my head. "I'll admit, he's extremely attractive and probably everything I'd look for in a man, except for one thing."

"What's that?" she questions me, drifting close enough that our blow-up floats bump into one another.

"He's emotionally unavailable."

I haven't been trying to dissect Caleb because I know he's so emotionally closed off. I know better than to get involved with someone like that again—but then again, this isn't even a situation where I should be thinking about getting involved with someone else.

"That can always change," she muses.

Caleb Ford is my boss and nothing more.

Never mind the fact that he's the literal image of perfection.

Since I started working for him, I've been seeing a different side to him. A warm, kind, and caring side. It's clear he cares about his daughter, she's at the fore-front of every decision he makes, but there's more than just that. He stocked his entire pantry with gluten free snacks because he knows that's all I can eat.

I'm not sure what that says, but it feels like it's a little more than just caring about his daughter.

"Why didn't I get the invite to the pool party at my own house?"

My heart stutters in my chest as I hear his voice carrying across the gentle fall breeze. I quickly move to sit upright, my raft teeter tottering beneath my weight as I shift quickly. "Oh shit," I say a little louder than intended as I catch myself before I fall in. I shoot a look at Caleb, my eyes rounding as I press my lips into a straight line.

Caleb's gaze lands on mine and he arches a brow. "That's a dollar for the swear jar, pup."

Pup?

"Pup?" Andi says, whipping her head to the side to look at him.

Caleb looks between the two of us, lifting his shoul-ders before letting them fall. There's a tint of red creeping across his cheeks and his throat bobs. "Sometimes her eyes look like a puppy dog's."

"Daddy!" Tella calls his name, splashing her way through the water into the shallow end. "Are you going to get in?"

"Yeah, Uncle Cale! Jump in!"

Caleb bites back a grin, mischief dancing in his expression. "I don't know . . ." His voice trails off as he slowly starts to walk around the pool. I don't miss when he kicks his shoes off, not bothering with his socks. "I don't have my bathing suit on."

"Who cares?" Tella yells at him, jumping up and down.

"Get in anyways!" Matteo joins her in the shallow end and they both start jumping up and down, creating waves with their bodies.

"Yeah, Caleb," Andi says, looking at me as she winks. "Take it off."

He rolls his eyes at her, turning back to the kids as he slowly starts to walk to the deep end, moving like he's stalking prey. Like a shark circling, about to attack. He pauses and pulls both of his socks off before tossing them into the grass. "I don't think either of you want me to get in."

"I think Mia does," Andi says in a quiet voice, only loud enough for the two of us to hear.

"Andi!" I scold her under my breath, my eyes flashing to her before glancing back at Caleb again as he walks toward the diving board.

"Shh," Andi shushes me, waving her hand dismissively. "It's our little secret, for now."

Caleb stops at the end of the diving board, his eyes drifting across the pool, stopping when they reach mine. He stares at me from where he's standing and I let myself drink him in. The white T-shirt is perfectly fitted around his torso, showing the lean muscles in his arms and his trimmed figure. My eyes head downwards to his shorts, where I see a small spot of black poking beneath the bottom hem of one.

I can't see what it is from here, but I know well enough that it's a tattoo. Black ink etched into his flesh. His tongue darts out to wet his lips and he runs a hand through his tousled waves.

"Come on, Daddy!" Tella calls out again, her voice almost sounding distant as I find myself locked in a trance. "Jump in!"

"Jump in, Uncle Cale!" Matteo urges again.

The two of them continue to chant as Caleb lifts one foot and then the other until he's standing on the diving board. His hands move down to the bottom hem of his shirt and my mouth goes dry as he grips it, lifting it up and over his head. He stands shirtless at the end of the pool, his muscles flexing as he tosses it over onto the grass by his socks.

"Mia, you have a little bit of drool on your bottom lip," Andi teases, tapping my knee with her foot.

I clamp my mouth shut, not even realizing that my lips were parted as I blatantly stared at him.

"For the record," she says, her voice low enough for just me as the kids keep chanting for Caleb to jump in the pool. "You can still have fun with someone who's emotionally unavailable."

"I've never been that type of person," I tell her.

"Yeah, well, different circumstances call for different things," she says simply with a shrug. "I didn't plan on anything with Carson either and look at me now." She lets out a soft laugh. "I'm just saying, it wouldn't kill either of you if you end up falling into bed together."

"I don't think that will ever be happening."

Caleb suddenly breaks out into a sprint, running and jumping off the end of the diving board. He takes perfect form, springing into the air as he dives in, plunging deep down toward the bottom of the pool. My breath catches in my throat and time is suspended as I anxiously wait for him to break through the surface once more.

He swims through the pool with perfect precision, not breaking through until he's in the shallow end, roughly two feet away from me. He comes up through the shimmering surface, both kids hooting and hollering as he gives both of them a dazzling smile.

He shakes his head, brushing his hair from his face as his gaze drifts to mine.

Andi snorts, shaking her head. "I'd put all my money on it."

Caleb's eyebrows pull together as he looks at her. "Huh?"

"Daddy! Daddy! Daddy!" Tella calls out, breaking through the confusion as she bounds toward her father. Caleb lifts her into the air, tossing her into the pool before doing the same to Matteo, careful to make sure he doesn't land on his cousin.

Caleb glances back at me, a smile drifting across his

lips before he goes back underwater, swimming after the two kids. He joins in with their games in the pool and every so often I catch his wandering eye. As much as I want to ignore it, it's undeniable that there's been some kind of a shift. Whether it's a shift into a friendship or some kind of a camaraderie.

Because surely, it can't ever be anything more than that.

CHAPTER FOURTEEN
CALEB

"Cale, wait up!"

I glance over my shoulder as my brother's voice calls out, slowing to a stop when I reach the door that leads out of the arena. We all came in for a morning practice, but thankfully we have off this evening. As much as I like games, I'm looking forward to having the evening to hang with Tella.

"Hey," he says a little breathlessly as he jogs over to me. I push open the exit door and hold it for him as he walks out ahead of me. "You seem like you're in a rush to get out of here. The guys were all talking about going and getting a late lunch or something. Did you want to come too?"

I shake my head, letting the door close behind us. The fall air is crisp as we walk through the parking lot to our cars. "I don't think so, not today. Tella has a riding lesson later and I want to take her instead of having Mia take her."

Carson raises an eyebrow at that. "How are things

going with that? I feel like I haven't really gotten a chance to ask you about it, but Andi told me about yesterday."

"Things are going well." I adjust my bag on my shoulder, keeping my gaze in front of me. "What did she say?"

Carson lets out a low chuckle. "Just that it looks like the two of you are getting along just fine." He pauses by my car and I feel his stare on the side of my face. "She said you're nicer to her than anyone else, except for T."

Reaching into my pocket, I press the button on my key fob to unlock the door and pop open the trunk, tossing my bag inside before closing it. "She's taking care of my daughter. Of course I'm nice to her."

Carson lifts his hands, an innocence smirk on his lips. "I didn't say anything," he says in a low voice. "I haven't been around the two of you to make my own observations yet."

I narrow my eyes at him as I walk to the driverside door and pull it open. "There's nothing to observe. She's my nanny and she's Landry's daughter. There's nothing more to it than that."

Carson steps closer, his hand grabbing the door as I get inside. "No one said she was anything more," he says, a frown tugging his lips downwards. "It's also not a crime if both of you are attracted to one another . . ."

"I'm not attracted to her." The lie falls from my lips with zero hesitation, the bitterness lingering on my tongue. "Not in the way that I would act on it."

Carson's face scrunches. "What does that even mean?"

"It means yes, she's attractive, but no, I won't be acting on it." I suck in a deep breath, my lungs expanding before I blow out the breath. "I—I can't."

"Why?" Carson questions me, his tone lighter.

My hands tighten on the steering wheel as I let my eyelids fall shut. "Because I don't think I can. I don't think I'm ready. I'm not sure if I ever will be."

Carson's silent as he lays his hand on my shoulder, giving me a gentle squeeze. "And that's okay too," he says softly, giving me another squeeze. "I think one day you will be, but only you will know when you are. Amelia wouldn't want you like this, you know that, right? She would want you happy, even if that means you're finding happiness with another person."

My chest constricts as his words seep through the spaces between my ribs.

"Being attracted to someone else isn't a betrayal to Amelia, and getting involved with someone else doesn't mean you're replacing her or forgetting about her." He pauses letting out a soft exhale. "She's not here, Cale. She's not coming back."

"I know that," I admit, my voice hoarse and thick with emotion. "Moving on just feels wrong."

"I can't pretend to know how you're feeling, but I promise you, it's not wrong. It's a normal part of the process of healing." He releases his grip on my shoulder. "Life continues on and the ones who are living need to keep doing just that. It's a disservice to the ones we've lost if we don't."

His words strike the organ beating beneath my ribcage. I slowly loosen my grip on the steering wheel, letting my hands fall into my lap as I turn to look at my brother. He's so right and none of this is news to me. I've gone over this with my therapist so many times, I could recite it word for word.

Although, this is the first time someone has given me this perspective. We truly are doing the dead a disservice by not living life to the fullest.

"Honor her by living your life, Cale." Carson's eyes slowly search mine. "Don't take a single moment or a single second for granted."

"Thanks, Cars."

His lips lift into a smile. "Always, bro. I'm here for you—to war and back."

"To war and back," I murmur the words back to him, dipping my chin. Carson mimics my actions, tapping his hand on my car door before he heads to his own vehicle. I pull the door shut, staring straight ahead for a few moments, replaying the conversation with him in my head.

Honor her by living your life.

I let my eyelids flutter shut as I tilt my head back to rest against the headrest. My mind wanders, attempting to conjure the image of Amelia's face behind my eyelids, but the memory is fuzzy. Her features aren't crisp like they once were.

Her lips lift into a smile. *It's okay, babe.* I hear her voice drifting through the darkness of my mind. *Find the joy in life. Laugh and love, always.*

I hold onto the moment for a few seconds before her face dissipates from my thoughts. Her words linger, long after I finally open my eyes and start the engine.

Amelia would want me to be happy, but what if I don't know how to be?

What if I'm too afraid to let myself feel that again?

What if I let someone in and lose them too?

———

As I walk through the house with two iced coffees in hand, I realize it's quiet—*too quiet*. My heart quickens in my chest, beating harder as my feet move faster. I head through the living room and kitchen, pausing by the back door to see if they're in the pool. I need to close it within the next few weeks and I make a mental note to remind myself to have the pool company come out then.

There's still no sign of Mia or Tella. I head back through the foyer to the stairs and make my way up to the second floor. I poke my head into all the rooms, my stomach flipping over itself when I don't find them in Tella's room.

Where the hell are they?

I slowly turn around and notice that the room Mia's been staying in has the door left ajar. I close the distance, walking directly up to it when I peer through the small space, catching sight of Mia and Tella. They're both sitting on the floor, Tella in front of Mia as she does some kind of a fancy braid with Tella's dark hair.

Relief washes over me, my lungs deflating, heart slowing as I see that they're both here, safe and sound. Lifting my foot, I tap on the door before pushing it open, gaining both of their attention. Mia glances over her shoulder at me as Tella does the same.

"Hi, Daddy," Tella says softly, smiling from ear to ear. "Mia is doing a fishtail braid in my hair!"

"I see that, T," I smile back at her, my eyes drifting to Mia's as she watches me carefully. Her eyes are rounded again, giving me those puppy dog eyes as something like uncertainty passes through them. "Hey, pup."

Blush creeps across her cheeks. "I'm not a puppy."

Tella giggles, but doesn't comment on it. She just settles back in front of Mia, patiently waiting for her to finish.

"How was practice?"

"Good," I tell Mia, walking deeper into the room, standing to the side of them to watch Mia's fingers move with precision to the ends of Mia's hair. "You're really good at that."

"Thanks," Mia says softly, grabbing a rubber band and wrapping it around the end of the braid. She releases Tella's hair. "There you go, kiddo."

Tella climbs to her feet, Mia doing the same as she turns around to face me. Tella speaks first as Mia's gaze drifts over me and down to my daughter. "Are you coming to my lesson? The time changed."

"Oh yes, her instructor called and asked if we could come at two. She had some things move around in her schedule and had time to do it earlier."

"I wouldn't miss it," I promise Tella with a wink. "Go get the rest of your things."

Tella smiles and nods before disappearing from

Mia's room. Mia's eyes move back to mine and I extend my arm, holding one of the coffees to her. "I stopped by the coffee shop and got you an iced vanilla latte with two pumps of vanilla and vanilla cold foam."

A smile crests Mia's lips as she reaches for the drink. Instinctively, I inhale a sharp breath as her fingers brush against mine. "You remembered my order?" she says, her fingers still warm against mine, sending an electric heat to my nerve endings. I let go of the cup as she wraps her delicate fingers around it. Her throat bobs as she swallows. "Thank you."

I clear my throat. "You're welcome."

"I'll get my things and get out of your hair, since you're home," she says, shifting her weight on her feet.

She moves to spin on her heel and my hand darts out, grabbing her wrist before she turns away. "Wait." The word falls from my lips in a rush, heat creeping up my neck as my hand lingers a second longer than it should on her wrist. Her gaze drops to my hand but she doesn't say anything about it as her eyes snap back to mine. "Do you want to come with us?"

Her eyes round again, her expression softening as I accidentally brush my thumb against the pulse point in her wrist. I release her, immediately feeling her absence, but I push the feeling away.

"Are you sure? I don't want to impose," she says, her eyes slowly searching mine.

"I'm sure."

She dips her chin, a sheepish grin tugging on her lips. "I'd love to."

The corners of my mouth twitch and I duck my head

as she steps out of her room ahead of me. Asking her to come wasn't exactly planned, but the thought of her not coming just didn't feel right.

It's a mindfuck I have no interest in dissecting right now.

Right now, I think I'm just going to try to live.

CHAPTER FIFTEEN
MIA

I'm acutely aware of how close Caleb is standing next to me and it's the only thing my brain can focus on at this moment.

We're both standing along the railing, watching Tella as she canters around the arena, but Caleb is standing a little closer than I expected. His warmth radiates from his arm, which is just nearly brushing against mine.

I attempt to even out my breathing, knowing I need to get myself under control here. It's just Caleb. My boss, Tella's father. I know I'm delusional, feeling this magnetic pull toward him, but goddammit, I can't help it. It's the little things that keep piling up. The way he stocked his pantry with gluten free foods, the way he remembered my coffee order.

The way he asked me to come to Tella's riding lesson, even though I should have just gone home.

I don't think he means anything by the way he looks at me, but my brain keeps transforming it into something more than it is. Caleb's a nice man, even if he may present a cold exterior to others sometimes. It's nothing more than him being friendly.

And him standing this close is nothing more than standing next to me while we watch Tella.

"So, do you still ride?" Caleb asks, breaking through my thoughts about him.

Blush creeps across my cheeks and I don't dare look at him. "Sometimes, but it's hard to find the time anymore. Since I don't have a rideable horse, I usually ride my best friend's or her brother's horse if I'm at the lake."

Caleb is silent for a beat. "Does her brother have a farm?"

"Yeah," I explain, nodding my head as I chance a quick glance at him from the corner of my eye. He doesn't look at me, keeping his gaze trained on Tella. But the muscle in his jaw tightens. "Well, it's their family farm. There was some extra stall space in their barn and he was kind enough to let me move Hank there for free."

"That's nice of him." The muscle twitches again. "Are the two of you close then?"

"Willow and me?" I ask. "Oh yes, we've been best friends for a long time."

"No," he says, his voice low and icy. "You and the brother."

I half snort, shaking my head. "Oh, no." I clear my throat. "I mean, we're friends, I guess."

"Hm," he says, letting out a breath, his shoulders relaxing. He slowly turns his head to look at me, his gaze immediately crashing into mine. "But not *close* friends?"

I swallow roughly, my stomach flipping over itself. "No."

He slowly nods, his eyes lingering on mine before he turns back to watch Tella. She slows her horse from a canter to a trot then to a walk as she begins cooling him down. "I think she's about done," he says, his voice still low. He doesn't move at first, his gaze transfixed on his daughter. "Amelia was afraid of horses," he whispers, his eyebrows tugging together. "At least, I think she was."

"They are huge animals and can be intimidating," I offer, my voice quiet, matching the same volume as his. "Tella is a very talented rider for her age, though."

"Sometimes I hate that she rides," he admits, his head cocking to the side as he looks at me. The back of his hand brushes against mine, sending an electrical current up the length of my arm. My heart stumbles over itself. "I can't help but feel like I'm putting her in such a dangerous position."

My heart pounds harder against my ribcage as his knuckles lightly graze mine. The first time could pass for an accident, but a second time? My mind swims. I shouldn't do it, shouldn't chance it.

The tips of my fingers twitch and extend backward, lightly skimming the sides of his. Caleb inhales sharply through his nostrils, the sound subtle enough that if I weren't paying attention, I would have missed it. My heart and lungs refuse to regulate themselves, but I ignore it. Time is momentarily suspended as I wait for him to make a move away from me.

His fingers move a fraction of an inch, pressing into the spaces between my own.

"Come on guys!" Tella calls to the two of us as she spins Sodapop around and starts walking toward the gate.

I immediately retreat, pulling my hand away from his, and I take a step back away from the fencing around the arena. Caleb doesn't move at first, his eyes slowly meeting mine as he turns around to face me. His gaze is intense and my lips part, the tension between us thick enough you could cut it with a knife.

And then he ducks his head, breaking eye contact, and walks past me, heading toward the gate where Tella is.

I fill my lungs with air, closing my eyes while I hold the breath, then release it. I give my head a swift shake, attempting to regulate my nervous system before I turn around to follow them. Caleb is standing by the gate, holding Sodapop as Tella dismounts. He smiles down at his daughter and my heart grows inside my chest as I watch her walk up to him.

He grabs her hand, leading her pony and her back toward the barn. He glances over his shoulder, his eyes surveying the landscape until he finds me. His expression immediately relaxes, a ghost of a smile cresting his lips and damn my heart for kicking into overdrive again.

And damn me for not being immune to this man.

———

"T, why don't you go get cleaned up and change while I start dinner?" Caleb says to Tella as we walk up to the front of the house. He unlocks the front door, holding it open for Tella and me to walk inside. Tella kicks off her shoes and heads up the stairs, leaving Caleb and me alone.

I turn back to look at Caleb as he shuts the door and moves to face me.

"I'm just going to grab my bag before I head home."

Caleb stares at me for a moment, tilting his head. "I know this is all temporary, but would it be better if you just stayed?" His eyes widen slightly. "I mean, instead of going back and forth."

My breath catches in my throat and I tuck a hair behind my ear while I look anywhere but him. "I don't want to impose and interrupt your alone time with Tella."

He swallows roughly and rakes a hand through his tousled hair. "No, no that makes sense," he says, his voice low as he nods. "I—uh. Tella likes you and it just seems like it would be easier." He pauses, letting out a shallow breath. "I could still have my time with her with you here."

My nostrils flare, my heart pitter pattering beneath my ribcage. "I'll think about it."

"Okay," he says softly, shoving his hands into the front pockets of his jeans. His eyes slowly search mine. "Thanks for coming to her lesson today. I know it meant a lot to her . . . and it was nice to have someone to talk to." He clears his throat and shifts his weight on his feet. "For so long, it's just been Tella and me."

His last comment hurts my heart. He's not completely alone. He has family, he has friends, but I know what he means. I know what is lingering beneath the words he actually speaks.

"Thank you for inviting me along," I tell him, my voice quiet as I give him a small smile. "I'm always here if you ever want to talk about anything." I take a breath, swallowing over the lump forming in my throat. "You're not alone, Caleb. You have a lot of people who care about you."

He pulls his hands from his pocket, taking a step closer. His throat bobs, eyes searching mine. "What about you?"

My heart climbs into my throat. "Well, yes. I care about you."

"No." He slowly shakes his head—another inch disappearing between us. "Who cares about *you*?"

Every cell in my body freezes. "I—I—" My eyebrows tug together. "What do you mean?"

"The other day," he says softly, his voice dropping lower. He takes another step closer so we're standing toe to toe. He lifts his hand, his finger crooking beneath my chin as he tilts it upwards. "You said you have to look out for you."

"We were talking about my celiac disease . . ." My voice trails off and I attempt to ignore the tugging feeling inside my chest. He's digging too deep, searching for answers I don't want to share with him.

His thumb rests against my chin and he slowly

moves it, stroking my skin in the softest, most tender way. "You're not alone either, pup." His lips part, a shallow breath escaping him. "You have people who care about you. People who want to look out for you."

I draw in my bottom lip, dragging it between my teeth as I stare back at him. His nostrils flare and the intensity of his gaze burns through my body. He drops his eyes down to my mouth and my insides melt.

"Mia . . ." he practically whispers, his voice strained, as if he's in pain. His eyes fall shut for a moment as the tension sizzles in the air between us. My stomach flutters and as he opens his eyes again, I'm met with a fire burning brightly inside his irises.

"I don't know how to act around you." A sigh escapes him, torment mixing with the lust.

"I don't know either," I admit, my voice barely audible.

He searches my eyes with desperation as if he wants me to tell him to stop. Like he wants me to be the one to shake some sense into him. I can't—not when I need this just as badly as he does.

He tilts his head to the side, his face dropping closer to mine. His warm breath drifts across my face and I catch one last look of the flames of desire burning inside his gaze. Just as my eyelids begin to flutter shut . . .

"Daddy!" Tella comes bounding down the stairs. She sounds like a herd of elephants and that's all it takes for reality to come crashing down around us. In a fraction of a second, Caleb's hand drops away from my face and he takes an exaggerated step backward. "Can I help you with dinner?"

Holy shit. I almost kissed my boss, who my father also coaches.

"Of course, T," he says, half choking out the words as he forces a smile onto his face.

"Mia! Are you going to have dinner with us too?"

Caleb doesn't look at me and I see that damn muscle in his jaw tic again. He adjusts his glasses, glancing at the kitchen, as if he's planning his escape. He's visibly uncomfortable and I feel like it's my fault.

I almost let him kiss me . . . and now I can't help but wonder if he would have regretted doing it.

"Not tonight, but I'll see you tomorrow," I tell Tella, smiling at her before turning to the front door. "Have a good night, guys."

"Bye, Mia!" Tella calls out to me, skipping past Caleb as she heads into the kitchen.

He slowly turns around, pain etched across his face as he meets my gaze. He clears his throat. "Drive safe."

I give him a curt nod before slipping through the front door. I don't bother turning back around to get my bag. Instead, I head out to my car and head home with nothing but regret building in the pit of my stomach.

I should have stopped him before we got to that moment.

Because that moment—it simply isn't meant for us.

CHAPTER SIXTEEN
CALEB

My heart pounds erratically and my body is coated in a cold sweat as I sit up in bed. The darkness surrounds me and I blink my eyes, my chest heaving as I reach for my phone on the nightstand. I grab it in a haste, the screen lighting up as I turn it toward my face.

Somehow, without even reading it, I know what the date is.

Amelia's birthday.

It's like my body knows, even when I try to block it from my mind. I knew this day was approaching, yet I've let myself get distracted. I've leaned into those distractions in an effort to keep my mind from wandering, from hyper-fixating. From spiraling.

Every year since I lost Amelia, her birthday has been the hardest day for me. The anniversary of her death sucks, but it's just a reminder of the day we lost her. Her birthday, however, has now become the start of another year for her, another year we're without her. Another year taken away that she doesn't get to grow old, watching our little girl.

And somehow, I neglected to acknowledge it coming on so quickly. I forgot to schedule my normal therapy appointment that I always do a few days before. I knew it was coming, but I chose to not think about it until this very moment.

I close my eyes, locking my phone and letting it fall onto the bed. A deep sigh escapes me, my chest deflating as guilt rolls through me at full force. There's no sense in trying to go back to sleep, as I know it will never find me now.

After a few minutes pass, I pull myself up out of bed and head directly into the bathroom, not stopping until I'm stepping beneath the hot water in the shower. Just for good measure, I turn it a bit hotter, feeling the scorching heat seeping through my skin as I stand directly beneath the stream, letting it flow over my body.

I stay in the shower until the water turns warm, until I've scrubbed myself three separate times, as if the action alone is going to wash away the guilt. Like it will wash away a single ounce of my pain.

Tella is still in bed, as she should be, so I get dressed, brush my teeth, and head down to the kitchen to make a pot of coffee. My appetite is nonexistent and I don't imagine it will come at all today. It feels weird for it to be another year passing. Amelia is frozen as a twenty-five year old. She's frozen in that year, not moving forward with the rest of the world as the earth continues to spin.

It's such a weird fucking thing, I hate thinking about it.

Leaving my coffee black, I grab my mug and head out onto the back deck, just as the sun begins to rise. Taking a seat, I stare out at the pool and lift my coffee mug to my lips as I watch the sunlight shimmer on the surface of the water. I don't know how I've lost count of the days, but the guilt seeps heavily into my soul, weighing on my shoulders. I've never once forgotten her birthday. I've never once forgotten the day that tears me apart inside.

I take another sip of my coffee, allowing the guilt to encapsulate me as I lift my gaze from the pool and up to the sky. It's a beautiful morning and it's quiet, which weirdly feels fitting for the day to remember Amelia. These kinds of mornings were always her favorite.

Reaching into my front pocket, I pull out my phone and open up my text messages. My eyes scan the names listed and their respective threads, pausing when they stumble upon Mia's name. She's supposed to be coming later for when I have to go to practice, but I'm not sure I want to see her—not on a day like today. I don't want her to see me like this, like a shell of a person.

I suck in a deep breath and instead tap on my therapist's name.

> I forgot to schedule an appointment.
> Do you have any time available today?

SANDY

Of course. Can you do eight thirty?

Virtual?

SANDY

I'll send you a link.

After closing out of her messages, I send a text to Andi.

Can Tella come over to your house today during practice?

She texts me back immediately.

ANDI

Anything you need.

Then it's followed by a separate text from Carson.

CARSON

Did you order a cake?

My throat bobs as I swallow hard.

Yes.

CARSON

Send me the details. I'll pick it up after practice.

My nostrils flare, emotion welling deep inside my chest. Three years ago, Carson decided we still needed to celebrate Amelia's birthday, even if she isn't here to celebrate with us. She was always the life of the party and if there was something to celebrate, she was putting some kind of an event together.

It feels weird, celebrating without her, but in a way, it's more for Tella than anything. For the last three years, Tella and I have been going over to Carson's to have dinner, cake, and spend the evening telling our favorite stories about Amelia.

She was detached from her family, so we were always all that she had.

I send the details for the cake pick up to Carson, then look back through my messages. My finger hovers over Mia's name. I should have given her a heads up. I should have made these plans before today, but here we are.

> Hey. T is going to Carson and Andi's this afternoon, so you don't need to come today.

Mia texts back in an instant and in the back of my mind, I remember her telling me how she used to hate mornings, but became a morning person over time.

MIA

> Are you sure? Is everything okay?

> Yes and yes.

She doesn't respond again, so I get up from my seat, heading back into the house. I need to wake Tella up, but that can wait until after. I turn my phone on "do not disturb" and head into my office, settling in front of my computer for my therapy appointment.

It's not something that offers a magical fix, but somehow, it truly does help.

———

I'm fairly certain I blacked out during my therapy appointment, but I end the virtual visit feeling a little bit lighter as I head up to Tella's room to wake her up. I pause by the side of the bed, my eyes traveling over the planes of her face. She looks so peaceful and innocent in her sleep. Her relaxed features look the same as Amelia's. My heart hurts as I stare down at her, reaching to brush her hair away from her face.

"Hey, T, it's time to wake up."

She stirs, her eyelids popping open as she stretches her arms above her head. "Can we snuggle for a second?" she asks, her voice filled with sleep as she rubs at her eyes.

"Of course," I murmur, climbing into her bed with her, pulling her into my arms. She nestles in against me. "You're going to go hang out with Aunt Andi and Matteo while I'm at practice and then we'll have cake for your mommy's birthday."

"Okay." Tella takes a deep breath. "Do we get to have vanilla cake again?"

A tender smile lifts my lips. "It was her favorite."

"I like vanilla too, but I don't think it's my favorite," she says, a frown tugging down on her lips.

"That's okay," I assure her, pressing my lips to the

top of her head. "Just because it was her favorite doesn't mean it has to be yours too."

"Do you miss her?"

"I do," I tell her, letting out a deep breath. I miss Amelia every damn day, but the pain has gotten lighter over the years. It doesn't feel as visceral as it once did, which also fills me with guilt. What kind of a husband does that make me if I don't miss my dead wife every second of every day?

What kind of husband does it make me if there are times where I don't think about her anymore?

There was once a period in my life after she died that it was all I could think about. All I could focus on was the fact that she wasn't here and I still was. That I had to continue on in life without her. As time grew on, those thoughts faded away. I began to move on in life with nothing left to hang onto but her memory.

And even now, as those memories become more and more distant, I find myself thinking of them less. *Thinking of her less.* Amelia's gone, but the rest of us aren't. We're all still here.

"It's okay, Daddy," Tella says softly, rolling to sit up as she pats the top of my head. "You'll get to see her again someday."

Guilt prickles beneath my ribcage. There was a low point in those first few days after her death where I wanted to end it all, just for the possibility of getting to see her again. But then, this little girl—our little girl—brought me back to reality. She needs me today like she needed me then, and she'll need me for the years to come.

I hate myself for ever entertaining the thought of leaving her alone.

"I know," I agree, smiling at her as she climbs over me and gets out of bed. I slowly sit up, watching her as she disappears from the room, heading into the bathroom. "I'll be downstairs, T," I tell her when I finally get up and head out into the hallway.

My footsteps feel heavy as I head back down to the first floor, stopping when I reach the island in the kitchen. I pick up my phone. It's still on "do not disturb" so I turn it off. As soon as I do, an unread message comes through, followed by another. My stomach immediately drops.

MIA

Did I do something wrong?

If it's about the other day, that's my fault and I'm sorry for that.

The muscle in my jaw tightens as I read over her messages two more times.

That was my fault, not yours.

And no, you did nothing wrong.

I suck in a deep breath, my lungs expanding before I let them deflate.

Today would be Amelia's thirty-first birthday. We celebrate it every year with my brother.

I'm so sorry.

Happy birthday, Amelia.

My throat constricts and my hands shake as I type out a one-word response.

Thanks.

And then I power off my phone . . .
And my mind.

CHAPTER SEVENTEEN

MIA

Caleb has barely looked at or spoken to me since his late wife's birthday last week. I'm not so sure I'm surprised, given his frosty exterior that I had grown accustomed to before I became his nanny. But that's the thing—there was a softness, a tenderness he had shown since then.

And now, it's like he took it all back.

I'm still sitting in my car out front of Caleb's house, dreading having to face him again. Every day that I've seen him, he stays hidden until it's time for him to leave, so I've been making it a point to only walk through the front door a few minutes before he's supposed to leave.

WILLOW

Are you still going to the game with
Steven tonight?

I stare down at my phone, the corners of my lips lifting as excitement dances in the pit of my stomach.

Steven is a friend of ours from college and we made plans a few months ago to catch a game together while he was in town for work. I haven't seen him since we graduated, so I'm excited to catch up with him.

Hopefully.

There's only one small problem.

Why hopefully?

I forgot to mention it to Caleb, so as of right now, I'm still supposed to watch Tella.

Shit. Is he still icing you out?

My lips turn down in a frown.

Yep.

I glance at the clock on my dashboard, opting to get out of my car an extra few minutes earlier than planned so I can talk to Caleb. An anxious feeling builds in the pit of my stomach as I drop my phone into my purse and head up to the front door. I let myself in, which still feels weird to do, but Caleb insisted when I first started that I don't need to knock.

Kicking off my shoes, I head through the foyer, my steps faltering in the doorway of the kitchen when I see Caleb. He doesn't notice me at first as he riffles through one of the cabinets with his back to me. I watch the way the chords in his arms tighten as he reaches for something up high.

He slowly turns around, setting the box of cereal on the counter before lifting his gaze to mine. He's silent, his lips parting like he wants to say something, but he immediately shuts them again, giving me a small nod.

"Hey," I say softly, mustering up the courage to walk into the kitchen. There's no room for small talk right now, so I'm just going to cut right to the chase. Caleb doesn't want small talk with me anyways. "Um, so I have a favor to ask, but you can totally say no."

"Okay," he says, his voice barely audible.

"So, a friend is in town and we made plans to go to a game months ago and I completely forgot that it's tonight. I can cancel them if it's an issue, but I didn't know if Tella could hang with Andi for a little bit."

Caleb stares at me, his gaze unwavering, his expression giving nothing away. "We can figure something out." He pauses, his throat bobbing, lips parting but then he shuts them once more. He pulls out his phone, fingers moving across the screen as he types out a message. He doesn't look at me, instead he scans the device.

"She said that's fine. She's not staying for the third period, so you could get Tella when she leaves." He drags his gaze up to me. "Is that enough time for you with your friend?"

I nod eagerly. "Oh, yes. That's perfect. I can drive separately, that way I can bring Tella home early."

"You can come with us. She can stay until the game is over."

"Are you sure? I don't want it to be too late for her."

Caleb dips his chin. "I'm sure." He rolls his wrist, checking his watch. "Tella is in her room playing. I need to go."

"Okay," I say, a smile pulling on my lips. "Thank you, Caleb."

His eyes linger on mine and he says nothing. He just gives me a curt nod once more before heading out of the room without another word. My lungs deflate and my shoulders sag at the sound of the garage door opening and closing.

Something inside him changed since we almost kissed. I don't know if it's because of Amelia's birthday and the reminders of her, or the fact that I didn't stop him. If Tella hadn't interrupted, I would have let him kiss me.

And I'm not sure which one of us would have felt worse for it.

———

"Momma Mia! Look at you!" Steven comes striding toward me, a smile lighting his whole face as he pulls me in for a hug. "It feels like it's been an entire decade since I've seen you!"

I wrap my arms around him, hugging him tightly as laughter escapes me. "It's only been like four months!"

"Whatever," he says, releasing me as he waves his hand dismissively. He loops his arm through mine, leading me in the direction of the bar. "Let's get some drinks and watch some hot men beat each other up."

Steven and I each grab a mixed drink and make our way through the crowds in the concourse before finding our section and heading down to the seats. We missed the national anthem but managed to make our way down just before the puck dropped. Steven pauses behind me, stopping in the middle of the row, eyes wide as he stares at me.

"We're right behind the bench?"

I managed to get us seats just three rows behind the Aston Archers bench. A smile breaks out across my lips and I laugh, nodding my head. "Come sit!" I wave for him to come with me as I sit down. He drops down beside me, his shoulder bumping into mine as he scans the players in front of us.

"This is truly a dream come true," he swoons, batting his eyelashes at me. "Do you think I'd get kicked out if I accidentally fell over the glass and onto the bench with them?"

Laughter escapes me once more and I raise my eyebrows at him. "Oh, without a doubt."

Steven, Willow, and I all became close friends while we were in college. Willow and Steven had a little friends-with-benefits thing going on for a few months, but then Steven started seeing this new guy who came during our junior year. And Willow . . . Well, she just moved on to the next hook up when she felt like it.

My eyes scan the backs of the players in front of us, running over their names and numbers before I direct my attention out to the ice. Play already started and I search the players, immediately finding him as I scoot forward in my seat. Caleb skates down the ice, following the play before the puck is overturned and moving back through the neutral zone.

"Which one is your boss?" Steven questions me, poking my arm with his elbow.

Caleb quickly heads over to the bench, his lips moving as he yells something and waves for the second line center to head out. He hops over the boards, his chest heaving as his gaze immediately collides with mine. His expression relaxes when he sees me, but only for a brief moment. He quickly looks at Steven, his brow furrowing.

"Him," I practically whisper, the sound tumbling from my lips as I stare back at Caleb. His eyes linger for a fraction of a second longer than they should before he tears them away from me, taking his seat on the bench. "Number 8."

"I didn't see his face," Steven says with disappointment. "There are two Ford players?"

My heart pounds erratically in my chest and I down more than half of my drink in a single gulp. "Yep. They're brothers."

"Woo wee, sister. That could be fun."

I snort, shaking my head at him. "Carson isn't single and Caleb is a widower."

Steven purses his lips then puckers them as he takes a sip of his drink. "Well, okay then. There goes that fantasy."

We get halfway through the first period before Steven abandons me to go get us fresh drinks. I shouldn't be drinking since I'm going to have to be responsible for Tella after the second period, but I swore to myself I'd only drink two during the first period.

That was before I realized how strong the bartender was making the drinks. And before I realized I'd have a bit of a buzz before even starting my second.

Steven finds me again, just before the second period starts and he settles back down into his seat just as Caleb is coming off the ice again. I haven't made eye contact with him since that first time and if I'm being honest, I've been actively avoiding any opportunity.

Until now.

He hops over the boards and I accidentally look at him. His gaze is hardened, his eyes moving to Steven and then back to me. They narrow the slightest bit, his nostrils flaring as he spins around and drops down onto the bench.

"Is he just an angry man or did someone piss in his coffee this morning?"

I suck in a deep breath, my chest rising and falling as I exhale. "He's not an angry person, he's just . . . complicated."

"A hot complicated person," Steven says, glancing at me with a wink. The horn sounds, signaling the period is over. "I'm intrigued."

"He's actually really nice and his daughter is such a little spitfire. I just think he's still hung up on losing his wife. It's almost like he hasn't figured out how to heal from it."

"Is that something you ever really heal from?" Steven questions me as the Zamboni pulls out onto the ice to clean it.

"I don't know," I tell him with a shrug, my mind drifting to my father. He's good, but thinking back now, I'm not sure if he ever truly healed. He dated other women, but he never brought them into our home or into my life. He never settled down. "I think in a way, you probably do."

Steven nods. "You're probably right. I'm sure it's not easy, but then again, what do I know?"

A small laugh escapes me as I shake my head at him then finish the rest of my second drink. Intermission feels like it passes by sooner than I thought it would, but perhaps it's from the alcohol in my system. I need this buzz to go away by the end of the second period or I don't think Caleb is going to be too happy with me.

The guys come back on the bench, Caleb glancing at Steven and me from the corner of his eye before he steps out onto the ice. The guys line up and the puck drops. Caleb wins the face-off, but there's a slashing penalty called on the other team within the first minute.

I glance up at the Megatron. They've turned on the kiss cam. A smile tugs on my lips as it jumps around the arena, flashing on different couples. And then it's me! My own damn face is on the Megatron, the camera zooming in on Steven and me.

"Oh! That's us!" Steven immediately turns toward me, his hands grabbing the sides of my face as he pulls me to look at him. We're both laughing, heat creeping up my neck and into my cheeks as he plants a wet kiss on my lips.

"Oh my gosh, are you drooling?" I snort, wiping my mouth with the back of my hand.

Steven laughs and winks. "Maybe it's you who is drooling over that hot boss of yours."

"Oh please," I chuckle, rolling my eyes at him as I slowly direct my gaze back out to the ice. Caleb stands just on the other side of the boards, his face stone cold as he stares back at me. My breath catches in my throat and my stomach tumbles onto the floor.

Caleb tears his gaze from mine and heads back to the center of the ice. My heart stumbles over itself and I watch him get ready for the face-off. The puck drops and he wins it, but instead of engaging in play, he drives his palms into the chest of the other team's center.

What the hell?

The guy looks visibly pissed off, shouting something inaudible to Caleb. In less than two seconds, both of them are throwing their gloves onto the ice and engaging in a full on fist fight. Instinctively, I rise to my feet, my hands covering my mouth in horror as the two men tousle, both of them throwing punches before going down on the ice with Caleb on top.

The refs break them up, hauling both players to their feet. Caleb glances over to the bench, eyes wild with blood dripping from his lip and eyebrow. I'm cemented in place, my heart forgetting how to beat and my lungs forgetting how to inhale and exhale properly.

Both of the guys are escorted over to the penalty box and I'm stuck standing motionless. Steven tugs on my arm, urging me to sit back down. "Mia, are you okay? You're pale as shit."

"Yeah, I—uh. It must just be the alcohol." I pause,

nervously tucking my hair behind my ears. My buzz vanished the second I watched Caleb drive his fist into another man's face. "I actually have to go."

Steven's eyebrows draw inward. "What?"

"I have to watch his daughter after the second period so I should go check on her." I swallow roughly, my heart pounding against my ribcage. "I'm sorry to run out on you. We'll catch up next time you're back in town."

Steven's eyes are filled with concern, but he concedes. He nods and pulls me in for a hug. "Okay. Text me later, okay?"

"Okay," I tell him, nodding as I rise from my seat as play stops again. I use the opportunity to quickly head up the stairs and back into the concourse. I find the nearest bathroom, pausing inside to catch my breath. I close my eyes and let my head tilt back against the wall as I focus on my breathing. After a few moments, my anxiety starts to settle. I walk to the sink to wash my hands, letting the cool water regulate my nervous system.

I don't know what the hell just happened.

And I'm not so sure I want to know what caused it.

I adjust Tella in my arms and she wraps hers tighter around my neck, a soft sigh escaping her as she settles against me. She fell asleep at the beginning of the third period. I scooped her up and carried her out into the hallway after the game finished. Most of the other families have already left so it's just Tella and me lingering near the exit, waiting for Caleb.

He comes out of the dressing room, hair damp from showering as he steps out into the hall. He pauses, his head on a swivel as he looks for the two of us, only stopping when he sees me holding Tella. His gaze fixes on mine, but as he strides over, he drops it down to the floor, as if he's avoiding eye contact.

"I can take her," he mumbles, extending his arms to take her from me.

I don't argue with him. I release her, letting him situate her in his arms. She doesn't even wake up from the shift and instead settles against his neck, her mouth opening as she yawns. My eyes trail over Caleb's face, over the cut on his eyebrow and the one in his swollen bottom lip.

"What happened out there?"

He doesn't look at me as he starts to walk to the exit. "It doesn't matter," he replies, his tone clipped and voice hoarse.

He pushes open the door with his foot and I immediately take it from him, squeezing my body between him and the door as I hold it open for him. "Thanks," he grinds out, skirting around me, as if he doesn't want to be anywhere near me.

My throat constricts, but I follow after him, heading in the direction of his car. "I can get a ride home, if you'd prefer," I offer. My car is at his house, but his body language tells me everything I need to know. He doesn't even want to be in the general proximity of me.

We both stop as we reach his car. He pulls open the

back door, his eyes falling shut as he inhales sharply. "Get in the car, Mia."

"It's not a problem."

"Mia," he breathes out my name. "Get in the fucking car." His throat bobs as he swallows hard, his eyes slicing to mine. "Please," he adds, his voice hoarse and just above a whisper.

My chest tightens and I give him a swift nod. "Okay."

Without another word, I climb into the passenger seat, my heart in my throat as I wait for him to get Tella strapped into her booster. Time stretches and it feels like an eternity as the blood rushes in my ears. Finally, he shuts her door and walks over to the driver's side, sliding in behind the steering wheel.

He's silent as he buckles his seatbelt and turns on the car, slowly easing out of the parking space. I swallow again, nervously tucking my hair behind my ear as Caleb drives us in complete silence, heading onto the main road in front of the arena.

I've been racking my brain for the last week, trying to figure out where I went wrong with us almost kissing. He said it was his fault, but what feels even worse is the fact that he regrets it and I don't. He's iced me out because of it and I don't know if it's my anxiety or . . .

"Did I do something to upset you?" The words tumble from my lips in a rush. I turn my head to look at him. "I'm at a loss for where I went wrong or what I did."

The muscle in his jaw clenches and I watch the way

his fingers curl tighter around the steering wheel. "I don't want to talk about any of this until we're home."

I straighten my spine, pressing it back against the leather seat. My anxiety peaks and I thread my fingers through one another in my lap. "Can you just tell me what I did?"

"You didn't do anything." He blows out a breath, working that muscle in his jaw once more. "I'm not mad at you." His throat bobs as he swallows hard. "I'm mad at myself."

CHAPTER EIGHTEEN
CALEB

ia is silent as she waits for me by the front door. Avoiding her gaze, I walk past, marching into the house where I kick my shoes off and head directly up to Tella's room. My blood is hot in my veins as it circulates through my body, carrying too many fucking conflicting emotions.

I get Tella settled in bed, pulling off her shoes before tucking her beneath the covers. Mia must have had a change of pajamas at the arena, because somehow Tella was already dressed for sleep when I found them waiting in the hallway.

Leaning down, I pull the covers up to her chin and press my lips to her temple. "I love you, T."

She stirs in her sleep, a gentle smile cresting her lips as she rubs her head against her pillow. I watch her for a moment, my eyes lingering on her perfect little face before I let myself out of her room. Leaving the door ajar, I head down the hallway and back downstairs. My heart pounds erratically, my stomach quickening when I don't see Mia in the foyer. *Did she leave?*

My strides are long, the anxiety creeping up my spine as I make my way into the kitchen. I pause to search for her. Movement through the glass door that leads out back catches my attention. She's standing on the pool deck, her head tilted back to stare up at the moon.

My breath catches in my throat as I take a moment to drink her in. The ends of her hair dance along her lower back. I memorize her curves, the way she looks right now as my feet begin to slowly move on their own, carrying me closer, like a man caught in a trance.

I reach for the door and slide it open, taking a step and then another onto the back deck. I try to slide the door shut without making a sound, but the plunk when it connects with the frame is audible. Mia doesn't turn to look at me, but I don't miss the way her back straightens a little. The way her chest rises and falls with shallow breaths.

I walk up beside her, letting the silence surround us as I, too, tilt my head back to look up at the moon shining brightly in the sky.

"Are you going to tell me why you were mad?"

My chest deflates as I blow out a breath through my nose in a huff, my eyes momentarily closing. "I'm still mad."

Mia turns her body to face me, her head no longer tilted up to the sky. "Why?"

I swallow roughly, my eyelids lifting as I move to her, my chin dipping down to meet her gaze. "Are you seeing him?" I chew on the inside of my cheek. "The guy that was with you at the game."

Mia's eyebrows pinch together. "What? No."

"You kissed him."

She cocks her head to the side, confusion pulling her eyebrows together. "Because of the kiss cam . . ."

I lift my hand, dragging it through my hair, pausing to grab the back of my neck as my eyes search hers. "I thought you were on a date . . ."

She stares back at me, her eyes round with her eyebrows still furrowed. "No, Steven is just a friend. It's never been like that between us."

I draw in a deep breath, my eyes falling shut again as I feel my chest expand. I hold it for a second, rolling my lips between my teeth before I open my eyes once more. My lungs began to expel the air, soft and slow as my gaze crashes into hers. "I saw you kiss him . . ." I pause, a ragged breath slipping from my lips as my hand falls away from the back of my neck. I take a step closer, closing the distance between us. "And all I could see was red."

Coach Landry is going to fucking kill me.

Mia closes the last two inches, stepping into my space. Her eyes slowly move between mine as she lifts her hand. She drags her fingertips just above the cut on my eyebrow. My gaze doesn't leave hers and I don't dare blink as she inspects my face.

She trails her fingers down the side of my cheek, drifting along the corner of my mouth before grazing my swollen bottom lip. "Is that why you got into a fight?" she whispers, lifting her eyes back to mine.

I swallow hard over the lump in my throat, bobbing my head up and down. Mia moves her fingers back to the side of my face, flattening her palm along my jawbone. My eyelids flutter shut, a deep sigh leaving me as I relax into her touch. "It was the only thing I could do."

"Caleb," she murmurs, her voice soft and tender. I lift my hand to cover hers, feeling the warmth of her skin beneath my palm "But why?" she asks. "Why would it matter if someone else kissed me?"

I drop my hand from hers, sliding it up her arm and along the base of her neck, curling my fingers around her spine. "Because it should have been me."

Mia's lips part, a soft breath escaping her as her eyes widen slightly, the moonlight catching the shimmering hues of her irises.

My face drops down to hers, my nose brushing the tip of hers. "Tell me to stop and I will."

She's my coach's daughter. I need to stop this somehow.

She drags her top teeth across her bottom lip as she shakes her head. "What if I don't want you to stop?"

Goddamn.

Any logical thought slips from my mind as my lips graze hers. I pause and the world around us slows down. Time is suspended between us and I feel the gentle exhale of her breath as it warms my lips. My heart beats faster, my left hand snaking around her hip as I pull her body flush against mine.

Mia circles her arms around my back, her fingers fisting the material of my shirt as my mouth sweeps across hers again. A groan rumbles in my chest as I sigh against her. Her lips move with mine, hesitant at first, but as the flames between us crackle, it's like her reservations disappear into the air around us, like smoke from a fire.

Mia's body melts into mine, the warmth of her slender frame pressing against me. My tongue slides along the seam of her lips, requesting permission, needing more. She parts them without hesitation, granting me the access I desire. My tongue moves against hers, touching and tasting her.

She tastes like red cherries and a bad decision.

My grip tightens on the back of her neck as she kisses me back with a tenderness that seeps into my soul. I can't stop the groan that I hum against her lips. She has been the most unexpected force to enter my life.

I breathe her in, the faint smell of lavender and vanilla infiltrating my senses, while I kiss her with a growing need. A warmth washes over me, blood rushing between my legs, the ache intensifying as I resist the urge to press my pelvis against her.

A breeze drifts through the air, shifting around us. One of the umbrellas by the pool creaks from the air as it puts pressure against the material splayed outward. It's an unwelcome distraction, however, it's the pull back to reality that I desperately need.

What am I doing?

I'm kissing Mia Landry.

My new nanny.

My coach's daughter.

My lips slow against hers, until we're breaking apart, both of us coming up for air. I open my eyes, searching her face as she carefully lifts her own eyelids. Her gaze collides with mine, the moonlight shimmering on her glassy eyes once more. I untangle my fingers from her hair, releasing the back of her neck as her hands fall away from the back of my shirt.

My left hand lingers on her hip, my eyes traveling to her mouth and back to her eyes. I crossed a line by kissing her, but there isn't a part of me that wants to take it back. "Mia," I whisper, my voice breathless and hoarse, throat bobbing as I swallow hard.

As much as I don't want to take it back, it doesn't extinguish the guilt that suddenly compounds inside my chest. I can't help but feel like I just betrayed the memory of my wife.

"It's late," she tells me, her voice soft. Her tongue darts out to wet her swollen lips. "I should probably head home."

"Are you okay to drive home?"

I saw her with a drink during the game, although she doesn't seem drunk or even like she's under the influence. Then again, I don't know. It's a difficult thing for me—to keep my mind from flashing back to the accident.

The corners of her mouth twitch. "I am."

Anything can happen in the blink of an eye.

"You'll let me know that you get there safely?"

Her expression softens, emotion engulfing her eyes as she bobs her head up and down. "Yeah, of course." She takes a step back and my hand falls away from her hip. Conflict mingles in her gaze as she stares at me for a moment. "Goodnight, Caleb."

The muscles in my chest tighten. "Goodnight, Mia."

She lingers for another second, her gaze still on me, her steps faltering before she quietly turns around, heading back into the house. There's a part of me that wants to call to her, to tell her to stay. To do anything other than watch her walk away.

But I know I can't.

Regret washes over me, but it's not the kind I expected to feel. I regret the conflict in her eyes, as if I'm the one who put it there. The last thing I want is for her to feel bad about that kiss, because it was anything but a mistake.

She's not the first woman I've kissed since my wife passed away, but she's the first I didn't pretend was her. She's the first person I've kissed without a single thought of Amelia and the guilt begins to creep in along the edges of my heart. Guilt because not once did she cross my mind and in a way, it feels like I'm letting go of the memory of her.

I run a ragged hand through my hair, blowing out a breath as I tilt my head to look up at the sky. I have to let go of the guilt. I can't betray someone who isn't here. Kissing Mia wasn't betraying Amelia's memory, even if it feels like it is.

A commitment to someone else will never be on the table, but maybe exploring whatever these feelings are isn't.

Even if it is with the one woman who should be off-limits.

CHAPTER NINETEEN
MIA

Sitting cross legged on the end of my bed, I lift my fingertips to my lips, my mind reeling back to last night as I read over Willow's message a second time. I'm transported back in time, back to the very moment when Caleb's lips crashed into mine.

Even though we had almost kissed before that moment, it was still unexpected. The last thing I expected was for that incident with Steven to trigger a reaction like that from him.

What happened?

I had to go get Tella from Andi so she could head home.

Noah had the game on and I saw your man get into a fight.

My heart crawls into my throat as two words glare back at me.

He's not my man.

What happened, though? The fight looked so unprovoked.

I roll my lips between my teeth, setting my phone down as I nervously tuck my hair behind my ear. There's a soft knock on my door, which interrupts me just as I'm about to come up with some answer that tiptoes around the real reason.

"Come in," I call out, knowing it can only be one person. The knob turns and the door slowly opens, revealing my father on the other side. He's wearing a pair of joggers and a hooded sweatshirt, his glasses adorning his face.

"Hey," he pauses, clearing his throat as he scratches at the stubble along his jaw. "I'm getting ready to head out and wanted to come check on you before I leave."

"Oh shoot," I mumble, climbing off my bed. "I didn't even realize the time. I need to get ready to go to Caleb's."

My father crosses his arms over his chest, a frown

tugging at his lips as he takes a couple measured steps into my room. I drag my bag back out from under my bed and start collecting outfits to put into it as my father takes a seat at my desk. "That's actually what I wanted to talk to you about."

"What do you mean?" I glance over my shoulder as I pull two sweaters from my closet. "About me heading to Caleb's?"

"Not exactly," he says, shaking his head as he purses his lips. "I wanted to talk to you about Caleb and this situation."

My movements falter and my throat suddenly feels thick. *Does he know about the kiss between Caleb and me? How?* I force my hands to work, folding my clothing in a rush now and tucking them into my bag as I swallow hard. "What about it?"

"Caleb's behavior on the ice seemed to be unprovoked by any of the players, but there was something one of the assistant coaches noticed that happened before the fight."

He pauses and I hold my breath, knowing exactly what is coming next.

"I wasn't paying attention to the Jumbotron, but apparently the last people it had on the kiss cam were you and Steven."

I swallow again and release a shallow breath. "Yeah . . ." I say, my voice trailing off as I zip my bag closed. It's not something I can deny and my father knows the kind of relationship Steven and I have. He knows there was nothing to that kiss.

"I know that kiss was just two friends having fun at

a game together." He raises his eyebrows as I finally turn to look at him. "Did Caleb know that was what that was?"

"I mean, I don't know," I say in a rush, my voice a touch higher than normal as I lift my shoulders and drop them. "He knew I was watching the first two periods with a friend."

My father lets out a sigh as he scratches his jaw again. He turns his head, looking out the window for a moment before glancing back at me. "Did Caleb start that fight because of what he saw and what he may have thought about it?"

Shit.

I don't know how I'm supposed to answer this question. Honestly, I didn't even think anyone would have noticed or put two and two together, but then again, Caleb isn't exactly known for provoking fights on the ice. Especially a fight that is completely unwarranted.

My father and I have always been close. The only things I've ever kept from him were things he didn't need to know, like when I lost my virginity or that time I drank too much at Grace Michaels' house the summer before my senior year of college.

If I tell him the truth, I will be blowing up Caleb's spot and for some reason, that just doesn't feel right. I can't help but feel like I'm throwing him under the bus if I say it.

"No."

The word doesn't come out nearly as strong as I pictured it would in my mind. Instead, it's barely audible. I quickly tuck my hair behind my ears, my gaze dropping to the floor before I look at my father again to catch him frowning.

"Meep," my father says, tilting his head to the side as he corkscrews his lips. "You've never been a good liar."

"Dad, please," I say back to him, letting out a breath as I shake my head. "I'm not the person you should be asking that question. And honestly, there's no reason for you to ask Caleb about it either."

He straightens his head and arches an eyebrow at me. "And why is that?"

"Because it was an isolated incident."

He holds eye contact. "It was, but I can't afford to have him fucking up on the ice, Mia. When Caleb's wife passed, I was certain he'd never step foot on the ice again. Surprisingly enough, he was back a month after. He blocked everything out, dug in deep and has been locked in ever since."

My eyebrows tug downward. "So you want him to operate like a robot, essentially."

My father purses his lips. "No. I want him focused." He runs his tongue over his top teeth. "I don't want him provoking fights."

"I don't control him."

"No, you're right," he says, nodding in agreement. "But perhaps you influence him in some way." He lets out a deep breath, running his hand through his hair. "You're an adult, so I'm not going to have a talk with you like you're a teenager, but Caleb is not someone you should be getting involved with."

Now *I* raise an eyebrow at *him*. "Are you saying this as my father or as his coach?"

He grabs his chin, his brow furrowing. "Both."

"I'm not getting involved with him, Dad," I say, shaking my head before disappearing into the bathroom attached to my room. I grab my toiletries and slip back into my bedroom, tucking them in the front pocket of my bag. "I think he and I wouldn't see eye to eye on what we want from another person."

"I just don't want you to get hurt, Meep." He pushes on his knees to rise to his feet and closes the distance between us. "I also don't need to have a scandal on my hands if something unsavory were to happen between the two of you."

"You don't have to worry about any of that," I tell him, not sure if I'm lying or telling the truth. Sure we kissed last night, but really that doesn't mean it will ever happen again.

I saw the conflicted look in Caleb's eyes last night.

But I also felt the way he kissed and touched me.

My father pulls me in for a hug, wrapping his arms around the tops of my shoulders. "Regardless of all that, at the end of the day, I just want you to be happy. You will always be my little girl and I will always be protective of you."

"Thanks, Dad," I murmur against his chest, hugging him back before we both release one another. "I promise, if there ends up being something you need to be worried about, I will tell you."

He raises an eyebrow at me. "I know how things go, Mia. I was young once too."

"Dad." I pause, staring at him as I purse my lips.

"Mia."

"I love you. Have a safe flight."

He chuckles lightly, shaking his head at me. "Deflecting, are we?"

"Nope," I retort, smiling at him. "Just making sure we both get to where we need to be on time."

He rolls his wrist, checking the expensive timepiece wrapped around it. "Shit." He glances back at me. "Okay. Be safe and if Caleb Ford *ever* gives you any problems, you let me know immediately."

Instinctively, I roll my eyes like a petulant teenager. "He won't."

"He'd better not," he says, shaking his head. "Okay, I'm off."

We say our goodbyes before he heads down the stairs as I get the rest of my things together. I grab my phone from the bed and it vibrates in my hand as soon as I pick it up, reminding me of my unfinished conversation with Willow.

And she's left half a dozen messages in my absence.

Do you know why he got into a fight?

Mia, you left me on read.

Did something happen?

Please tell me the fight was because of you, omg.

Mia.

Mia, so help me God, you'd better answer me or I'm heading to your house now.

Sorry, I was talking to my dad while getting ready to head to Caleb's.

Excuses.

Let's skip to the good part.

The kiss cam landed on Steven and me and you know how Steven is.

Showy motherfucker. He kissed you on the screen and Caleb got pissed, didn't he?

OMG MIA! This is huge.

Yeah . . . lol

What happened afterwards? Did you talk to him?

Well, yeah.

AND?!

We kind of kissed.

Mia Evelyn Landry. What do you mean kind of?!?

Okay, not kind of. He said it should have been him who kissed me, not Steven and then we kissed.

Holy shit, I am living for this right now.

Well, don't because I'm pretty sure it won't be happening again.

Oh no, why?

If my dad gets ahold of him and has a talk with him, I'm fairly certain he'll never look in my direction again. My dad doesn't want a scandal on his hands.

I swear to God, if your dad messes this up, I will skin him alive.

I don't know, it was just kind of weird after the kiss. We stopped and he just had this look in his eye. Not like he regretted it necessarily, but almost as if he felt guilty.

I have faith, Mia. One of us has to.

He's so emotionally unavailable and I've never done just casual with someone.

Well, now might be your chance.

Everyone who comes into your life isn't meant to stay. It's not always supposed to be that deep or that serious. Just let yourself have a little bit of fun.

And what if he doesn't want that? What if he doesn't want anything with me?

Then fuck him, that's his loss.

Go sleep with his best friend or his
brother or something.

You're such a menace.

☺ I gotta go, but we'll talk later.

Love you!

Locking my phone, I tuck it into my pocket, collect my bags, and head downstairs to get ready to go to Caleb's. Anxiety rolls in the pit of my stomach as I think over my conversation with my dad, what Willow said, and how last night came to an end.

In a way, I feel foolish for how I responded to Caleb and the way I kissed him back. I know that Willow is right and this doesn't have to be anything serious. It might not be anything more than a kiss, and the thought of trying to pursue anything with him after that literally makes me feel like I'm going to break out in hives.

I can't control Caleb anymore than I can control the outcome from us kissing last night. He let me walk away and maybe he was feeling just as confused by it as I was.

The concept of anything casual is borderline foreign to me. I've never done casual with anyone before and I'm not so sure Caleb is the person I want to test it with.

He's so hot and cold, it gives me whiplash. One minute he's warm and kind and the next, he's shutting down and blocking me out.

I'm not good at reading other people and I'll be

damned if I'm the one who approaches him about this situation.

If he wants this to be anything else, he can be the one to come to me.

CHAPTER TWENTY
CALEB

"You all right, Ford?" Rowan asks as he slides into the seat beside me. "You've been extra quiet all night."

I slowly turn my head to look at my brother's best friend. I'm not extra close to any of the guys other than my brother, but if I had to pick a close second, it would be Rowan Taylor. I watch him as he lifts his water bottle, taking a sip of it before resting it against his thigh.

"I'm good," I tell him, tipping my chin before looking back at the TV ahead of us. "I just have a lot on my mind right now."

Like clock work, Carson comes strolling over, plopping onto the couch next to me. We all finished a morning practice session and were taking turns going over film with the coaching staff. I already sat down with them and went over mine, so I decided to watch the replay of last night's game while I wait for the rest of the guys.

"Hey, Cale," Carson says, knocking his knee against mine. "What did I miss?"

"Not much," Rowan tells him with a shrug. "Just trying to figure out why your brother's so quiet today."

I can feel Carson's gaze searing the side of my face and I resist the urge to dig my elbow into Rowan's side. "It's nothing."

It's not nothing, but it's not something I particularly feel inclined to talk about. Motion over by the door catches my attention. It's Coach Landry coming to grab another player. His eyes meet mine and something unreadable lingers in his gaze. They narrow just a fraction of an inch, assessing me like I caught him doing earlier when it was my turn to go over film.

I don't know why the hell he keeps looking at me like that, almost like he knows I kissed his daughter three nights ago.

"Taylor." Coach says Rowan's name in a clipped voice as he waves him over. The couch shifts as Rowan gets up, heading in the direction of the door. Coach Landry glances at me once more, his Adam's apple bobbing as he swallows and turns away.

"Something going on between you and Coach?" Carson asks, his voice dipping low so only I can hear him.

"Nothing that I know of. He seemed fine when I talked to him." I run my hand through my hair, letting out a deep breath as I turn to look at my brother. I don't know if Mia would have said anything to him. I don't know if he noticed the kiss cam before my little temper tantrum on the ice. He hasn't said a single thing to me that signals he's mad or having an issue with me, but I'm not blind. I've seen the little looks he's been giving me all morning. "I think I'm just being paranoid."

Carson's eyebrows draw closer together. "Paranoid about what?"

Shit. I didn't realize I said that aloud. I know I can trust my brother, but saying the words out loud seems like a betrayal to Amelia. And what's fucked up is, it's not in the least bit.

I tried dating three separate times about two years ago. The three different women were nice and the dates were set up by some of the guys from the teams families. Even one of them was Gloria's niece. I made a whole-hearted attempt to connect with someone else for the sake of everyone pressing for me to do it.

It's like everyone else was afraid for me to be alone forever. Like they were afraid I'd never move on from losing Amelia. Part of me didn't want to and a part of me didn't think I ever would. I still don't know if any part of me today thinks I ever will, but something has changed.

I've begun to feel the loneliness everyone was worried about. Human connection is a huge part of life and I didn't realize it was something I was missing until Mia. Until she offered that sense of safety, of comfort, of connection.

And that's what makes it feel like the biggest betrayal of all. None of the other women made me feel like it was something worth my time, worth investing in. I only kissed one of them and it left me feeling numb. The entire kiss just felt forced and not right.

Everything with Mia feels different. It makes my heart race and my stomach flutter. It makes me forget what I've been missing in life.

"A few nights ago, after the game, the one where I got into that fight…" I pause, sucking in a deep breath before letting out an exaggerated exhale. "I kissed Mia."

Carson is silent, his eyes widening as I turn to look at him. "Wait . . . what?"

"Yeah." I chew on the inside of my cheek. "That entire night was just a mental fuck for me and it just kind of happened after we got back to the house."

Carson stares at me. "You kissed Coach's daughter? Your nanny?"

I roll my lips between my teeth, biting down as I nod my head.

"I think your paranoia is probably justifiable."

My eyes narrow on him. "The only way he would know is if Mia said something to him."

"Do you think she would?"

"I don't know," I tell him, lifting my shoulders and dropping them. "It was just a kiss and nothing more. I had a moment of weakness, a moment of vulnerability."

"But you still did it," Carson says, his voice dropping lower. His eyes slowly search mine. "If you're worried, I think you should ask her about it." He pauses, tilting his head to the side. "You know what they say—it's better to ask for forgiveness than to ask for permission."

I purse my lips. "I think that might apply to anyone other than Coach." I rub the back of my neck. "It's not like it's going to happen again."

Carson raises an eyebrow at me. "Why not?"

"This was different than when I kissed Gloria's niece." I sigh, shaking my head at him. "When I kissed Mia—for those few moments, I was consumed by her— I completely forgot about Amelia. I forgot about what we had and what I lost."

Carson's expression softens, his lips lifting into a sad smile. "You know, Amelia wouldn't want you alone. She wouldn't want you miserable and by yourself for the rest of your life."

"I'm not miserable," I counter through a mumble.

Carson rolls his eyes. "You know what I mean. You're not betraying her by moving on. You're not forgetting her or replacing her."

My stomach sinks. "It feels like it."

"You're not, Cale. Amelia was an amazing woman and we both know that no one can replace her. There's no way any of us could ever forget her. But that doesn't mean you can't let yourself have feelings for someone else. It doesn't mean you can't enjoy being with someone else. You're allowed to be happy."

I stare at my brother for a moment, his words sinking down into my chest. I know he's right, but it's such a hard concept to wrap my mind around, even if it's slowly happening without me realizing.

"One day, you're going to fall in love again. One day, you're going to love someone just as much, if not more than you loved her," he says, staring at me intently. "And it will always be different, because it's not her. And that love will never replace the love you had for Amelia."

A ragged breath escapes me, my heart pounding erratically in my chest. "How can you truly believe any of this?" The thought of falling in love again is something I've refused to even entertain. The thought of that vulnerability. The thought of taking that chance with someone else. Risking it all, only to have the possibility of losing someone the same way I lost her.

It's absolutely terrifying to even consider.

"Because I refuse to believe that there isn't more for you, Cale. I refuse to believe that we live in a world where my brother doesn't get his happily ever after." He pauses, corkscrewing his mouth while he considers his next words. "Even if that means that it wasn't with Amelia."

The door opens once more, Rowan breezing through as he glances at my brother. "Your turn, Carsy."

Carson grabs my knee, giving me a soft squeeze. "It will all be okay, Cale. What's meant to be, will be, as long as you're not stubborn enough to fight against it forever."

Sadness wells in my chest, creeping up my throat. I turn my head to look back at the TV with his words ringing in my head long after he disappears through the doorway. I always thought Amelia was it for me and with her being gone, I never thought there could be someone who came after.

The possibility still seems so farfetched to me, but maybe my brother's right.

Maybe letting myself feel again isn't wrong, after all.

CHAPTER TWENTY-ONE
MIA

Slowly sitting up in bed, the sheet and comforter pool around my waist and I turn my head to look at the alarm clock on the bedside table to my right, checking to see what ungodly time it is in the middle of the night. A groan escapes me and my eyes linger for a second longer before I decide to throw the covers away from my body.

It's almost four o'clock in the morning and I need to be up in almost three hours to get Tella out of bed and ready for school. It feels a little senseless to try and fall back asleep now, especially when I feel wide awake.

The last few nights have been spent tossing and turning, haunted by those grey eyes every time I close mine. I've been avoiding Caleb Ford since the night we kissed, which has been easy with him on the road for some away games.

He's FaceTimed every day, but only to talk to Tella. As soon as their conversations were over, the call would end. He never once bothered to try and have a conversation with me other than to ask how she's been and if he could talk to her.

It's clear that the kiss was a momentary lapse in Caleb's judgment. He has yet to bring it up and I'll be damned if I'm the one who says anything to him about it. If I acknowledge it, that means it happened. And if it really happened, that means he most likely regrets it.

My bare feet hit the wood floor and I press up from the bed, grabbing my sweatshirt from the bottom of the bed and tugging it over my head. I grab my hair, pull it out, and let it cascade down my back, then adjust my sleep shorts and tuck my feet into my slippers. I head over to the bathroom to relieve myself and end up washing my face and brushing my teeth while I'm in there.

After I finish, my feet carry me over to the window and I push the curtains back, separating them as I peer up at the moon. It's massive tonight, bright and white as it appears closer than it actually is. The full moon was last night, but we're still blessed with the intensity of it tonight. It's inching closer to the horizon and it won't be long before it will be hidden by the trees in the distance. I stare up at it, inhaling deeply before letting a breath escape me. There's something calming about the moon, just like the ocean. It's unexplainable, but I feel the peacefulness drifting down my spine.

Down in the backyard, the pool shimmers with the lights beneath the surface. I overheard Caleb telling Tella that he has the closing scheduled for next week, but with how cold the weather has been getting, it's probably best if she stays out at this point.

We're nearing the end of October now and being in Maine, most of the warm days are behind us. I let my eyes continue to wander along the patio, past the hot tub and inching closer to the back deck when I see the outline of someone walking toward the pool.

My body becomes rigid in an instant. My heart stalls in my chest. The person pauses and turns back toward the house. When I catch sight of their features, my body sags with relief, although there's a touch of confusion. It's Caleb.

I didn't think he was supposed to be home until tomorrow morning. I guess they ended up flying in earlier than anticipated.

Either way . . . It's four o'clock in the morning and he's wandering around his backyard in the dark.

He doesn't look up at my window and instead, he walks over to one of the lounge chairs, lowering himself down onto its edge. He positions his elbows against his thighs, his fingers threading together.

I should crawl back into bed. I back away from the window, close my eyes, and let out a deep breath. I'm not sure what he's doing down there, I should just leave him alone. But I feel drawn back to the window.

Caleb lifts a hand and runs his fingers along his forehead. Time hangs heavily in the air as he lifts his other hand, cradling his head as he lets it hang.

Go back to bed, Mia.

He's not your problem.

An exaggerated sigh escapes me as I walk over to my dresser, pulling out a pair of sweat pants and quickly swap out my sleep shorts for them. Giving my room and my bed one last lingering glance, I slip out the door. I keep my steps light so I don't wake Tella as I head down the stairs.

I wasn't planning on going back to bed anyway.

I'm not so sure I ever stood a chance.

The alarm on the sliding glass door beeps twice as I ease it open, making my entrance known as I step out into the cool crisp air of the early morning. Caleb lifts his head as if it weighs a ton, slow and deliberate. My breath ceases as his gaze meets mine. His hands hang between his legs and the muscle in his jaw relaxes as he sighs out a breath.

My heart shifts into overdrive and I suck in a sharp breath. My feet carry me across the deck, not stopping until I sit down on the lounge chair that is next to his. Caleb's head turns and I can almost feel him studying the side of my face for a moment.

"Did I wake you?"

I shake my head, slowly turning to look at him. Even in just the glow from the pool, the dark circles underneath his eyes are evident. "No," I whisper, then clear my throat since it's the first time using my voice today. "I haven't been sleeping well."

He's silent as his eyes scan my face. His lips part, as if he's going to say something, but his mouth falls shut again. He drops his gaze, lowering it down to his hands again as he rubs his thumbs together.

"I thought you weren't getting in for a few more hours?"

"Earlier flight. We landed around two."

I roll my lips between my teeth, nervously tucking

my hair behind my ears as the cool fall breeze drifts between Caleb and me. It feels like the distance grows, even though in reality we're shoulder to shoulder.

My gaze drifts to his hands. He steeples his fingers before threading them back into the spaces between. "Are you okay?"

The muscle in his jaw flexes as he clamps his teeth together and then releases. Moonlight outlines his side profile. Tense and hard, almost as if he's holding something inside, but there's a lingering softness just beneath it all. A tenderness in the curves of his eyebrows and in the way he drags his teeth over his bottom lip.

Ever so slowly, he turns his head to the side. His gaze starts on the bottom hem of my worn sweatshirt, traveling up my torso, my neck, along my jaw, only stopping when it reaches my eyes. "I don't think I am, pup."

"Want to talk about it?" I question him, turning to angle my body toward him more.

His brows pinch together and his lips turn down in a frown. "I'm sorry for the other night."

My stomach tumbles to the floor as the air leaves my lungs in a rush. There it is. The one phrase I had been hoping I wouldn't hear from him. The single phrase that changes the trajectory of things between us. I thought I saw a hint of regret in his eyes that night and here is the confirmation.

I swallow hard over the lump in my throat, my spine immediately straightening. "It's okay. I'd prefer to just forget that it happened, if that's okay with you?" The words fall from my lips in rapid succession. "If you no longer feel comfortable having me watch Tella, I also understand that."

"No, none of that is okay with me," he says, his voice quiet as his eyebrows pull tighter together. He slowly turns to face me, leaning forward as he grabs the leg of my lounge chair and pulls me closer. He drags it across the stamped concrete until the corner of mine is between his legs. He scoots to the edge, his knees pressing against mine. "I'm sorry for letting you walk away. I'm sorry if I led you to believe it meant nothing to me."

My heart skips a beat and my breath catches in my throat. "What?"

"I don't regret kissing you, Mia." His throat bobs, his eyes slowly searching mine. "I regret letting you think I did."

"But you've been avoiding me," I tell him, my voice barely audible as his admission sinks deep into the fibers of my being. "You've barely spoken to me since that night."

His nostrils flare. "Because all of this is fucking with my head, pup." His tongue darts out to wet his lips and he pinches them together momentarily. "When I'm around you, I don't think about her as often and I'm not sure what to do with that."

My eyes bounce back and forth between his. This is the moment where I should walk away. Caleb Ford is the furthest thing from healed and I have no business thinking I can be the person to help guide him through that. I've never lost anyone in my life, I don't know the first thing about how it feels to try and move past the grief and guilt and all the emotions that come with it.

"I don't want to be a problem for you," I whisper.

"That's not what I meant," he says in a rush. He lets out a breath, running a ragged hand through his hair. "I tried dating about two years ago and it just wasn't for me. But with those women, it felt different than whatever this is between you and me," he says, dropping his hands to his knees. His fingers brush against my own, which sends a tingle up my arm. Warmth radiates off him through the material of my sweatpants. "I'm not ready for anything serious and honestly, I don't know if I ever will be."

My mind plays back what Willow said. *It doesn't have to be serious. It can just be for the plot, for the fleeting moment passing through time.* Caleb doesn't have to become a permanent fixture. Instead, he can just be a short chapter. A piece of my past.

And for some reason, that feels like a complete disservice to this broken man in front of me.

"I've never done casual before," I admit to him, tucking my hair behind my ears again. I drop my own hands to my thighs, my fingers reaching toward Caleb's. The tips of his find mine and he slides them against the pads of my fingers until my hand unfurls for him. When our palms touch, he laces our fingers together and gives my hand a little squeeze . "But it's not something I'm against trying."

The corners of his mouth twitch as he rolls his wrists, moving his other hand to cradle mine. "I can't stop thinking about you, pup." A shiver slithers down my spine. "I need you, but you need to know—I can never give you more than stolen moments when I'm home. It can never be anything more than physical."

My stomach flutters, my heart racing inside my chest. "I'm not interested in anything serious," I tell him what he needs to hear, the words tasting foreign on my tongue. *Will I be able to keep it casual?*

His eyes burn into mine, his throat bobbing as I inch to the edge of my lounge chair.

My knees press against the insides of his thighs. He breathes out, a low groan vibrating in his throat as my tongue darts out to lick the lies from my lips.

"I don't want anything more."

CHAPTER TWENTY-TWO
CALEB

Any logical thought evaporates my mind when my hands reach for the sides of her face as I lift myself from my lounge chair. Mia reaches for me, her hands grabbing at my sweatshirt as I slip my hands behind her head, my fingers plunging through her hair. It's so soft and slips through my fingers like water.

Mia leans back, tipping her chin up to look at me with lust filled eyes. I pause to take her in. A ragged breath escapes me as I take my time to search her irises. Looking for any sign of hesitation.

"We shouldn't be doing this," I murmur, my voice barely audible as my gaze drops down to her plump pink lips with their perfect Cupid's bow.

"No," she breathes before she glides her tongue along those perfect lips to wet them. Her hands push up the bottom hem of my sweatshirt, and I suck in a sharp breath when her fingers dance across my flesh, sending goose bumps up my torso. "We probably shouldn't."

My eyelids fall shut, a groan vibrating in my throat. There's no place for rationality right now. If I'm going to live my life, I can't second guess every move I make. That defeats the whole purpose of just living. I take another slow deep breath through my nose to try to calm myself down.

Opening my eyes, they immediately meet her hooded gaze. "Fuck it," I growl as I lower my mouth to hers. She inhales sharply and there's a moment of hesitation as I begin to move my lips against hers before she responds. She works her lips against mine, kissing me back as her fingers continue to trail along my skin.

I inch closer, lips locked together as I begin to lower her down onto the lounge chair until she's lying flat on her back. I crawl over her, settling between her legs as my tongue slides along the seam of her mouth. Mia doesn't hesitate this time and they immediately open, granting me access inside.

Warmth builds in the pit of my stomach and I feel blood rushing between my legs, my already hard cock throbbing against her center. I can't help myself as my body reacts to the warmth between her legs. A low moan sounds from my chest and I shift my hips forward, pressing my erection against her.

Mia nails dig into my back, biting into my flesh as she moans against my mouth. Her tongue is like silk, tangling with mine as she winds herself inside the fibers of my very being.

She kisses me with an intensity that has my toes curling, body trembling. The cool air of the early morning skates across my skin, a stark contrast to the heat blooming inside my body as she pushes my shirt up farther.

As her hands move up along my shoulders, I break apart from her, coming up for air as I rock back to sit on my heels. Mia's breathless, her hair splayed out around her head, the bottom of her shirt pushed up above her belly button. I stare down at her before pulling both of my shirts off and tossing them onto the ground beside us.

"Should we go inside?" she murmurs, lifting herself up as she reaches to touch my stomach. A shiver dances down my spine, more goose bumps breaking out across my skin as she trails her fingers along the ridges of my abdomen.

"Are you cold?" I ask, my eyes slowly searching hers. "We can go in if you are."

She drags her top teeth over her bottom lip. "Not so much anymore."

The corners of my lips twitch. "What are we doing here, pup?"

"I don't know," she replies. She's out of breath but her fingers slip beneath the waistband of my sweat-pants. Her lips tip up in a coy smile. "What do you think we're doing here?"

My cock twitches in my pants. "Whatever feels good," I tell her, my hands dropping down to her stomach as I mimic her, pushing her shirt farther up. "I'm—uh—" I pause, running my tongue over my top teeth. "It's been a long time since I've—"

I pause, the words dying on my lips because I can't bring myself to speak them out loud. Not now, not here.

It will only sever the moment and I'm not letting that happen.

Call me selfish, but I'll deal with the feelings that come with this afterwards.

Her smile softens. "No one is in a rush, Caleb," she says softly, her fingers abandoning my waistband. She rests her hands on the tops of my thighs. "I think it will be better for both of us if we just take it slow."

"How slow?" I ask as I begin to lower both of us back down onto the lounge chair. Her hands creep up to my body, circling around my back, nails raking along my flesh.

"We don't have to decide right this second," Mia says, her eyes searching mine. "If it begins to feel like it's too much, we can stop."

I hover above her, taking her in. She's so beautiful lying on her back, her hair like a halo around her head, the light emanating from the pool making her glow. She stares back up at me without regret or judgment. She's being genuine and considerate of my situation. Honestly, after knowing her only a short time, I wouldn't expect anything different. Mia Landry is steady and strong, caring and kind. She doesn't waver and I find solace in that predictability.

Unable to hold off any longer, my lips crash into hers. Mia holds me close, bending her knees and caging my hips in with her thighs. One of my hands makes its way down to her thigh, gripping her through her sweatpants as I slide my other along the side of her neck, plunging my fingers through her silky hair to cradle the back of her head.

Mia kisses me back with a tenderness that mixes with a blazing heat, seeping through every cell in my body. Her nails dig into my flesh again but it feels so good. Her thighs tighten against me as her tongue dances with mine. I breathe her in, savoring the way she smells, the way she feels, and the way she tastes, just like this, lost in this moment with me.

My cock strains against my pants, throbbing as I lower my hips and press against her. Mia lets out a soft breathless moan when I grind against her clit. I swallow the sound, pressing harder into her. One of her hands moves up my neck to the back of my head to pull me down more, her tongue sliding over mine. The way she responds ignites a fire inside me. It spreads rapidly through my veins and I can't help but wonder how she might look coming undone beneath me from my touch.

"Fuck, Mia," I groan against her mouth, pulling her bottom lip between my teeth as I clamp down. She whimpers, lifting herself up against me. I release her lip and run my tongue over the indents I left in her flesh.

Releasing her hip, I glide my hand along her torso. My fingers dive beneath her shirt and slide up until they graze the underside of her breasts. I suck in a sharp breath and hold it as my thumb caresses her soft, supple skin. My cock throbs at the knowledge that she's not wearing a bra.

I pull back from her so I can search her eyes, desperate for her words. Her eyes shine through the darkness, and she licks her lips again. "Is this okay?" I ask, my voice low and hoarse.

She drags her teeth over her bottom lip, nodding as she stares up at me. "Yes."

"Tell me what to do, pup," I say, my voice gravely.

Her slender throat bobs. "Touch me, Caleb."

A low moan vibrates in my chest and I slowly slide my hand up and over her breast, appreciating its fullness in my palm as I cup it. She stares up at me through a hooded gaze, lips parting as a shallow breath escapes her when I brush the pad of my thumb over her nipple.

"Oh," she breathes out. My heart stutters in my chest from that soft sound falling from her lips. I move my thumb again in a sweeping motion over her tender flesh. Mia shivers, her hands drifting along the waistband of my pants as her gaze burns into mine. I drag my forefinger along her skin, stopping to pinch her nipple with my thumb and pointer finger, rolling it between them.

"Caleb," she moans, withering under my touch as she begins to push her fingers a little farther beneath the waistband of my boxer briefs. Warmth builds in the pit of my stomach and goose bumps break out across my skin as the tips of her fingers graze my flesh, creeping closer to my throbbing erection. "Is this okay?"

A shiver travels down my spine as she pauses and waits for my response. "Yes," I admit, my voice thick with lust. "Go lower, pup. I want you to feel exactly what you're doing to me."

A quiet laugh falls from her lips as her fingers travel lower, her hand pushing farther into my pants. Her warm palm sends an electrical current through me as she grazes my cock. She pauses, a sheepish grin dancing across her lips. "You too," she murmurs, sliding her other hand to mine that lingers on her chest. She wraps her delicate fingers around my wrist. "I want you to feel what you're doing to me."

My cock throbs as she releases my wrist and I begin my descent down her abdomen. I slip it beneath the waistband of her sweatpants, and push beneath the elastic of her panties to find her soft, hot flesh with my fingertips. Her eyes are locked in on mine, her lips parted as she pants just from my fingers at the top of her mound. I slip my hand between her legs and drag my fingers against her pussy.

"You're so wet," I growl at the moisture collecting on my fingers. I tease her clit, moving past to linger against her center. I could push my finger inside and feel the depths of her. Feel how tight and wet and warm she is inside.

I can't take my eyes off of her, my body still as I watch the way her throat moves as she swallows. Her eyes widen a little, her pupils dilating and nostrils flaring as I give in to the temptation, slowly pushing a finger inside of her. Her cunt constricts around me.

My heart pounds against my ribcage as I focus on how tight she's wrapped her hand around my cock. The tips of her fingers don't touch around my girth. "Goddamn, Mia, I want to feel my cock inside of you."

"I—I don't know." She pauses, a breathy laugh escaping her. "You're big. Like really big."

"Don't worry, pup, you'll be able to take it," I growl, pressing against her center as she slowly slides her hand down my length and back toward my groin again.

"Not now though," I tell her, my eyelids fluttering shut as I revel in the way she feels, stroking me in such a teasing way as I lazily push my finger in and out of her. "I want to have an entire night to take my time with you. I want to taste and touch every inch of your skin. I want to fuck you until we're both satiated. And then I want to fuck you again."

The gentle breeze drifts past us and a wind chime sounds in the distance. I freeze. They sound just like the ones Amelia had hanging on the front porch of our old house. I stare down at Mia, my heart crawling up my throat, my cock throbbing as I feel a cold sweat rolling over me. My lungs constrict as panic licks at my veins. She said we could take it slow, that she felt it would be best for both of us, yet here I am with my fingers inside of her and her hand wrapped around my cock.

This is too much, too fast. And I'm a fucking asshole for letting it go this far.

Mia's eyebrows pull together, her hand releasing me as she pulls it out of my pants. My face screws up and a ragged breath escapes me as I drag my fingers from her. "Hey," she says softly, her hands coming up to cup the sides of my face. "It's okay. It's okay."

"I'm sorry," I say in a rush, lifting myself from her, reaching for my shirts as I sit back on the edge of the lounge chair. "I—" I pause, closing my eyes as I drag my hand down my face. I blow out a deep breath. Shame washes over me at the way I just pulled away from her.

"Caleb," she says quietly, sitting up as her eyes search my face. She reaches for me, her hand wrapping around mine as she gives me a gentle squeeze. "Please don't apologize, unless you didn't actually want to do any of that." She swallows roughly. "I think we both got a little carried away there."

"No, I did," I say in a rush to assure her. The last thing I want is for her to question any of this because of my inability to get my shit together. "I don't know." I let out a breath, frustration washing over me as my gaze drops down to her hand on mine. "I don't know what I'm doing."

"And that's completely fine," she says with a tenderness that seeps into my soul. She gives my hand another squeeze. "You don't have to know what you're doing. I meant what I said, about not being in a rush. You're setting the pace here."

"I just let myself get into my head sometimes," I admit, my voice barely above a whisper. "Sometimes it's like a goddamn prison in there. I forget about things and then as soon as I'm reminded, it's like I'm trapped again. Paralyzed almost."

"I got you, Caleb." She releases my hand and inches closer, her leg brushing against mine. I turn my face to hers and she stares at me with an intensity that has my heart beating harder inside my chest. "If you get lost in your head, I'll come find you."

Emotion lodges in my throat. I stare back at her, then brush the hair away from her face. "Yeah?"

A tender smile lifts her lips as she slowly nods. "Yeah."

CHAPTER TWENTY-THREE
MIA

Two days of silence and I feel like I'm going insane.

"How do casual hook-ups work?"

"What do you mean?" Willow questions me just as Steven also begins to talk.

"Who are we talking about?"

I let out a breath, pressing my foot down on the brake pedal as I pull up to the red-light. I'm currently on my way to Caleb's house to watch Tella for most of the day. The other night has played on repeat in my mind since I drove home that morning.

"We're talking about her and that gorgeous hockey player who hired her as his nanny."

"Wait, wait, are we talking about the one I think we're talking about?" Steven asks, his voice coming through the speakers in my car as soon as Willow stops talking. "Momma Mia, where art thou?"

"I'm here," I say quietly, letting them have their

moment. "Is it normal to have an intimate moment with someone and then just not talk for a few days after?"

"Oh, honey," Willow says softly. "Yes. Neither of you owe the other anything more than what happens in that moment."

"I think it just depends on the person or the hook-up, honestly," Steven adds in. "I've done 'casual' with a few people who ended up being clingy as hell."

I purse my lips, pressing on the gas when the light turns green. "So, all this could be perfectly normal?"

"I mean, what's going on?" Willow asks.

I shrug, even though neither of them can see. "Nothing really. We—um—we were together the other night and haven't spoken since. I mean, he texted me about what time to come today, but that was it."

"Sounds normal to me," Steven says.

"Let him adjust and acclimate. This is new for both of you," Willow says, chiming in as the voice of reason. "If he acts like you don't exist in person, then fuck that, but if you're just talking about when you're apart, then I think it's normal."

"Is there anything really normal with casual flings?" Steven chuckles. "Just go with your gut, Mia. If it feels wrong, it probably is."

"Okay, okay," I tell both of them, turning on my turn signal. "I'm pulling up to his place now, so I'll keep you posted."

"Are we still going to get drinks for your birthday tonight?"

"Caleb has a game tonight, so if I don't get out of here too late," I tell Willow. Steven isn't in town anymore, so Willow and I are going to go get drinks to celebrate without him. I meant to say something to Caleb the other night, but it slipped my mind.

"Okay, let me know. Love you!" Willow says as Steven says bye and we end the three way call. I thought maybe I'd feel better after talking to the two of them, but I don't. I don't want to seem clingy or desperate. I don't need to hear from him every single day, but I can't help feeling like I'm in a vulnerable place.

We shared an intimate moment, a moment that felt deeper than the purely physical he spoke of before. I can't let myself read into it and make it seem like it's more than it was. I have to mean what I said to him.

I have to convince myself that I won't ever want anything more with him.

After parking in Caleb's driveway, I slip out of my car and make my way to the front door. It's already unlocked, so I let myself into the foyer. The soft sound of music drifts down the hallway from the kitchen.

I kick off my shoes, setting my bag on the bench by the front door before I head deeper into the house. As I walk up to the kitchen, I pause in the doorway, my heart crawling into my throat as I see Caleb standing over by the oven. He bends forward, the muscles in his back stretching as he leans down to look just beyond the glass as he tilts his head to the side.

I look at him for a moment, watching as he pulls open the door and the sweet aroma of chocolate chip cookies wafts through the air. My stomach unleashes a grumble in protest and I remember I forgot to eat a full breakfast.

A chuckle bubbles in my throat as I glance at the clock and then back to Caleb as he slowly stands upright.

"Cookies for breakfast?"

His shoulders relax and he slowly turns around to face me. The corners of his mouth twitch when his gaze meets mine, and he tucks his hands into the front pockets of his grey sweatpants. They hang a bit low on his hips, showing the black waistband of his boxer briefs that hide the lower half of the *V* shape that disappears beneath them.

He's wearing his glasses this morning and my God, he's a sight that would break your damn heart. Tousled hair, damp from an early morning swim, low hanging sweatpants, the perfectly chiseled torso, and those grey eyes that burn brighter than the sun.

"I didn't want to mess up baking a cake and I didn't have time to order one."

I slowly tilt my head to the side, moving away from the doorway as I enter the kitchen.

"Tella told me you like chocolate chip cookies," Caleb says, his voice low as he meets me halfway. His fingers trail along the side of my face as he brushes my hair away. "Happy birthday, pup."

Heat creeps up my neck before spreading across my cheeks. I can't stop the smile that takes over my face. "You didn't have to bake me anything."

"I know I didn't," he half whispers, his eyes searching mine as he tips my chin up. "But I wanted to. You should have told me it was your birthday."

"It didn't feel like an important thing to mention."

Caleb's face dips down to mine, his lips softly brushing against my mouth. He kisses me with a tenderness that doesn't require any words to be spoken. His lips move against mine, gently coaxing them open as his tongue slips inside. He feels like silk and tastes like chocolate as his gentle kisses turn to pecks before pulling back. "It's important to me."

My heart is lodged in my throat. He releases my face, taking a step back before he turns around to head back to the oven.

"Do you have any plans or anything to celebrate?"

"I—uh." I pause, shaking my head to chase away the dazed feeling he leaves inside my brain. My fingers hover over my lips, while I scan the back of his body. "My best friend Willow wants to go get drinks after your game, if I have time. It's not a big deal though."

The timer on the oven begins to beep. The cords in Caleb's muscles tighten as he presses the off button and grabs two oven mitts. His fingers tease the opening and he slowly pushes them into the mitt, one by one.

How does he make everything look sexy?

Caleb pulls the cookie tray out, setting it on the stove top before he turns back to look at me. "You don't have to wait until after my game."

My eyebrows tug together. "What do you mean?"

"When Tella told me about your birthday, I talked to Andi and she's going to keep Tella tonight."

Emotion washes over me. It's such a simple gesture, but it hits me hard inside my chest. He had no idea I had plans. He also took the word of a five year old, who could have gotten her days confused. But he went ahead and made other arrangements so I could have the evening off. "You didn't have to do that," I say, my voice barely audible.

"I don't do things I don't want to do, pup."

Tella comes bounding into the kitchen, severing the moment as she wraps her arms around my legs. "Happy birthday, Mia!"

I catch Caleb's gaze, the way his expression softens and a warmth enters his eyes as he watches his daughter. I stare down at her, waiting for her to release my legs before I crouch down and pull her in for a hug. "Thank you, Tella! Did you come down for the cookies?"

"Duh, silly!" She giggles and hugs me back. When she pulls back, her blue grey eyes meet mine. "And because it's your birthday! Birthdays are the best days ever."

"They are, aren't they?" I smile back at her, tapping the tip of her nose with my finger. My gaze shifts past her, colliding with Caleb's as he watches me from across the room. His throat bobs with a rough swallow, a ghost of a smile dancing across his perfect lips and I could swear his eyes are a bit misty.

"The cookies should be cool enough to move to the cooling rack in a few minutes," Caleb says, his voice catching in his throat as I stand back upright and Tella marches over to the oven. "Wait until they're cooled before you eat them," he tells Tella.

"Aw, Daddy. You're not even going to stay and eat Mia's birthday cookies with us?"

I stifle a laugh, walking over to the two of them. "He has to go to practice, babe."

"I promise I'll eat one when I get home," he says as he leans down to plant a kiss on her forehead. "You be on your best behavior for Mia."

"Yes, daddy," she says, nodding her head at him as she steps around him to head over to the fridge.

"Thank you, Caleb," I say just loud enough for him to hear me. "Thank you for this."

He studies my face and he takes a step closer, lifting his hand to cup the side of my face. "Thank you," he counters, his voice barely above a whisper. The pad of his thumb runs along my jaw and he immediately drops it away as Tella closes the fridge. "Happy birthday, Mia."

His eyes linger on mine for a fraction of a second longer before he leaves the two of us in the kitchen and heads out the door to the garage. I touch the side of my face, feeling the warmth of his fingers once more. My own fingers move down to my lips and I bite back a grin, still feeling the softness of his mouth pressed against mine.

Caleb Ford is inching deeper and deeper into the organ beneath my ribcage and he doesn't even know it.

And I'm not so sure I'll ever tell him how much any of this actually meant to me. But I swore this could just be casual. *Who am I kidding?*

CHAPTER TWENTY-FOUR
CALEB

As I walk into my house, it feels weird, walking into the silence. There's no one here and it just feels . . . off. Tella fell asleep at Andi's, so Andi just said to come get her in the morning. Mia left early this afternoon after I got home from practice. It just doesn't feel right coming home and not even seeing her.

I kick off my shoes, walk deeper into the house, and pause when I walk into the kitchen. On the center of the island in the middle of the room is a Tupperware with the cookies I made for Mia this morning. A smile pulls on my lips as I walk closer, noticing a note she left for me.

These were the best cookies I've ever had.

I don't know what the secret ingredient is that you put in them, but I promise I won't tell anyone if you decide to share it with me.

Yours,

Mia

Popping off the lid, I pull out one of the cookies and sink my teeth into it. The sweetness of the chocolate and the almond flour blend so well, it doesn't even taste like it's gluten free.

After finding out she has celiac disease, I found out everything I could about it. I know it's not necessarily a food allergy, but anything that can do internal damage is worth exercising safety from. The last thing I want is for my home to be a danger to Mia and her health.

Everything in my house is completely gluten free now, just so there's no risk to her.

Pulling out my phone, I open my messages app. My finger hovers above Mia's name. It's her birthday and she's out with her friend right now, but I feel compelled to text her. I don't know if it's the note she left or the loneliness and silence creeping in.

I just want to talk to her.

> How's your night going?

MIA

It's going well.

I'm actually waiting for the car I ordered to get here.

> Where are you at?

The Bellvue.

> Where is Willow?

She's in the bathroom.

The hair stands up on my arms. It's almost midnight and they're at a bar, so why aren't they together?

Is she not riding with you?

Oh, no, she is.

She had to go to the bathroom, so I came out to wait for the car. I don't know why it looks like they're driving to the other side of town though.

Popping the rest of the cookie into my mouth, I shake my head at my phone and type out my next message.

Cancel the ride, I'll come get you guys.

No, you don't have to do that.

Mia.

Caleb.

Cancel the damn ride and go find Willow.

I'll be there in ten minutes.

Thank you.

Tucking my phone in my pocket, I head back out to the garage. I know exactly where I'm going, so I don't bother with directions. I would much rather be the one driving Mia than having her fucking around with ordering a car that is clearly not coming to where she is.

I don't know if she's drunk, I have no idea what I'm

really walking into here with her and her best friend, but I can't sit here idly and hope she gets home safely.

It's one thing I can control. It's one thing I can do to ease my worried mind.

I slow down as I pull up to the bar, coming to a stop along the curb out front. Putting the car in park, I push open my door and immediately climb out to scan the street for the two of them. Just along the front of the brick building, I find her leaning against it.

She doesn't see me at first and I allow myself the moment to drink her in from this distance. Her hair is pulled back in a slick high ponytail. The red dress she's wearing hugs every curve of her body, stopping at the middle of her thighs. In one hand, she's holding a small clutch and in the other, her heels dangle by the ankle straps.

It's not warm enough outside for her to be out here without a coat or shoes, but she doesn't seem to mind the cold air. Must be the alcohol keeping her warm and I can't help but wonder how much she had to drink.

Next to her stands another woman with strawberry blonde hair and a similar dress, although it's in a dark mahogany shade.

I walk up to the two of them. Her friend doesn't notice me, her attention glued to her phone screen, but Mia's eyes immediately meet mine. Her lips curl upwards into a lazy grin, and her eyes lower as she tilts her head to the side.

"Hey, you," she says, slurring the words together a bit.

"Hey, pup," I say in a calm voice. With the swipe of

my tongue, I wet my lips and inch closer. I reach for her hand, relieving her of her heels. "You ready to go?"

"Is this our knight in shining armor?" Her friend says as she stumbles, knocking her shoulder into Mia's. "Oh shit, he's hot."

Blush creeps across Mia's face and she bats her eyelashes at me. "Caleb, this is Willow."

"Hello, Willow," I respond, dipping my chin at her before my gaze flashes back to Mia. "Let's get you both in the car."

Willow begins to walk past us and Mia pushes away from the wall, clearly unsteady on her feet as she sways. I step closer, sliding my arm along her back to guide her over to where I'm parked. Willow walks right past the car, not paying attention to anything.

I stop at the passenger's side, opening the door as I help Mia in. She calls to her friend, who whips her head around and stumbles back in our direction. Mia smiles up at me as she leans her head back against the seat and her eyelids flutter shut.

"You're my hero."

I brush some hair from her face and stare down at her for a moment, memorizing the way she looks. I don't drink really anymore and I can't fault her for enjoying her early twenties as a single woman out with her friend. I just feel so much better having her in my car right now, knowing that she's safe.

Willow pauses by the backdoor and I push Mia's door closed before opening the back for Willow. She gives me a smile, her eyes rolling slightly. "Thanks," she half hiccups and flops into the backseat. I watch her for a moment, making sure she gets strapped in before she folds over to the side.

I let out a breath, shutting the door behind her. I swear to God, she'd better not throw up in there. I walk around the front of the car, climbing in behind the wheel and turning to look at Mia. "Where to?"

She doesn't say anything as she sits with her head back against the seat. I stare at her for a moment, my eyes widen and my heart races in my chest. The rise and fall of her chest captures my attention for a moment before I let out my own breath of relief.

"Mia."

She clears her throat and whispers, "Yeah, love?"

Love? I can't get hung up on that word right now. Maybe she uses it with everyone when she's been drinking. I give my head a slight shake to knock those thoughts from my head and refocus on the task in front of me. "I need your address, pup."

"I'm not ready to go there," she half mumbles.

I swallow the lump in my throat, glancing at her sleeping friend in the backseat before looking back at Mia. Her head rolls as she turns it to face me, but her eyelids don't lift.

"Take me home." She pauses, letting out a soft breath. "With you."

My throat constricts as my eyes travel over the planes of her face. Leaning forward, I reach across her and grab the seat belt to pull it across her body. "Okay," I whisper, my voice strained as I secure her seatbelt before sitting back in my own seat.

The drive is silent, except for both of them snoring

as I head back to my house. Neither of them stir as I pull up the driveway and into the garage. I kill the engine, glancing at Mia and then back at Willow. Turning away, I sigh and climb out of the car, making my way to the back. I pull open the door, not sure how the hell I'm supposed to wake her up.

"Willow," I say loudly, poking her shoulder. "Willow, wake up."

Willow lifts one eyelid to peer at me. "What?"

"I need to get you inside."

She runs her tongue over her top teeth. "I need a drink."

"Okay. I'll get you water as soon as I get you inside."

"Yeah, okay," she sighs, pulling herself into a seated position. She struggles with the seatbelt for a second before she undoes it. She's a bit unsteady as she attempts to climb out of the car, so I hold my arm out for her in an effort to help. "I can see why Mia likes you."

I stare at her for a moment, not commenting on her remark as I feel the familiar twisting in my chest. Willow gets out of the car and I help her into the house, immediately walking her to the couch where she flops down across it. She's snoring before I get the chance to get her water, so I grab one anyway and leave it on the coffee table for her.

I toss a blanket over her body before heading back out to the garage to get Mia. I grab another bottle of water on the way and tuck it in my back pocket for her. She's still asleep when I open the front door.

"Pup, we're home," I say softly as I unbuckle her seatbelt. "Let's get you inside, yeah?"

She turns her head to face me, a smile lifting her lips as she raises a hand and cups my cheek. Her eyelids crack open, but I can see the colors of her irises peeking through. "You're a good man, Caleb Ford. The best man, really."

"You're sweet when you're drunk," I chuckle as I grab her clutch and loop her heel straps with my finger.

"I'm always sweet."

"You are," I murmur, my eyes traveling down to her perfect pink lips. My nostrils flare, a shiver trailing down my spine as her thumb brushes against the corner of my mouth. "Lean forward."

Mia slowly sits up straight as I slide my arm behind her back. I slip the other beneath her bent knees and lift her into the air in one fluid moment. "Oh," she breathes as I hold her against my chest, her arms moving to link around the back of my neck. "I can walk."

"I'd rather carry you," I whisper, reveling in the way she feels in my arms. I know she can walk, but she's tired and drunk. The last thing I need is for her to fall and get hurt. I know I can keep her safe if she's in my arms.

Mia nestles her face into my neck and I kick the door shut before heading deeper into the house. I glance over at the couch where Willow is still asleep and thankfully hasn't thrown up. I carry Mia upstairs to the second floor, walking right past the guest room she's been occupying.

I carry her straight to my bedroom and quietly shut

the door behind me. Dropping her heels on the floor first, I then set her clutch down on my dresser and carry her over to the side of my bed.

Mia lifts her head, and pulls back a little so her eyes can meet mine as I slowly lower her down onto her mattress, pushing the covers out of the way. "This is your room," she says softly, her voice barely above a whisper.

"I know," I murmur, as I kick my shoes off and pull off my sweatshirt. Emotion wells in my throat as I stare down at her for a moment. Her mascara is smudged under her eyes, her cheeks a little flushed still from the alcohol, her lips still bear the fainted tint of lipgloss, and I can just make out her faint pulse flickering in her slender neck. I haven't had anyone else in my bed since Amelia passed, it never felt right. But for some reason, nothing about this feels wrong.

She rolls over, shifting her body into the center of the king sized bed as she reaches for me. "Sleep with me?"

Her sleep laden voice is so sweet, like honey dripping from her tone. I can't walk away from her, instead I remove my glasses, and set them down on the nightstand. The bed shifts beneath my weight as I lower myself onto it, scooting closer to her as she pulls the covers over both of our bodies.

I'm hesitant at first, but once my hands find her beneath the blankets, my arms encircle her and I pull her flush against my side. Her head rests against my ribcage, the sound of my heart pitter pattering beneath her ear.

She snakes her arm around my torso, her warmth seeping into my flesh. "I'm afraid when I wake up, this will all be a dream."

My breath catches in my throat as I lift my hand to run it over her hair. "I'll be here when you wake up in the morning."

"Promise?" She murmurs against my chest, her jaw widening as she yawns. She holds me a little tighter.

I lower my face to her head, burying it in her hair as I breathe in the scent of her, wanting to memorize every piece of this woman. "Promise."

I know I'll be here in the morning, but I can't promise her any more than that . . .

CHAPTER TWENTY-FIVE
MIA

Something warm and heavy tightens around my waist. I'm surrounded by heat as I peel my eyes open. The light shining from the window burns my eyes. I squint against it, immediately shutting my eyes once more as my mind registers that the hot thing behind me is another body.

My eyelids fly open again, the harsh light forgotten as I take in my surroundings. My mind plays back over the events of last night. Willow and I met up at my dad's house and then we ordered a car and went out to dinner. We ended up going to two different bars, and I don't remember having that many drinks, but judging by the pounding in my head, I know I drank more than I should have.

I remember the car wasn't coming and Willow was in the bathroom and then Caleb texted me.

Caleb.

I'll be here when you wake up in the morning . . .

I'm in his bed with his arm wrapped around my

waist, holding me firmly against the front of his body. I slowly stir against him and attempt to turn around to face him but his arm tightens a little more.

"Go back to sleep, pup," he murmurs, his breath warm against the back of my neck as he nuzzles his face against me. "I'm not ready for it to be day time."

My body protests. "I hate to ruin the moment, but I need to go to the bathroom."

"Fair," he murmurs. "I'll only let you go if you promise you'll come right back."

I giggle, wiggling against his arm as my bladder screams at me to get the hell up. "I promise."

"Good girl." He presses his lips against the nape of my neck before untangling his arm from me. I slip out of bed, sprint into his bathroom, and shut the door behind me. I quickly relieve myself and head to the mirror, my eyes widening in horror as I take in my appearance.

My once slicked back hair is still pulled back in a pony-tail, but it's looser and all the little short pieces form a halo around my head. My makeup is smudged around my eyes and I look like a goddamn mess. I take a minute to wash my hands and my face and adjust my ponytail before pulling open the door a crack. "Do you have any spare toothbrushes?"

"I don't care about your morning breath, pup."

I wince against the thought of the stale alcohol on my breath. "I drank quite a bit last night."

He chuckles as he rolls over in bed to face me. "Under the sink. Help yourself to whatever you need."

I smile at him, then close the door again. I walk back

to the vanity and look under the sink where I find a pack of toothbrushes. I take one out and find his toothpaste in one of his drawers. I quickly brush my teeth and swish some mouthwash. *There. Now I feel a little better.*

I open the door to step into the room, but I almost collide with him. With a smirk on his handsome face, he winks and heads into the bathroom without a single word. I walk back over to his bed, climb into it, and settle in the center of his mattress once more. As soon as I get cozy, the toilet flushes, followed by the sink running.

He spends another minute or two in there before he steps back through the doorway, pulling his shirt up over his head. My mouth is instantly dry as my gaze travels over the muscles I've been recently acquainting myself with. "Got some toothpaste on my shirt," he mumbles as he discards it on the floor. His eyes flash back to mine as I lie on my side in the center of his bed. The heat in his gaze smolders as he prowls across the room. "Goddamn," he breathes, his throat bobbing as he swallows hard.

"Come here."

"Yes, ma'am," he groans, climbing back onto the bed. Instead of sliding in beside me, he climbs directly over me, hovering above me as his eyes search mine.

I pull my bottom lip between my teeth, dragging the top row over my flesh. "I thought you wanted to go back to sleep?"

He presses his knee between mine and they part for him with little resistance from me. Lowering himself between my thighs, he plants his forearms on the bed by the sides of my head to cage me in. "I changed my mind," he breathes against my lips, nipping at them. His fingers trail along the top hem of my dress, his gaze following. "I love you in this dress, but—fuck—I want to see it off you instead."

My heart skips a beat before falling into a rapid, unsteady rhythm, knocking away at my ribcage. "Then take it off."

Caleb inhales sharply, his eyes flashing to mine and burning with desire. "Mia . . ."

"Or don't," I breathe, lifting my hands to slide my fingertips along the sides of his naked torso. He shivers beneath my touch, and his lips part as a ragged breath slips out. "The choice is yours."

Time is momentarily suspended, his eyes locked on mine. I can practically see the thoughts warring in his head. "Fuck," he groans. The muscles in his arms flex as he slips a hand beneath my back and pulls me to sit up with him. His gaze is transfixed on mine as he slides the zipper down my spine. With a gentle touch, he grazes my shoulders as he slides the straps off, his fingers following them halfway down my arms before sliding back up to trace the top hem over the swell of my breasts. My chest heaves as he peels the dress away from my body. My nipples turn to hardened buds when the cool air dances across them.

Caleb shifts to the side so he can drag the material down my legs before tossing it onto the floor. I'm left in nothing but my panties. "My God," he murmurs, his fingers trailing along my legs as he inches closer. His hands find my hips and he rolls himself onto his back, pulling me onto his lap. My knees fall on either side of his thighs, my hands planting on his chest. His hard cock presses against me through the three layers separating us.

His hands are warm against my flesh as he begins to slowly slide them up my thighs. The cords in his throat move with each clench of his jaw. His eyes follow his hands as they touch every inch of my abdomen until his fingertips are grazing the undersides of my breasts.

"You're so perfect," he murmurs as his hands cup each breast and he brushes his thumbs over my pebbled nipples. "So fucking beautiful."

"Caleb," I breathe, his name falling from my lips like a quiet plea. With a mind of their own, my hips shift, grinding against his erection as he takes my nipples between his forefingers and thumbs, rolling them over the tender flesh. "Oh my God."

"You like that, pup?" he murmurs, a low moan vibrating in his chest as I circle my hips, desperate for the friction of his cock rubbing against my clit. Warmth builds in the pit of my stomach, a dampness growing between my legs as he presses his hips up against me. "Fuck, you're so goddamn sexy."

I rock my hips again, my hands sliding along his chest, trailing down his torso as I let my head fall backward, my clit throbbing harder, desperate for release. Caleb presses up against me, grinding his rock hard erection against me. "Please, don't stop," I moan. My eyelids flutter shut as the warmth spreads into a ferocious heat rippling through my body.

Straightening my head, I begin to move my hands over the muscles in his abdomen, my fingers splaying out across his chest as I memorize every inch of his skin. The low moan that Caleb makes as my hands slide over his throat and push my fingers through his hair, is the sexiest sound.

"I want you to come for me, Mia," he groans, his hands abandoning my breasts as he slips them around my back, urging me closer.

He rolls his hips, his cock a delicious friction against my pussy as my face drops down to his. His hands drop down to my hips and his fingertips dig into my flesh. My fingers are tangled in his hair, my mouth crashing into his as the pressure becomes borderline unbearable. I'm a mess on him, our colliding tongues tangling.

He's consuming me in the best way possible and I'm not sure I ever want to come back from this high.

Caleb devours my mouth while his cock grinds against me. It's too much and sends me over the edge. I moan into his mouth, my orgasm hitting my body like a tidal wave. He kisses me deeper, swallowing my sounds as I come apart on top of him. I feel wrung out, shaking and quivering on top of him. His movements slow until his cock jerks against my sensitive center.

A deep, guttural moan escapes him before his body stills beneath me as I feel a wetness growing between my legs. And it's not just from me. I slow our kiss and draw away from him. We're both left panting, gasping for air.

I bury my face in his neck and breathe in his scent. His hands move away from my hips, sliding along my spine until they're spread across my back to hold me tightly against his chest. "How are you feeling?"

"Amazing," I breathe, my eyelids fluttering open as I pull back to look down at him. Heat creeps up my neck, spreading across my cheeks. "And a little embarrassed."

"Why?"

"Because I just came from rubbing against you."

A chuckle rumbles in his chest. "You're not the only one who came." He drags his fingertips along my spine. "And I'm not embarrassed about it."

My lips part to say more, but there's a knock on his bedroom door. My eyes widen as I stare down at him. Were we that loud? He cocks an eyebrow, a smirk lifting the corners of his lips.

"Mia?" Willow says from the hall. "I know you're in there."

"Shit," I murmur, peeling myself away from him to climb off the bed.

"I hate to ruin your fun, but I need to get back to your house. I overslept and should have left like two hours ago."

"We'll be right out." Finding my dress in a pile on the floor, I pull it on in a haste. When I look at Caleb, he's still lying on the bed, his body stretched out, hands tucked beneath his head as he watches me. He's clearly not in a rush. "Get up. You're our ride home."

A lazy grin pulls across his lips as he rolls out of bed and stands up. "I should probably change," he chuckles, glancing down at the glaringly obvious wet spot on his pants.

"Yeah, probably," I say, trying to hold in my laugh, a smile cracking across my face.

Caleb walks over to his dresser to grab a new pair of underwear and shorts. He looks back at me, his eyes shimmering from the sunlight coming through the window. I like seeing him like this—like he's actually happy.

"I'll meet you downstairs?"

"I'll be right behind you, pup," he says with a wink before disappearing into the bathroom. I linger for a moment, taking a deep breath. We really just did that. I smile at the bathroom door, imagining him half naked behind it, then force myself to leave his room.

And already, I know, it's far too late for my heart.

Because somehow, it belongs to him now.

CHAPTER TWENTY-SIX
MIA

The water bubbles around me, pushing up over my shoulders as I sink deeper into my seat. The jets hit all the right spots in my back and it feels amazing. Tilting my head back, my eyelids fall shut as I soak up the heat. Tella went to bed earlier this evening and now I'm just waiting for Caleb to get home from his game.

It's my first time using the hot tub and now I'm wondering why the hell I haven't used it sooner. This is the only option now that he closed his pool last week since the weather is getting cooler.

Lifting my arms, I extend them along the outside of the hot tub and let my head fall back as I let the water sooth my muscles. Soft music plays from my phone that I left sitting on the table nearby. I slowly open my eyes and look up at the stars sparkling in the sky above.

It's a cool fall night and there isn't a single cloud in the sky. The visibility is great and if I wait long enough, I might get the chance to see a star falling.

"There you are."

His hoarse voice sends a shiver down my spine. Removing my arms from the sides of the tub, I turn in my seat to watch Caleb walk over to the hot tub. He stops when he reaches the side, his gaze crashing into mine.

"I was looking for you."

"I hope you don't mind," I say, staring up at him through my lashes.

His throat bobs and his nostrils widen as his gaze travels down across my chest. The water dances just above the top of my bikini. "I don't mind at all."

"Are you going to come in?"

His eyes drift back to my face, slowly searching my eyes as he reaches for the bottom hem of his shirt. He lifts his sweatshirt and T-shirt over his head and tosses them onto the chair behind him. "I already planned on it when I saw you from the window." He runs his fingers along the waistband of his black swim shorts that I didn't notice he was wearing until now.

He walks up the steps and reaches the edge of the hot tub. I can't help myself as my eyes begin to wander, traveling over the flexing muscles in his torso. As he bends his knee, his swim shorts hike up farther and I see the black ink etched into his thigh.

I lift up, trying to get a better look to study the art he has tattooed on his skin. It's Tella's birthday.

"I've been wondering what your tattoo was after I first caught a glimpse of it," I admit, my voice hoarse as I watch him lower himself beneath the surface of the water.

He settles back into the seat next to me, his thigh brushing against mine under the water. My breath catches in my throat and his eyes find mine, the corners of his mouth twitching. "You saw it before?"

"I noticed it when you were jumping into the pool," I say, my voice sounding breathless as his body shifts, his thigh pressing harder against mine.

"Hmm," he murmurs softly as his fingers dance through the water, dipping them below the surface before poking them back through. He slowly turns to face me, resting his right arm against the edge of the tub as he leans forward to tuck my hair behind my ear. "Do you have any tattoos?"

I suck in a sharp breath at the contact, a shiver trailing down my spine again. "I don't."

"That's okay." He trails his fingers along my jawline and down the side of my neck. "I like you with or without tattoos."

"Yeah?" I breathe out as he flattens his hand along my collarbone.

"Yeah, pup," he says quietly, his right hand lifting to stroke the side of my face. "I love you just the way you are." His jaw clenches immediately after the sentence slips from his lips.

My eyes widen as the words hang heavily in the air around us. He meant it in the same way he said he likes me with or without tattoos. He doesn't *love me* love me. "How was your night?"

"It was good," he says, his fingers toying with the strap of my bikini top. "Better now that I'm here with you." He pauses for a moment, goose bumps erupting across my skin as his fingers drift lower. "I don't know why, but I can't seem to get you off my mind."

A soft laugh sounds from my chest. "That sounds slightly problematic."

"It is," he murmurs. His hands find my waist under the water and he lifts me to set me down on his lap. "I'm not sure what to do about it."

"Maybe I'm just something you need to get out of your system," I whisper, my arms circling around the back of his neck as my fingers slip through his hair. He's the one who said he couldn't give me anything more.

"Maybe," he says, his voice hoarse and thick with lust. He slides his hands along my torso and over my shoulders until he's pushing his hands through my hair to grip the back of my head. I don't protest as he urges me forward until my lips graze his. "I think it might be worth trying, at the very least."

"Yeah?" I breathe, the warmth and hardness of his arousal pressing against the apex of my thighs.

He chuckles, pressing up against me. "Yeah, pup," he groans as his mouth captures mine. There's nothing gentle or tender about the way he kisses me. It's fueled by a deep seated need. Lust and desire, passion and pleasure. Warmth floods me as his tongue pushes past my lips, tangling with mine in a frenzy.

His lips are bruising, his tongue a tease as he draws the air from my lungs. My toes curl, my fingers gripping his hair as he kisses me deeper, like he's trying to fit himself inside me in any way he possibly can. He consumes me and I surrender to the desire driving my own actions.

"I need you out of this hot tub," he moans against my mouth as his fingers trail over my nipples hidden beneath the thin material of my bikini. "And out of this bathing suit."

I'm powerless against him. I wrap myself around his body as he lifts me out and carries me onto the patio. The air is cold on my wet skin, but I pay no attention to it as he pauses to kiss me deeply again. He gently lowers me to the ground, hastily grabbing a towel from the table before wrapping it around my shoulders.

"Come with me," he whispers, his fingers threading through mine before he pulls me behind him. He leads me to the back door, stepping out of the way as he pulls it open and lets me step inside. I walk in first, but as the door clicks shut behind us, his hand snakes out, wrapping around my wrist to stop me and pull me back to him.

My body crashes into his and he drops my hand so he can push the towel away from my shoulders with both of his hands. His fingers dance across my skin as the towel pools around my feet. One hand wraps around my hip as the other slides around the back of my head.

I lift my chin, my eyes drifting between his eyes and down to his mouth. With my arms wrapped around the back of his neck, I pull his face down to mine. Our mouths crash into each other like a cosmic collision. I can't catch my breath, our lips locked together as we suck and nibble each other in a constant battle for control. His hips press forward, his cock pushing against my stomach, rock hard and ready.

My hands abandon his neck and slowly descend down his body, taking note of every hard ridge and soft valley of his chest and abdomen. He shivers beneath my touch, a low moan rumbling deep inside his throat.

He's panting, his mouth hovering just over mine as my fingers plunge beneath the waistband of his swim shorts. "Mia," he whimpers, the sound altering my goddamn brain chemistry. "Touch me, please."

"Because you asked so nicely," I murmur, smiling against his mouth before nipping at his bottom lip. Both hands slide down into his pants and I find the base of his cock, wrapping my right hand around it as my left shimmies his pants down a little farther.

He moans into my mouth again, his entire body quivering as I slowly start to stroke his length. As I reach the head, I roll my thumb over the tip, feeling the precum already there. "Goddamn, Mia," he pants, withering beneath my touch. I slowly move my face away from his, my eyes searching his as I tug on his cock again.

"May I?" I ask him, my voice quiet as I begin to lower myself down onto my knees in front of him. "I want to make you feel good."

"Holy fuck," he growls, his hands moving to cup the sides of my face as I bring his cock closer to my lips. "You're going to be the end of me."

I stare up at him, my hand still moving along his length. "Tell me what you want me to do, Caleb."

He lets out a breathy whimper, drawing his bottom

lip between his teeth before releasing. "I want you to suck my cock."

"Good boy," I murmur, opening my mouth wide as I guide him inside. He lets out a low, guttural moan as I wrap my lips around him. He's too big and my gag reflex is overreactive, so I'm only able to fit half of his cock inside my mouth while wrapping my hand around the rest.

He slides his hand around the back of my head, his fingers fisting in my hair as I start to move. "Fuck," he growls, his head tipping backward, eyelids falling shut. I stare up at him, savoring the way his face contorts as I suck him. The way the cords in his throat tighten and flex. I pump my hand in tandem with my mouth, sucking him in and out, taking him as deep as I can, even though it makes me gag.

Tears spring to my eyes and saliva dribbles from the corners of my mouth as I keep moving, sucking him in and out. Caleb's grip tightens on my hair and his hips shift, thrusting his cock deeper into my mouth. I gag around him again, my lungs burning as it momentarily restricts my flow of oxygen, but I don't falter.

"That's it, pup," he breathes, tipping his chin down as his eyes meet mine. "I'm gonna come."

I hum around his cock, my own wetness pooling between my legs. Seeing him like this, so needy and desperate, is driving me insane. I love seeing him come apart at the seams and I love knowing that it's my doing. He stares at me through hooded eyes, growing darker with lust as I fuck him with my mouth.

I need to feel him everywhere, filling me wholly.

"Do you want me to come in your mouth?" he asks in a low, barely audible voice. He's so close. There's a moment where his eyes search mine, desperate for me to tell him what I want. I can't talk around his cock, so I stare back at him, dipping my chin as I murmur around in, urging him to continue.

My hand tightens around him, pumping him harder as he picks up the pace with his hips. He's unable to control himself, jerking into my mouth as his body bucks. He thrusts in deeper, hitting my uvula as I choke around him. My other hand dances along his thigh, only stopping to cup his balls and massage them in my palm. I give them a gentle tug.

"Oh fuck," he growls, his hold tightening on my skull as his body tenses. He lets out a string of curses and screws up his face as he tips his head back again. His muscles go rigid for a split second, his hips giving a final jerk, before he relaxes and his release floods my mouth. I immediately swallow, continuing to suck him, pumping my hand until there's nothing left for me to swallow.

Caleb releases my hair and I pull him from my mouth with an audible pop. He hauls me to my feet with his hands under my arms, then his hand slides back along the nape of my neck. He surprises me when he kisses me. His tongue sweeps along the seam of my mouth, urging them open before it slides against mine, surely tasting what remains of his release on my tongue.

"You're so perfect, Mia," he breathes against my mouth. His fingers tug at the tie of my bikini. With a quick flick of his wrist, the ties come loose and the material falls to the ground. "Let me take care of you now too," he murmurs, his fingers sending a series of shivers across my body as he strokes the sides of my body, over my breast and down to the hem of my bikini bottom. "I want to taste you."

My breath catches in my throat as he slides his hands beneath my butt, lifting me into the air in a rush. My legs instinctively wrap around him as he carries me through the house, but we don't make it past the kitchen.

Caleb carries me over to the island, lying me down on the cold marble as he stands up right. Mischief and desire burn in his eyes as he drags his fingers down over my bare breasts. I lie flat on the counter, staring up at him as he lowers himself down to me, his mouth meeting mine once again. He kisses me with a tenderness that has my toes curling, his tongue dancing with mine before he abandons my mouth.

He trails his lips along my jaw, peppering kisses down the length of my neck and over my chest. He nips and bites and licks my skin as he makes his way down my torso. Hooking his arms beneath my knees, he moves me to the edge as he lowers himself down to the floor. His fingers splay along the insides of my thighs as he pushes them open.

"My God, look at you," he murmurs as he trails his lips along my legs, pulling down my bikini bottom. He breezes past my pussy, kissing every inch of skin around it. He pulls back, lifting a finger as he drags it through my lips. "You're so fucking wet."

My heart pounds against my ribcage to an unsteady beat as he circles his finger around my clit. My head falls back against the marble and my hands reach between my legs as I thread my fingers through his hair.

His lips are soft, his tongue warm as he lowers his face between my thighs and runs his tongue right where I want him, along my pussy. He flicks the tip against my clit and a shiver of pleasure races down my spine as my hips buck against his face. He chuckles against my flesh, licking his way back to my clit again.

Caleb plants his forearms against my thighs, holding me down so I can't buck or squirm as he licks and sucks, teasing and tasting his way to the finish line. I'm a mess of moans, my hips fighting to lift up as he flattens his tongue against my clit, rolling it in precise circles. He knows exactly what he's doing and in this position, I'm ready to give him everything he wants from me.

My body is on fire, the heat spreading rapidly through my veins. I was already aroused while I sucked his cock and felt him coming down my throat. Knowing I was the one who was driving him over the edge had me close to my own orgasm at that moment.

A groan vibrates in his chest as he continues to feast upon me, driving me absolutely insane with the way his tongue teases my clit and then slides along my pussy. He pushes it into my pussy, taking a second to fuck me with his tongue. A low moan sounds from him, mixing with my own moans as he moves back to the most tender spot between my legs.

My grip tightens on his hair, tugging on the strands as I feel my orgasm approaching quickly. "I'm going to come," I breathe, a moan following. As soon as the words fall from my lips, I can feel it as it crashes like a tidal wave against the shore, fast and all-consuming.

My body quivers beneath his touch as my orgasm washes over every part of my body and floods my brain. My face screws up, his name falling from my lips like a breathless chant, my eyes shut. Stars dance behind my eyelids and I'm so lost in this moment, in him. Lost in the way his tongue feels as he laps at my pussy, drinking every last drop of my orgasm.

I can't dissect a single thought swimming in my brain as I drift into a peaceful state of ecstasy. He slowly stands up, taking his warmth with him. I lift my head to see what he's doing. His gaze is still on me as his fingers trail along the waistband of his pants.

"I need you, Mia," he breathes. There's a bit of pain mixed with the passion in his eyes.

"Take whatever you need," I say and I mean it. Though my voice is filled with nothing but desire as the last remnants of my orgasm dissipate in my limbs, I want him to find comfort in me, in my body. *Just casual, right?*.

"I need to get a condom," he tells me, his voice barely above a whisper. "I don't even know if I have any."

"I'm on birth control." I stare up at him, my body splayed out on the island in the center of his kitchen. "We don't need a condom . . . as long as there's nothing else to worry about."

He shakes his head. "No. Absolutely nothing to worry about."

"Then we don't need anything."

His nostrils widen, his pupils dilating as his eyes roam over my body. He pushes his pants down, taking his boxer briefs down with them. They fall down his legs and he steps back between mine, pushing my knees apart as he positions himself against my center.

"I don't know if you're going to fit, though."

A smirk tugs on his lips. "I promise we can make it fit, pup."

He holds my gaze as his fingers skate along my skin and he brings his face closer to mine. He shifts his hips, slowly sinking into me, stretching me wide as his cock fills me inch by inch. I lift my legs, granting him deeper access as I wrap them around his lower back.

"Fuck," he breathes out, the sound low and gravely as his eyelids droop.

"Caleb," I moan, breathless as he fills me to the brim. He stills, scanning my face to make sure I'm okay before he lowers himself down to me. His hands cup the sides of my face, mouth claiming mine in a fury of passion.

His tongue parts my lips, plunging into my mouth to dance with my own. My muscles constrict and a wave of pleasure washes over me as I clench around him. Caleb moans into my mouth, shifting his hips as he presses deeper into me, until it feels like there's nowhere else he can possibly go.

He slowly starts to piston his hips, dragging his cock in and out. He's so thick, stretching me as he massages my insides with his length. His kisses are slow and tender, his tongue tangling with mine in lazy strokes, his fingers plunging through my hair as he grips my head. His other hand falls onto my hip, his grip digging into my flesh so hard it's bound to leave bruises.

He's consuming me, piece by piece, inch by inch and I'm so lost in him. At this point, there's no question about it—if this is what it's like with him, I never want to be found.

Caleb starts to move faster, his breathing growing labored as he picks up the pace. He moves his hips, drilling into me over and over with only the sounds of his skin against mine and our moans filling the air around us. It's a sweet, delicious torture and I can feel myself already approaching the edge of ecstasy once again.

"Fuck, Mia. I'm not going to last long," he moans against my mouth, nipping at my bottom lip before he pulls away. He moves his body so he's standing upright, hands gripping my waist.

"Come for me," I say, my voice filled with nothing but lust and need. I reach for his arms, my fingernails digging into his wrists as I hold onto him. "Let go, love."

Urgency simmers beneath the surface as he thrusts into me even harder. He releases my hip, sliding one hand between us as he presses his thumb against my clit. He rolls it over and over, applying the right amount of pressure as he sends me spiraling over the edge.

My body quakes, my pussy tightens around him, his hips jerking. A wildfire of pleasure spreads through my body, pulling me into the depths as I cling to him, moaning his name as he continues to pump into me, unrelenting.

"Mia," he sighs, my name falling from his lips in the softest breath. A low moan follows as he thrusts into me, filling me with his warmth as he loses himself deep inside of me.

His movements slow as he empties himself, filling me with his cum. He doesn't stop until we're both coming down from our highs, then his hips still. He stares down at me, his expression soft, eyes warm and hooded as he lifts his hands to stroke the sides of my face.

"Mia," he says quietly, his voice cracking around my name as his eyebrows pinch together. There's a moment where a twinge of panic passes over his face. His eyes dart around, like he's needing to figure out a way to get out of this.

My heart cracks, I can feel him pulling away. I fight against the rejection and slowly lift myself. "Hey," I say softly, reaching for him. "Hey." He pulls out of me, leaving me empty and aching, but he doesn't move away. I slowly sit up, pushing off the counter until I'm on flat feet. His cum drips down the insides of my thighs. "It's okay. I'm sorry if I let that go too far."

He stares at me, eyes slowly searching mine before he lets out a breath. He leans forward and presses his forehead to mine as his eyelids flutter shut, breathing me in. My shoulders relax, the rejection fizzling as he lifts his hands to hold the sides of my face.

"I'm sorry," he murmurs, lifting his head from

mine to press his lips against my forehead. "You did nothing wrong. I just had a little moment of panic there."

"It's okay," I assure him, my hands circling around his waist. "I don't want any of this to be too much for you."

His throat bobs as he swallows hard, pulling back to look at me. "It's not. It's everything I want." He pauses, stroking my cheek with his thumbs. "This is just . . . new and different for me."

"I know," I tell him, lifting up on my tip toes to press my lips to his. "I think everything you're feeling is normal."

He slowly rolls his lips between his teeth, biting down as he nods. The sound of a bedroom door opening upstairs immediately severs the moment. "Shit," he breathes out, his eyes widening. "She's up early."

"Shit is right."

The corners of his lips lift and he lets out a soft laugh, shaking his head. "I'll distract her if you want to get your bathing suit and sneak upstairs."

"You're a life saver," I tell him, pressing my lips to his once more. He slides his hand behind my head, his tongue pushing past my lips as he deepens the kiss. His hips shift forward, pressing his hard cock against my stomach. "You'd better stop, sir," I laugh. I lightly push him away, taking a step back as I bend down to grab my bikini bottom.

"I fear I haven't had my fill of you, pup."

I grab my towel and bikini bottom, wrapping the

towel around my body as I smile at him. "We'll have to take care of that issue later."

"It's a deal," he says with a wink before he disappears into the foyer, heading upstairs to Tella.

I wait until I hear the two of them going into the bathroom before I sneak up into my room. As I shut my door, I lean back against it, clutching the towel around my body as I let my head fall back against the door. I suck in a deep breath, my eyelids falling shut as the memory of him inside of me, his hands and lips on my skin still so vivid.

Caleb Ford is going to be the end of me.

And there's nothing I can do to stop it now.

CHAPTER TWENTY-SEVEN
CALEB

"Turn left on the next road," Mia tells me, her voice soft as she turns her head, her eyes gazing out the window as we head down the winding backroads. Sugar Hill Hollow isn't a long drive from Aston and since I don't have any games today, I jumped at the opportunity to drive Mia and Tella.

Tella's been bugging Mia about getting to meet her horse ever since Mia brought him up. Mia asked me a few days if I minded if she took her today, as long as the weather was cooperative. The sun's been shining bright all morning without a single cloud in sight. The air has a bit of a chill to it, which isn't surprising since we're deep into the fall months now, but it's a nice warm day considering.

As we approach the road, my eyes roll over the sign and I flip on my turn signal, waiting for a truck coming the opposite way to pass. Following Mia's directions, I turn the car onto Lavender Lane, slowly making our way down the road. Bright white fences line the right side and there are a few horses out in the center of the field.

"That's Willow's family's farm," she says, glancing at me, a soft smile pulling across her lips. "The driveway is down between those two trees." She points ahead. We near the two massive maple trees with an opened black iron gate situated between them. I pull off the road, the gravel beneath the car kicking up from my tires as we head down the drive lined with trees and the same bright white fencing.

As we reach the end of the lane, there's a house situated on the left with the back of it overlooking the lake. If you turn to the right, there's a barn with the grey exterior matching the house.

"They have a really nice property here," I tell her as she points to where I can park alongside the barn. Just beyond what looks to be the horse stable is a small riding arena and another barn.

"Don't they? I just love coming here. It's so peaceful and quiet, tucked away from the rest of the world," she adds with a smile.

"It's got a great view of the river," I say, turning off the engine as I glance at Tella in the rearview mirror. She's already unbuckled with her hands on the door. Her eyes are wide as she stares out at the field with half a dozen horses occupying the space.

"Which one is yours, Mia?"

Mia smiles, glancing over her shoulder as she looks at my daughter. "Come on, I'll show you."

I grab the bag of apples we brought along and Mia gets out of the car before I have the chance to open it for her. I stop by the back, opening Tella's. She climbs out with excitement rolling off her in waves.

She doesn't even bother to stop by me. Instead, she breezes past, skipping over to Mia. I close the car door, slowly turning around to catch sight of the two of them. Mia tips her chin to look down at Tella as Tella lifts hers. Their gazes are locked and a tender smile tugs on Mia's lips as Tella slides her hand into hers. Just two horse girls.

My grip on the bag of apples tightens, my throat constricting as my heart swells. I never really worried how Tella would take to Mia, but seeing the two of them like this is indescribable. It hurts my chest while simultaneously filling it to the brim with joy.

I shelve the conflicting feeling as I let myself enjoy this moment with just the two of them. Tella tugs on Mia's hand and Mia lets out a soft laugh that tugs on my heart. It's the sweetest melody I've ever heard and I soak in the warmth that washes over me.

She warms my soul like the sun upon my skin.

I follow behind them as they lead the way, heading down the gravel lane that wraps around the back of the barn. We stop at the gate by the meadow.

"Do you see the bay one out there?"

Tella lifts on her tip toes, pointing out to the field. "The one over there?"

"Yep," Mia smiles at her. "That's Hank."

"Can we go get him?"

"I have a better idea," Mia says with a wink. She releases Tella's hand, bringing both of hers to cup around her mouth as she whistles loudly. The sound has two beats and I watch in amazement as the gelding lifts his head quickly, his whinnying carrying across the breeze.

He drops his head, breaking out into a trot and then a lope as he heads across the field, not stopping until he's reaching the fence where we are. He slows to a stop and snorts out a breath when he drops his head, a low knicker escaping him as he comes right up to Mia.

"Hey, old man," she murmurs, scratching her nails against the whorl in the center of his forehead. "I brought a new friend for you to meet."

As if he understands what she's saying, he drops his head down to Tella. She holds her hand out to him, letting him smell her. He bobs his nose, blowing his breath against her hair as he lets out another soft sound.

"I think he likes you, babe." Mia smiles down at her. "Should we get him out? We can take him into the barn and give him a good brushing. He loves that."

"Oh, yes, please!" Tella says, bobbing up and down. She looks back at me, remembering I'm here. "Can we, daddy?"

"Whatever Mia says, T," I say, meeting Mia's eyes as she glances over her shoulder at me. "She's in charge here."

Mia's gaze lingers for a moment before she grabs a rope halter and lead rope from the hooks next to the gate. Tella takes a few steps back beside me, both of us watching as Mia lets herself into the pasture. I watch her carefully as she steps up next to her horse.

Her lips move as she says something quietly to him, too quiet for either of us to hear. I'm mesmerized by the way the horse responds. It's as if he's completely tuned in to her, dropping his head, waiting patiently as she slips the halter on. He stands beside her, waiting for her to move as she pushes open the gate.

The horse doesn't try to lead her or pull away. His movements are deliberately slow and careful as he walks with her and beside her, not ahead of her. Tella's pony operates in the same fashion. It's clear he's a well trained animal that is in tune with his rider.

Mia leads him through the gate and I step up, pushing it closed behind her and making sure it's securely shut. As I turn back around to see them, I find Mia handing the lead rope to Tella, falling in step beside her as she leads Mia's horse toward the stable.

My heart crawls into my throat once more. Carrying the bag of apples, I follow after Mia Landry like a lost puppy. She's doing things to me I never imagined would be possible again. She's making me feel things I never thought I'd be capable of feeling again.

And suddenly, I can't imagine not looking at her the way I do now.

As we walk up to the barn, an older white truck pulls up alongside the barn and parks close to mine. Mia pauses, her horse stopping beside her as she lifts her hand to wave at whomever is sitting behind the wheel. I slow to a stop next to her and Tella as a man slips out of the driver's door.

"Hey, Noah!"

He looks to be in his mid to late twenties. Dirty blonde hair curls around the edges of his backward baseball hat and a smile lifts his lips as he raises his hand to wave back to her. "Hey, Mia."

He shuts the door of his truck and walks around to the back as he pulls something out of the bed. I watch him for a moment, assessing the situation as he drags a bail of hay from the tail gate. His hands grip the twine, the lean muscles in his arms flexing as he carries it to the front of the barn and tosses it on the ground.

Something tightens around the base of my throat, my stomach sinking as I watch him walk over to Mia. His black T-shirt and light jeans are dusty, undoubtedly from a day of work but he doesn't hesitate to pull Mia into a hug.

"How are you doin'?"

"I'm good," she says, smiling brightly as they release and take a step away from one another. "I wasn't sure if I'd run into you or not today." My jaw tightens, my teeth clamping together. The pressure is significant and it feels as though my molars could crumble beneath it.

This must be Willow's brother—the one who now runs the farm.

"Noah, this is Caleb and Tella," Mia says, motioning to me. Her eyes quickly scan my face, eyebrows tugging together. "This is Willow's brother, Noah."

Noah looks down at my daughter, offering her a warm smile. "Hello, Tella."

"Hi, Mr. Noah!"

Noah lifts his gaze to me, immediately closing the distance between us and extends his hand for me to take. I release my clenched jaw, the jealousy still boiling in the pit of my stomach as I take his hand. "Nice to meet you," he says, giving me a firm shake and a swift nod.

"You as well," I tell him, my voice low in warning. I don't like the way he and Mia embraced and I sure as hell don't like the jealousy that's wrecking havoc inside of my mind. I know he's her best friend's brother, but did they ever have a thing?

Mia's past doesn't matter to me, but at the same time, she's drop dead gorgeous and to my knowledge, this man isn't blind. It's hard not to be blinded by her light.

He lets go of my hand, his green eyes assessing me with a raised eyebrow before he slowly bobs his head. "I'll let you guys get back to it. It was nice meeting you," he says to me and looks at Mia. "If you need anything, I'll be down by the dock."

"Thanks, Noah," Mia smiles at him, placing her hand against Tella's back. "Come on," she says softly as she guides her toward the barn.

"Bye, Mr. Noah!" Tella says, waving at him. The muscle in my jaw ticks once more and my knuckles are undoubtedly white as I tighten my grip around the bag of apples. Noah looks between Mia and me once more before he heads in the direction of the lake.

I catch Mia's gaze as she looks over her shoulder at me. "What was that?" she half whispers as she lets Tella lead Hank into the barn. We follow behind as she leads him to the wash stall.

"I don't like him."

Her face scrunches. "You don't even know him."

"I don't need to."

She grabs a brush for Tella, handing it to her as she quickly ties the horse and gives him a pat on his neck. The horse drops his head, eyes closing as if he's falling asleep. I walk to the side of the stall, just around the corner as I set the bag of apples down.

Mia appears in front of me and corners me against the wall, stepping into my space. I look past her. Tella has her back to us, paying us no mind as she sings to Hank.

Mia slides her arms up around the back of my neck, lifting onto her tip toes. "Are you jealous, Caleb Ford?"

A grumble vibrates in my chest as I slip my hands around her waist, pulling her flush against my body in a rush. "Maybe."

"Well, I promise, you have nothing to worry about with him," she says under her breath, her lips softly grazing mine. "Or anyone for that matter."

I capture her mouth with mine, my lips moving torturously slow against hers as I draw the air from her lungs. Mia half sags against me, her lips parting, tongue slipping out to tangle with mine. My tongue dances with hers, before I'm pulling away with both of us breathless.

Lips parted, breathing shallow, she peers up at me through her long dark lashes. "What was that for?"

"Assurance," I murmur as her gaze burns through mine.

"For what?"

My fingers tighten on her hips. "That you're mine."

She slowly tilts her head to the side, her fingers

threading through the hair along the nape of my neck. Her lips part as if she's going to say something, but the words dissolve on her tongue as Tella's voice severs the moment.

"Mia! Am I allowed to try and clean his hooves?"

A slow smile pulls on her lips as she stares up at me. "Grab the hoof pick from the grooming box," she tells my daughter as she drops her arms away from the back of my neck. "I'll come help you."

My fingers linger on her hips, pulling her back to me once more. "This isn't over," I murmur, my mouth claiming hers in a hasty kiss. "This is far from over," I assure her, letting my hand fall away from her hip.

"I'll reassure you later tonight," she says with a wink before spinning around to head back into the wash stall.

My chest constricts as I watch her walk back over to my daughter, Tella greeting her with excitement. I walk to the wash stall and lean against the wall as I cross my ankles, pushing my hands into the front pockets of my pants. I savor the moment, my heart stumbling over itself as I watch the two of them together.

And as swiftly as a soft and gentle exhale, I let the realization wash over me, settling deep beneath my rib cage. Mia Landry has a hold on me. It tugs on my heart strings as I watch the tenderness she has with my daughter. My daughter, who looks at her as if she hung the sun and the moon and all the stars in the sky.

And perhaps she did . . .

Because I know my skies shine a little bit brighter with her in it.

CHAPTER TWENTY-EIGHT
MIA

Stripping down to nothing, I slowly slide open the glass shower door to stick my hand into the water to check the temperature. Caleb is getting Tella into bed and anticipation has been building in the pit of my stomach all evening after we were at the farm.

I hadn't originally planned on spending the night, but since Caleb has an early morning skate tomorrow, it makes more sense to just stay here. Not to mention the promise Caleb made to finish whatever it was that we started at the farm earlier this afternoon.

As much as I want to initiate things and go to him, I know I can't. I know that he needs to be the one who decides this is what he wants. Caleb's still fighting something inside of himself and I won't be the one who pushes him too far. I need him to be the one to tell me what it is that he wants or he needs.

He's not fragile by any means, but I know he doesn't trust anyone with his heart. And I'm not asking for it, even if he's been slowly creeping into mine. My heart crawls into my throat at the thought as I take a slow step into the shower and pull the glass door shut behind me.

Falling for Caleb Ford was not part of my plan. Hell, not falling for him was part of my plan. An emotionally unavailable man is the last thing I want. But falling for him was beyond my control. There was nothing I could do to stop it from happening and now here I am, hanging onto every single word he says to me like it's a promise or a prayer.

The water pelts my body and I tilt my head back, letting the hot water rush down the length of my hair. I know I can't get hung up on anything that happens between Caleb and me. It's a recipe for disaster and I need to remind myself that to him, this is just sex.

There's no way it could possibly be more to him.

Grabbing some shampoo, I work a lather into my hair, pushing the negative thoughts from my mind as I scrub my scalp and rinse it out. Whatever this is with Caleb, I knew what I signed up for the moment we kissed. I don't regret that at all, even if I know my heart will be the one to suffer in the end.

I finish washing my hair, applying conditioner next before I grab my washcloth and work a lather into it with some body wash. I start to scrub myself, my mind drifting back to earlier in the day. The way Caleb looked at me, the way he pulled me aside and kissed me in the barn.

He's been driving me insane and dare I say, I'm loving every minute of it. No one has touched me the way he does—with such a tenderness coupled with an intensity that has my toes curling.

Warmth spreads through me and as I run my washcloth between my legs, a tingling sensation breaks out through my body. A shiver trails down my spine, my nipples instantly hardening as I let my eyes fall shut, imaging Caleb when he was between my legs in the kitchen.

I slowly circle my fingers as the memory washes over me. He touched me like he was a skilled musician, like he was trying to figure out the exact keys he needed to hit to make my body play his melody. Like he wanted my pleasure to be his and only his.

There's a soft knock on the bathroom door and for a moment, I think I'm hearing things. My body stills, my hand still between my legs as I look over at the door. My breath catches in my throat. I'm silent, waiting to see if I hear it again.

And then the knock sounds again, a little louder than the first time.

My heart stumbles over itself, knowing damn well that he can hear the shower running. Curiosity washes over me, my stomach doing a somersault. "Come in," I call out to him, my voice hitching a touch higher than normal.

The door quietly opens and Caleb steps in. The fog that's built in the shower creates a film on the glass, making it impossible to fully see him on the other side.

Tension hangs heavily in the air, so thick that it wraps itself around my body. A shiver trails down my spine as the outline of his body turns to face the shower and leans back against the counter.

Heat creeps up my neck, spreading across my cheeks as I can feel his eyes staring at me though the fogged glass. Can he see my hand between my legs? Does he know I was thinking about him and touching myself?

I slowly pull my hand away, ignoring the throbbing between my legs. "What are you doing out there?"

He's silent for a moment. "What are you doing in there?" He counters, his voice gruff.

I swallow roughly, my face burning. "Showering."

"Don't lie to me, pup," he says, his voice low.

"I—" My voice catches, heat coursing through my veins as my clit throbs, desperate for attention. "I was just washing my body."

"Yeah?" he asks, his voice rough. He pushes away from the counter, stepping closer to the door. "From where I'm standing, it looked like your hand was lingering between your legs."

My heart pounds erratically against my ribcage.

"Were you touching yourself?"

I inhale sharply, goose bumps erupting over my skin.

"Who were you thinking about while your hand was between your legs?"

I swallow again, my nostrils flaring. "You," I admit.

He groans, the sound subtle, yet I feel the way it vibrates against my eardrums. "Tella's asleep," he tells me, his voice low. "Come to my room when you're

done," he says, desire woven into his words. "And don't touch yourself anymore."

My heart skips a beat, my stomach doing another flip as moisture builds between my legs and it isn't from the water rushing down my body.

"I'll be waiting for you."

He doesn't say another word before he slips out of the bathroom. His words echo in my brain and I quickly rinse the soap from my body and the conditioner from my hair before getting out. My movements are rushed as I dry my body and my hair, running my hair brush and products through the long strands.

Anticipation builds in the pit of my stomach and I exit the bathroom, not bothering to change into any clothes as I clutch my towel around my body and pad down the hallway to Caleb's room.

His door is left ajar and I slowly push it open, slipping into the darkness of his room before I close it behind me. He stands across the room, the top half of his body is naked and his arms hang by his sides as he stares out the window at the night sky.

I take a few steps into his room, pausing to watch him for a moment, drinking in the sight of him as the moon casts its light across his body. He slowly turns around to face me, his eyes raking up and down the length of my body.

"Come here," he murmurs, his voice gentle, yet demanding as his gaze fixes on mine from across the room.

My heart quickens and my feet immediately move without my command, closing the distance between us until I'm standing directly in front of him. He dips his chin, staring down at me for a moment, his eyes searching mine as his breathing picks up.

Lifting a hand, he slides it along the side of my face, fingers diving through my damp hair as he moves to cup the back of my head. "It feels like I've been waiting an eternity to touch you," he breathes, his face dipping down to mine. "It's been utter torture."

"So stop wasting time," I breathe, his mouth sweeping across mine. "Touch me, Caleb."

A low groan sounds in his throat just as his lips crash into mine. He kisses me slowly at first, his lips soft and gentle against mine as he breathes me in. There's a tenderness, as if he's caressing my tongue with his own. Like he's afraid he might break me.

And then I reach for his hand, covering it with my own as I lift it to the top of my towel. His moan vibrates through my body as I use his hand and tug on the fabric, letting it fall away from my body and to the floor.

His hesitation vanishes and his hand drops down to my hip, pulling my body flush against his and kissing me with an intensity that has my core melting.

He holds me close to his body, mouths fused together as he spins me around. His leg presses between mine as he pushes me backward until the backs of my legs meet his bed. Sliding his hand around my lower back, he guides me down onto the bed, shifting me to the center of the mattress.

His mouth leaves mine and we're both breathless as he stares down at me. His eyes search mine as a fire burns brightly in his irises. His lips part as if he's going to say something, emotion washing over his expression, his eyebrows tugging together. A ragged breath escapes him and his mouth drops back to mine again.

There's something else lingering in his kiss this time. Something deeper than the lust, deeper than the desire. He doesn't give me the chance to try and decipher it as his tongue swipes across my lips and then he's pulling away again.

"Look at you," he murmurs, fingers trailing down the length of my body as he slowly lifts himself off the bed. "I can't get enough of you, pup." He lets out a ragged breath as he walks around the side of the bed, his fingers trailing along the insides of my thighs. "You're all I think about. All I see. And seeing you like this . . . I'm fairly certain you're going to be my undoing."

I can't look away from him. Electrical currents roll through my body in waves, every nerve ending lighting on fire beneath his touch.

He walks over to his nightstand, pausing before he slowly flicks on the light. "That's better," he murmurs, hooking his fingers beneath the waistband of his pants before he drags them down the length of his legs. Stepping out of them and his boxer briefs in one fluid movement, his cock hangs heavy between his legs "I want to be able to see you. I want to watch you while I make you come."

He moves to the end of the bed, pushing my legs apart as he drags the tips of his fingers over my flesh.

"But first, I want you to show me how you were touching yourself in the shower."

My mouth instantly goes dry, my lips parting as a shallow breath slips from me. "I—" I pause, my throat bobbing as I swallow roughly. Heat creeps up my neck, spreading across my cheeks again.

"Don't be ashamed, pup," he murmurs, his eyes bouncing back to mine. "I fucking love that you were thinking about me as you played with yourself." He lowers himself onto the bed, his hands inching closer to the apex of my thighs. "Did you touch yourself like this?" He questions me, sliding a finger along my wet pussy. He completely avoids my clit, a frustrated groan rumbling in my throat as he passes by it again. "Oh, I'm sorry," he smirks, mischief dancing in his eyes. "Am I not doing it right?"

Excitement bubbles inside of me, mixing with the embarrassment. "Like this," I tell him as I move my own hand between my legs. Caleb's gaze flickers downward, his eyes transfixed as I begin to work my fingers over my clit.

"Fuck," he moans, reaching down between his own legs as he starts to stroke himself. He wraps his large hand around his length, working his fist around his erection as he starts from the base and moves to the tip.

A moan falls from my lips as I slide a finger inside, pressing my thumb over my clit as I stare up at him, lost in the way he's looking at me right now. Like the sky could be falling around us and he still wouldn't be able to look away.

It's like we're playing a game right now to see who's

going to fold first. He strokes himself in long, drawn out movements, like he's savoring every last second as I move my hand against my pussy, drawing my fingers in and out as I play with my clit.

"Don't you dare come," he growls. He releases his cock, folding first. His movements are rushed as he pushes my legs farther apart, his hand circling around my wrist as he pulls it from between my legs. He lifts my arm, pinning it to the bed beside my head. The tip of his cock presses against my center as he hovers above. "I want your pleasure. I want to be the one to drive you over the edge."

"It's yours, Caleb," I breathe, lifting my hips as he slides in a fraction of an inch. "Take whatever you want, whatever you need."

He lets out a low moan, lowering his hips as he pushes into me, filling me to the brim in one fluid movement. "I want it all," he breathes, sinking deep into me before he begins to move, his cock thrusting in and out of me. He grabs my other hand, dragging them both above my head as he pins my wrists to the bed with one hand as the other trails down my torso, gripping my waist. "I want all of *you*."

My heart jumps into my throat, the inner corners of my eyebrows softening as I stare up at him. His gaze penetrates mine, burning directly through me and into my soul. My lips part, the words hanging on my tongue, but he silences me as his mouth crashes into mine again.

His tongue fills my mouth and his fingers dig into my skin as he thrusts in and out of me, the sweetest pleasure rippling through my body. He takes every-thing I have to give, siphoning my soul as he continues to rock into me, filling me deep with every thrust until I'm a mix of moans, coming apart at the seams beneath him. My eyelids flutter shut as I feel my orgasm approaching.

His fingers tighten around my wrist, his mouth breaking apart from mine as he continues to shift his hips, stroking my insides with the length of his cock. "Look at me, Mia," he breathes as I open my eyes, meeting his fiery gaze. He moans, the sound low and guttural as I begin to clench around him. My orgasm slams into me, pushing me over the edge as ecstasy floods my body. "That's it," he groans. "Come for me," he pants, thrusting into me. "Come with me."

His eyes never leave mine as he loses himself deep inside of me. I'm lost in the moment, lost in him as we ride out the waves of euphoria together, falling into the abyss. His mouth drops down to mine, kissing me again as his hips begin to slow, drawing out every last ounce of pleasure either of us have, until we're both panting, breathless and fully satiated.

He slowly pulls out and rolls off me in one swift movement before he slides his arms beneath my legs and behind my back. He lifts me into the air effortlessly as he tucks my body against his, carrying me across his bedroom and into the bathroom.

Caleb is careful as he lowers me onto my feet, walking over to the tub in the corner of the room as he turns on the water. I watch him carefully, my legs like jello as I'm still riding the high of him. He walks over to me, wrapping his arms around my body as he pulls me flush against him.

I press my face against his chest, reveling in his warmth and the familiar scent of him as I link my own arms around him. I'm hopelessly addicted to him.

He's silent as he holds me with only water rushing into the bathtub echoing in the room. We stay like this, wrapped up in one another until he's pulling me over to the corner of the room with him. He shuts off the faucet, stepping into the hot water as he leads me in with him.

He turns me around, positioning me with my back to his chest as he lowers both of us beneath the surface. His legs part and I settle between them, his arms sweeping around the front of my body to hold me against his.

His breath is soft and warm and he brushes my hair to the side and buries his face in my neck. His lips brush against my skin, his mouth moving closer to my ear. It sends a shiver down my spine.

"I don't know what we're doing, pup, but I don't think I can stop whatever this is."

My heart skips a beat. "So don't."

"I don't think I could even if I tried," he whispers as his arms tighten around me, his hand lifting to turn my head to look at him. I shift in front of him, turning in his arms until I'm sliding up the length of his body, mouths melting into one another again.

We stay exactly like this, wrapped up in one another until the water grows cold. He lifts me out, dries us both and carries me back to his bed where we spend the greater part of the night losing ourselves in one another. And only after he's fallen asleep with his head on my chest, arms wrapped around me like he's afraid I'll slip away in the night, do I let my mind drift back into the thoughts that creep in the dark corners of my brain.

I'm falling for him and it hurts knowing whatever this is will never last. Not when he's so closed off to the thought of letting someone else in. Not when he's too afraid to let himself feel such intense emotions.

I know one day this will end and I'm going to hold onto it—onto him—for as long as I possibly can.

CHAPTER TWENTY-NINE
CALEB

"Thanks again for coming so last minute," I tell Willow as I open the door for her and she steps inside. I didn't want to make things obvious and ask Mia for her information, so I tracked her down on social media and sent her a direct message.

Willow lets out a low whistle as she steps into my foyer, kicking her shoes off. She gives me a once over, her eyes dropping down to my feet and back up to my face. "Well, you look rather dashing, Mr. Ford."

A chuckle vibrates in my chest. I've only met Willow once before, but she strikes me as the kind of person who has no issues talking to anyone. Just from my small interaction outside of her spending the night on my couch last week, she doesn't come off as standoffish or reserved at all.

"Where are you taking Mia?"

"Willow," I say, waving her to come farther into the house. "I haven't told her yet, so I don't know how this is going to go over." I pause, corkscrewing my lips. "I suppose there's a chance I might come back early, if she doesn't want to go out."

Willow stares at me for a moment, lifting a perfectly arched brow. "If you think that, then you really don't know Mia."

I bite back my grin, dipping my chin at Willow. "Touche." Willow follows me into the kitchen and I motion for her to sit at the island in the center. The sound of car doors shutting draws my attention over to the window and I glance out at the driveway. "That's them," I tell her, watching as they make their way toward the house.

Mia took Tella to her riding lesson this afternoon while I was at practice. The side door opens and their voices carry through the mudroom as they both kick off their shoes. Tella comes out first, her eyes meeting mine before she sees Willow sitting at the counter beside me.

Mia follows after her, her footsteps faltering when she sees the two of us, confusion washing over her expression. "Hey?"

"Hey, girl," Willow says, waving at Mia. "I'll let your man explain what I'm doing here."

I chuckle softly, closing the distance between the two of us as Mia walks deeper into the kitchen to meet us. "T, this is Willow, Mia's best friend. Why don't you go change?"

"Hi, Miss Willow!"

"Just Willow." Willow smiles at her, laughing as she shakes her head as she gets off her stool. "I'll, uh, go make sure my car is unlocked."

Willow and Tella both disappear from the kitchen, leaving Mia and me alone. I step into her space, my hands finding hers, fingers threading together as her eyes slowly rake up the length of my body. "I want to take you out to dinner, pup," I tell her, my voice hoarse as her eyes meet mine. "I want to take you out on a date."

Her lips part, eyes widening as she stares at me for a moment. "I—" She stops, her throat bobbing as she swallows hard. The inside corners of her eyebrows pinch together and rise, her eyes rounding as she stares up at me. "Are you sure?"

I roll my lips between my teeth, biting down momentarily as I bob my head. "I've never been more sure."

"I thought you don't go on dates," she says quietly, stepping closer until our bodies are just nearly touching. She tips her chin up, her eyes holding mine.

"That was before you," I admit, my voice quiet like hers. My thumbs stroke the length of hers as I spend a few moments getting lost in her eyes. "Can I take you to dinner?"

The corners of her lips slowly lift. "I'd like that."

"Good," I say softly, my face dipping down to hers as I find her lips with mine. It's a gentle kiss and I keep it brief, allowing myself a second to revel in her familiar warmth before I pull away. "I found a place that is 100% gluten free and celiac friendly. I made a reservation for six, so we should probably leave in thirty minutes. Is that enough time for you?"

"I'll make it work," she tells me, lifting up on her

toes to kiss the side of my mouth. When she lowers herself back down, her fingers linger against mine as she begins to pull away. I let her go, immediately feeling her absence, a smile tugging across my face as she disappears from the kitchen.

Change is scary and not something I normally welcome, but seeing that goddamn smile on her face makes this all worth it . . . even if it might not go any further than this.

———

"I still can't believe you reached out to Willow to watch Tella."

I lower my fork, chewing a bite of food before swallowing it down as I look at Mia. She lifts her glass of water, shaking her head before taking a sip. "Why is that so unbelievable?"

"Why her? You had to track her down through social media and she doesn't even know Tella." She tilts her head to the side, her expression softening. "I know it's hard for you to trust people with her."

My throat constricts and I make an attempt to clear it before forcing down a mouthful of my own water. "Trust is something I'm trying to work on," I say, my voice low. "I didn't want to ask any of my friends or family because of your father." I pause and wet my lips. "He doesn't know about any of this, does he?"

Mia's silent for a beat. "Is there something here he should know about?"

"Maybe," I admit, the word shocking me as it falls

effortlessly and without a second thought from my lips. "I don't want to disrespect him and I don't want him to be pissed off if he finds out about anything between us." I pause, blowing out a shallow breath. "I can't make you a single promise about my future or even what this is between us, but I know I have no interest in anyone other than you."

"Neither do I."

"After I lost Amelia, I never thought I would ever be able to move on. I resigned in life and was perfectly content with being alone . . . until you came along." A ghost of a sad smile dances across my lips and Mia leans forward, pushing her nearly empty plate forward as she folds her arms on the table. "I do feel guilty when I think of her sometimes. Like I'm betraying her by being happy. She's dead and here I am, moving on in life, spending time with another woman."

A frown tugs on Mia's lips. "I can't pretend to know what you're feeling and I never really knew her, but I think if she loved you, she would want you to be happy."

Chewing on the inside of my cheek, I slowly nod. "I'm beginning to think that maybe she would too." I push my own plate forward, extending my arms as I reach for Mia's hand. "Things are easy with you and I like that. A lot."

"Good," she says softly, her eyes shining brightly as she threads her fingers within mine. "That's how it should be—easy and comfortable, like a safe place where you can rest at the end of a long day."

Her words tug the edges of my heart. "Things with

you just feel . . . right and natural. Like it's the way it's supposed to be."

"I never want to be a complication in your life, Caleb," she says quietly, her eyes slowly searching mine. "If you want me to tell my father, I can."

"I think it's something I need to do," I say, dipping my chin. "I'm the one who is technically in the wrong so I think it would be better if he heard it from me."

"There's nothing wrong about any of this," she retorts, her eyebrows tugging closer together. "We could have never predicted that anything would happen between us."

"It was beyond either of our control," I agree, my voice barely above a whisper. My feelings for her—I still refuse to dissect them because of my fear. My fear of just how deep they run and how strong of a grip she has on my heart.

I tried to fight this as long as I could, but my resolve is fractured and Mia Landry has infiltrated my heart. She's crept into the cracks carved in my heart and dare I say, she's been slowly putting me back together without me even realizing.

"Some things are just meant to be," she says. "Sometimes we find people when we aren't even looking."

I've fallen for her and I'm certain there's no way I can backtrack now.

I'm too far gone and I'm in too deep.

I stare back at her, her eyes burning into mine.

"And sometimes they become more important to you than you ever expected them to be."

CHAPTER THIRTY

MIA

"You did so good during your lesson today, T," I tell Tella as we walk to my car parked beside the barn. I open the back door for Tella and she climbs in, plopping onto her booster seat.

"Can we ride together sometime?" she asks as she pulls the seatbelt across her body. I let her do it herself and double check it after she gets it buckled. "Maybe you can ride one of Miss Magnolia's horses or something."

"I would love that," I tell her, smiling brightly as I linger by the back door. "I can ask her. Or maybe we could go to my friends farm where Hank is and ride there. He has a few horses that would be quiet enough for you to ride."

"Can we do it soon?"

A laugh bubbles in my throat. "Yes, of course. I'll ask Noah when we get home and I'll ask Miss Magnolia when we come for your next lesson."

"Yay!" Tella claps her hands together with exuberance. "Thank you, Mia! We're going to have so much fun."

"You know it, babe." I smile and wink at her before shutting the door. I quickly walk around the back of my car, heading to the front where I climb in behind the steering wheel. I press the engine button and glance back at Tella once more.

Tella's humming in the back seat, looking out the window as I pull my car from the parking spot. "Maybe my daddy will ride with us too."

"Has he ever ridden before?" I ask her as we make our way down the drive, heading in the direction of the road. We're only about fifteen minutes from their house, so it's a relatively short trip.

"No," Tella says with a sigh. "Well, he never did with me."

I look back at her in the rearview mirror just before I pull out onto the road. "We will have to see if we can change that."

"Maybe he's afraid."

Focusing on the road, I grip the steering wheel and nod in response. "He might be, but you know what? Fear isn't always real. Sometimes it's just a thing our brains make up. Fear can be good at times because it keeps us safe, but sometimes it can stop us from doing things that might be scary. Sometimes it can get in the way of living our lives."

"Are you scared of anything?"

I laugh softly at the irony of this conversation. "Of course I'm scared of things," I tell her, meeting her eyes in the rearview mirror. "I'm afraid of eating at some restaurants because I'm afraid I might get sick and then it will hurt my body."

"Because of the gruben, right?"

I laugh a little harder. "The gluten, yes," I say, correcting the word. "I have a lot of different things I'm scared of, but that's normal. I think what is most important is to not let the scaries keep you from doing fun things in life."

"I don't like the scaries, but my daddy usually helps me feel better when I get scared."

A smile tugs on my lips. "You have a really good daddy."

"He's the best." Tella smiles while staring back out the window again. Caleb is such a good dad to her. Truly, I don't think she could ask for a better father. Even though he has a demanding career, you would never know with the way Tella talks about him and the bond the two of them share.

I'm in awe of Caleb's quiet strength. In his devotion to his daughter and giving her the best life possible. I'm completely captivated by him—the man who has made a home for himself in my heart.

Falling for Caleb was never part of my plan, but I already know it's too late. He occupies my thoughts and I constantly find myself looking forward to being around him, even if it's just in passing before a game or a practice.

I'm addicted to him. To his smell, his touch, his taste, and just his presence.

I gave my heart to him without even trying and all I can do now is hope he doesn't give it back.

We pull onto the familiar busy street that leads us deeper into Aston and closer to Caleb's house. He lives on the outskirts of town, but because of where the horse stable is located, we have to cross through one of the busier sections of the small city.

I personally don't like driving during these hours. It seems like everyone tends to be in a rush, most likely trying to get home from work. I'm very patient and not an aggressive driver, so I just take my time and let traffic dictate how quickly I'll be getting home.

Safety is always my first concern, especially while I'm driving with Tella in the car.

"Can you turn up the music?" Tella asks me from the backseat as we sit at a red light. I glance at her through the rearview mirror, my lips lifting as I see her swaying back and forth, quietly singing the song to herself.

"Absolutely!" I smile, reaching forward to increase the volume. The popular pop song plays louder through the speakers and it isn't long before I start singing along with Tella.

The light turns green and I step on the gas, moving my car along with the traffic as we start to head down the road again. I bob my head along, listening to Tella singing over the music and laughter spills from my lips as she breaks out into the solo part of the song.

The upcoming light is red, so I press the brake pedal in anticipation of having to stop at the light. But it turns green again before we're fully stopped, and I let us coast into the intersection.

Movement to my left catches my eyes and the air

leaves my lungs in a rush as I whip my head to the side. A silver car breezes through the red light and it's heading directly toward my side of the car.

I react as quickly as I can, stomping down on the brake pedal. The car jerks and the sound of my tires squealing slices through the air. "Oh no, hold on, Tella!" I yell out to her as my fingers grip the wheel so tight that my knuckles turn white.

The car coming directly at me sees me at the last second. The driver swerves in an effort to avoid hitting me. But he doesn't.

The entire vehicle lurches. Tella yells out but the sound of her voice is drowned out by the sounds of crunching metal. My body jerks violently, my head bouncing against the side window just as the airbags deploy. The force of the blow to my head immediately silences everything.

There's a harsh ringing sound in my ears and I blink twice, my eyes rolling back in my head as everything goes black.

"Mia!"

Her voice is what pulls me back from the darkness. I'm not sure how long I was out, but with immense effort, I lift my head. It throbs and there's still a faint ringing in my ears. Something warm trails down the side of my face and I lift my hand to it, smearing the stickiness beneath my fingertips.

"Mia! My seatbelt is stuck."

"Hold on, T. I'll get you out." I look down at my hand, my face scrunching when I see its blood. Hastily wiping it on my pants, I fight with my own seatbelt, getting it undone as I push past the airbags and climb into the back seat with Tella. "Are you okay? Are you hurt anywhere?"

Her chin quivers and she shakes her head. "No, I don't think so."

"Okay, good." I let out a deep breath, my head swimming. I blink rapidly in an attempt to refocus my vision. "Let's get you out." I push down against the seat belt buckle and it takes some wiggling and a lot of force to get it undone, but it eventually pops open.

A knock on the window grabs my attention. As I turn to look, my vision immediately goes blurry. It looks like a man on the other side of the door. He tries to open it, but the door is locked.

"Come on, babe," I murmur, scooping Tella into my arms as I scoot closer to the door. My fingers fumble with the lock, my heart an erratic mess as I finally pop it open. The man pulls the door all the way open and I stumble out, clutching Tella against my chest.

"Whoa, are you okay?" the man asks, reaching for the two of us. "Shit, you're bleeding." He shakes his head, raking his hand through his hair. "I'm so sorry, I didn't see that the light was red."

I wave my hand at him dismissively, barely able to register a single word that he's saying. My head throbs in protest and the dizziness is consuming me. Abandoning my car, I turn to walk over to the side of the road, but my legs refuse to cooperate. Traffic is stopped and other people are getting out of their cars just as emergency services begin to surround the area.

A paramedic walks up to the two of us. I lower Tella

to the ground and collapse onto my hands and knees. My head hurts and I feel sick as the darkness floods the corners of my vision. "Please, get her off the road," I say to the paramedic. I lift my head to look at her. She's crouched down in front of Tella.

Tella looks at me, eyes filled with fear. I can feel myself about to pass out again. "It's okay, babe," I tell her, rolling onto my side just as the darkness pulls me back under.

CHAPTER THIRTY-ONE
CALEB

"Hey Coach," I call out to Coach Landry as I step into the hall on my way to the rink. The rest of the guys are already on the ice, which is where I'm supposed to be. Except here I am, about to drop a goddamn bomb on him.

I originally planned on approaching him after practice, but as soon as I saw him, I panicked.

"What's up?" he asks, not taking his eyes off his tablet as he falls into step with me. "Is everything okay?"

"Yeah, yeah," I say, pausing to chew on the inside of my cheek as I nod. "I-uh-I wanted to talk to you about Mia."

Coach's footsteps slow as he turns his head to look at me, arching a brow. "Okay . . ."

I mull over the words in my head, unsure of the proper way to get them out. I should have rehearsed or had some kind of a script to follow because now I'm just floundering.

The last thing I need to do is say something out of line or even just the wrong thing.

"I'm not sure how to say this and I know it's probably something that would really be frowned upon."

"Caleb," he says, his voice stern as we both stop by the boards. "Spit it out."

"Mia has really been helping me with Tella and just to work through some of my own shit." I pause and blow out a breath. "I would like your permission to date your daughter."

He stares at me, his face giving nothing away. The sounds of the guys on the ice fills the air, but I can't hear any of it, not with the way Coach Landry is looking at me right now.

"You are interested in dating my daughter?"

"Well, yes," I say in a rush, half stumbling over the words.

"And if I say no," he starts, raising an eyebrow. "Would that stop you from pursuing her?"

I chew on the inside of my cheek, shifting my weight on my skates. "If I say yes, I will be lying."

He clicks his tongue, shaking his head. "Make good choices, Ford. You have my permission because she is an adult who is free to live her life how she chooses. However, if you hurt her or this turns into some kind of scandal, I will not hesitate to have you traded at the first opportunity."

"Yes, sir," I say, nodding my head as my heart accelerates inside my chest. "I understand."

He lifts his phone, his eyes diverting away from me

as he glances at the screen. His face contorts, eyebrows tugging together. "I need to take this."

He doesn't give me the chance to respond as he immediately answers. When I turn around and open the door to the rink, I hear him say, "Hello?" After a pause, "Yes, this is her father."

Just as my foot touches the ice, he calls out.

"Caleb, stop." His voice is demanding. "We need to get to the hospital."

I spin on my heel, my stomach tumbling to the floor. "What?"

"Mia and Tella," he whispers and his throat bobs on a hard swallow. "They were in a car accident."

———

The glass doors barely slide open before I stride through them, entering the waiting room with panic rolling through my body. I straighten my spine, every vertebrae stacking over top of the other as my eyes scan the room. There's a handful of other patients and family members sitting, but my vision refuses to focus. They're all blurry, all insignificant.

A vise-like grip tightens around my chest and neck. It feels as though there's barely any room for air to pass through my trachea. Sweat clings to my skin as my heart beats to an erratic, unsteady rhythm. My strides lengthen, my feet carrying me directly to the front desk.

"Hello. What can I do for you?"

"My daughter is here. She was brought in from a car accident."

According to Coach Landry, another car hit them, but only hit the front. Tella was left uninjured and they determined Mia had a concussion.

My body is operating on autopilot. I'm not so sure how I'm even standing here right now. The last time I was at this hospital was when Amelia was killed. Another car accident, except that one had a different outcome. Amelia didn't survive. But supposedly, Tella is completely fine.

I can't wrap my mind around it and refuse to believe it until I see her.

"May I have her name please?"

"Estella Ford," I blurt out, my voice hoarse and thick with worry as I shift my weight. There's movement beside me, but I don't bother looking over. I hear Coach's voice as he talks to the other woman at the desk, giving her Mia's information.

Mia . . . fuck.

I'm torn between the two, desperate to know if Mia is okay, but knowing that my daughter needs me. Estella is my top priority, as she always is.

Coach Landry glances at me, worry etched in his expression. "Mia's okay," he tells me softly. "I have a friend in the emergency room here and he said it's just a concussion and they don't plan on keeping her except for observation." He lets out a breath, grabbing my shoulder and giving it a squeeze. "They're both okay, Ford."

The muscle in my jaw tightens, my throat constricting with emotion as I dip my chin at him. There's a touch of relief with his assurance, but it doesn't chase away the panic. It doesn't eradicate the deep seated fear I harbor inside my heart.

"Mr. Ford, come with me please," the woman behind the desk says, immediately severing my thought process. I step away from the desk, following her as she holds her badge up to a pad by the next set of doors. They slide open and the moment I step across the threshold, I'm transported back in time to the worst day of my entire life.

The ticks of the wall clock echo throughout the small family room. My body is rigid, my heart barely beating, my lungs hardly expanding as I dig my fingers into my thighs, gripping onto them for support. The air filling the room is cold and laced with a sterile, chemical smell.

I can still hear the phone conversation with the police officer ringing inside my mind. Tella had just fallen asleep and I was waiting for Amelia to get back from running errands. Carson came over for a beer and I can't get the look on his face out of my head.

The way the color drained from his flesh as he heard the police officer speaking urgently to me. Amelia was in an accident. She was hit head on by a drunk driver. The other driver died on impact, but when the ambulance left the scene, Amelia was still alive. It didn't look good but she was still alive.

I was on my feet within a fraction of a second, rushing out the door to get to her. Carson told me to go, he told me Tella would be fine with him, so I got in my car and raced here in the hope that this was all just a cruel fucking joke. A nightmare I can wake myself up from.

Because I've been sitting here for the last five minutes,

preparing myself for the worst from the doctors. When I got here, they immediately brought me back to this room and told me that someone would come talk to me about my wife. The last five minutes have felt like a fucking eternity.

"Mr. Ford."

My eyes slice to the door as a man in dark blue scrubs enters, pulling a surgical cap from his head. I don't rise to my feet as I stare at him, his shoulders sagging in defeat. My heart begins to crumble inside my chest, ice settling through my veins as I know what he's going to say before he even speaks another word.

"I'm so sorry, but we did everything we could to save her," he says, his voice low and quiet as he comes to sit in front of me.

The floor falls out from under my feet. My surroundings fade, the noises, the smells, even the light above me no longer feels real.

"She coded in the ambulance and they were able to revive her, but she sustained significant internal damage and massive blood loss. We lost her again in the emergency room as we were getting ready to transfer to the OR and unfortu-nately, we were not able to get her back."

I stare back at him, completely paralyzed and frozen in place. The edges of my vision begin to blur and I can't form a single fucking word. The pressure on my chest is insur-mountable. The loss rips my beating heart directly from my chest.

This can't be real. She can't be gone.

"Mr. Ford."

I blink my eyes rapidly, turning to look at the

woman as she stares at me with concern in her eyes. "Sorry."

"She's down this way. We have her in one of the pediatric bays, but that was just as a formality until you were able to come get her."

She pauses when we get to the small room toward the end of the hall.

"The nurse will be in with her discharge papers because they did look over her just to make sure she was okay. I'm happy to report that they found nothing wrong, not even a scratch."

Relief floods me. Tella is okay. This is nothing like Amelia's accident. Tella isn't hurt and I get to take her home with me.

The woman pushes back the curtain to the small bay and tears spring to my eyes as I find Tella sitting on the center of the bed, watching a small TV screen on the wall across from her. Her head whips to the side, her eyes widening when she sees me.

"Daddy!"

Tella climbs off the bed and I rush into the room, catching her as she runs into me and lifting her up into my arms.

"Hey, baby." I choke out the words as I wrap my arms tightly around Tella and hold her flush against my chest. I pull her away so I can quickly scan her, making sure with my own eyes that she's unharmed. "Are you okay?"

She nods, reaching for me to pull her back against me. "It was just really scary, daddy. And you weren't there."

Burying my face in her hair, I breathe in her familiar comforting scent, reveling in the fact that she is okay. She's in one piece. "I'm so sorry, T," I murmur, holding her even tighter. "I'm sorry I wasn't there to keep you safe, but I'm here now. I promise I will never ever let anything happen to you, okay?"

"What about Mia?"

Emotion wells in my throat as I pull away from my daughter again, tears blurring my vision as I scan her face. There isn't a single mark. "We can go see her before we leave."

"Her head was bleeding and she fell asleep on the ground after she got me out of the car." Tella frowns, tears welling in her eyes. "Can you keep her safe too?"

"Yes, of course, baby," I murmur without a single beat of hesitation. It's not the truth though. I can't keep Mia safe anymore than I could have kept Amelia safe. The thought alone sends a spark of panic through my body. My chest hurts at the thought and my heart fights against the conflicting feeling.

Falling for Mia happened without me even realizing it but I don't think I can do this again. I barely made it through losing Amelia and I know that there's no way I could survive it again. If something happened to Mia, it would destroy me.

I have to let her go. She deserves to find someone who can love her without fear.

Because I know now that I can't.

CHAPTER THIRTY-TWO

MIA

An emptiness settles over me, a coldness seeping into my bones as I stare down at my phone, reading over the message Caleb sent me the day after the accident.

CALEB

> Hey. I know none of this was your fault and I'm glad that you're going to be okay. You should take the time to recover. Andi and Nova offered to watch Tella, so it's probably best if you just focus on yourself getting better right now.

Rolling my lips between my teeth, I clamp down on them, my jaw hurting as my eyes grow wet. I'm such a stupid, stupid girl. I knew better than to let him in. I knew better than to trust that he wouldn't hurt me. I knew that Caleb's heart was fragile and that he still had a lot of healing to do on his own. Yet I handed him my own heart, thinking he would be able to keep it safe.

I never wanted him to hand it back and that's exactly what he did. He shut me out, without giving me a chance to even rebut it. He brushed it off, as if everything was transactional. As if I were just his nanny and nothing more.

I should have expected it, especially after the way he acted when he brought Tella to check on me in the emergency room . . .

My chest expands as I suck in a deep breath, ignoring the throbbing in my knee as I adjust on the thin mattress. I'm ready to get out of the emergency room and go home where I can rest without the sounds of beeping monitors echoing down the hall.

A soft knock on the ajar door has me sitting up straighter, forcing my eyes to open as I see Tella's small frame lingering in the doorway. "Can I come in?"

"Of course," I breathe, relief washing over me to see her in one piece. She was fine when I last saw her before I passed out, but this confirmation that she's okay sends a wave of comfort through me.

"Hi Mia," Tella says, her hand clutching onto Caleb's as they stand just inside the doorway.

"Hi Tella," I smile as the corners of my eyes burn from the tears I'm holding back. "Caleb."

His eyes don't meet mine and he dips his chin. "We wanted to come make sure you were okay."

"I'm fine," I say, my eyes searching Caleb's ashen colored face in an attempt to will his gaze to meet mine. He stares at the end of the bed, his eyebrows knitted close together. "Just a little headache and some soreness in my knees."

"My daddy is taking me home. Can you come with us?"

My heart constricts. "Not right now, babe. The doctors said I'll be able to leave in a few hours."

"But you get to come home?"

"Where did your father go?" Caleb asks, his voice low and hoarse as he interjects before I get the chance to answer Tella.

"He had to step out to make a phone call. Did you need him for something?"

Caleb shakes his head, the muscle in his jaw tightening. "Is he taking you home?"

He still refuses to look at me. A heaviness settles on my chest, anxiety rolling in the pit of my stomach. Why won't he just look at me?

"Yes," I say, my voice barely audible. "I'm sorry for what happened."

Caleb's eyes flicker to mine. His eyebrows momentarily relax, his nostrils widening as he shakes his head. "It wasn't your fault," he says softly. "I don't blame you." His eyes are filled with so many emotions, I can't decipher a single one.

His forehead creases again and in a haste, he pulls his gaze away from mine, glancing back down at Tella.

"I'm glad you're okay, Tella."

Tella looks at me, a tender smile drifting across her lips. "I'm glad you're okay, too. Even though your head hurts."

I return her smile, although mine barely lifts my cheeks. "I'll be okay."

"We should let Mia rest, okay?" Caleb murmurs to his daughter.

"I don't want to leave her," Tella says to him. My throat constricts as emotion stacks on my chest.

"We'll see her after she's all better."

Caleb releases Tella's hand and she strides across the room toward me. She pauses at the side of my bed, her hands reaching for mine as she gives me a gentle squeeze.

"Feel better soon, Mia. I love you."

My vision blurs as tears fill my eyes. My heart easily grows three sizes as I squeeze her hands back.

"I love you too, T."

She releases her grip on me and I bend down, ignoring the pounding in my head as I open my arms wide to her. She steps into them, wrapping herself around my torso as I hug her tightly.

Lifting my eyes, I find Caleb standing even closer by the door, almost as if he has one foot through the doorway as he watches the two of us. His gaze is cold and distant as it meets mine and it feels like miles stretch between us.

His throat bobs, that muscle ticking again as he drops his eyes down to Tella's back. "Come on, T," he calls to her. "Get some rest, Mia."

Tella untangles herself from me, smiling at me once more before she walks back to her father. Caleb doesn't look at me again as he reaches for Tella's hand and the two of them step out into the hallway, leaving me by myself.

It felt like they were stepping out of my life when they walked out of the hospital room and I think I knew it at the time, I just didn't want it to be true.

He said I wasn't to blame for the accident, although for some reason, it feels like maybe he does blame me. I was the one driving, I was the one who had his daughter in my care. Thankfully, she was perfectly fine, although that still doesn't change the fact that she could have been injured.

If I would have just looked to the left a little sooner, I

would have seen the car coming and we could have avoided the entire situation.

It's been almost a week since he sent me those messages and I still haven't said a single thing back to him. His words were bullshit. He's putting as much distance as humanly possible between the two of us and I can't help it but I want to know why. I need to know why.

However, that need isn't great enough to put my heart back on the line after he just handed it back to me, bloodied and bruised. My fear keeps me frozen in place, glued to the couch at our house at Sugar Hill Lake. My father took me home from the hospital after the doctors cleared me with a concussion. I asked him to bring me here instead and he agreed, but only on one condition.

I wasn't to be here alone until I was healed.

A ragged breath escapes me. I don't know if I'll ever fully be healed . . .

"You're up early," Willow says softly as she steps out onto the back deck. She walks over to where I'm sitting by the railing, holding two mugs with steam rolling from the tops. She hands me one as she sits down in the seat next to me. "Did you watch the sunrise?"

"Yeah." I lift the mug to my lips, the liquid burning my tongue as I take a small sip. "I couldn't sleep."

Willow frowns as she looks out at the shimmering surface of the lake. The sun is nestled just above the horizon, the hues of pink and yellow and orange melting in the morning sky. "You haven't been sleeping well this whole week. How are you feeling?"

Mentally drained. Emotionally exhausted.

Willow came to stay with me for a few days and has been hovering like a damn helicopter.

"I feel much better, actually. It seems like my headaches have gone away and everything's pretty much back to normal."

She looks at me. "Except for your sleep."

"It's hard to sleep when he's all I can see when I close my eyes."

"Shit," she says softly, blowing out a breath. "He still hasn't said anything else to you?"

I slowly shake my head at her. "Whatever it was, is clearly done." I pause, my gaze dropping down to my coffee for a moment before I look back at her. "I knew better than to get involved with him. I knew this was most likely what would happen in the end, but it still didn't prepare me for how bad it would hurt."

"Because it's not what you wanted to happen," she tells me, her expression softening as she stares at me. "I doubt you were anticipating it actually happening."

Tears burn my eyes and I quickly blink them away, directing my gaze back out to the water. "I think I just need to try and forget about him."

"Do you think it's worth trying to talk to him?"

I slowly shake my head from side to side. "He was pretty clear in his messages." Disappointment and hurt prick my skin as my brain wanders over the messages. He didn't come to me in the hospital, which I wasn't fully expecting him to because of Tella. But not once did he try to see me after the accident. Not once did he actually check in on me except to send me a message to break my heart.

And the worst part? He couldn't even be direct about that.

Instead, he leaned into our working relationship, claiming it was better if Andi and Nova watch Tella. I had a damn concussion, not a serious injury that would require months of rehab.

"Listen, this isn't me sticking up for him at all, but maybe show him a little bit of grace," Willow suggests, her voice quiet. "Just think about it for a second. He lost his wife in a fatal car accident and then you and his daughter end up getting into an accident. That had to be triggering for him."

Her words sink into my mind and I mull over them. It's a thought that has already crossed my mind. Caleb has already shown what his fear can do to him, but at some point, you have to let that go, right?

"It is what it is," I tell her, lifting my shoulders with indifference as I shrug it off. "Even if it were triggering, he could still be honest with me. He could have told me that, instead of making it seem like I'm no longer capable of watching Tella. He didn't have to go and replace me."

Willow blows out a deep breath. "I know," she agrees, slowly bobbing her head. "I don't disagree with you at all. I'm just trying to look at it objectively and from both sides." She pauses, running her tongue over her teeth. "I wish I had a solution. The only thing I can suggest is for you guys to have a real conversation."

Emotion compounds in my chest. My resolve is

wavering and the pain and the rejection roll over me in waves. I just want to see him. I want to feel him and hear his voice, but I can't. His last message didn't leave room for me to respond, really.

"I don't think I can," I admit, my voice cracking around my words. "Not right now at least."

Willow turns her head to look at me. "You love him, don't you?"

I swallow hard over the lump in my throat, tears burning the corners of my eyes. "I do." I let out a shallow breath and allow the tears to fall while simultaneously wiping them away with haste. "I know I shouldn't, but I do."

"Fuck," Willow swallows, a frown tugging down on her lips as her forehead creases. "We don't get to choose who we love, babe," she says. She reaches for my hand and gives it a squeeze. "And it has an uncanny way of happening when we least expect it."

"I never should have let him in."

Willow tilts her head to the side. "The time you had with him though, was it good?"

"Yes."

"Did he make you feel loved, even if he didn't say it?"

"Yes," I say again, swallowing back my emotion. "No one has ever looked at me the way he does. No one has ever made me feel the way he does."

"Then I think it was worth letting him in," she says, her voice barely above a whisper. "Not all good things are always meant to last. He had a purpose in your life and I think that's at least worth something."

"Even if it ends with my heart in a tattered mess?"

A soft smile crests her lips. "There's always beauty in the pain, babe. Maybe the beauty of it was just having the opportunity to experience the love you both felt. Maybe it was you opening up your heart to someone you knew was unavailable and for him to just feel something with someone after losing his wife. You taught him love was worth experiencing. It's not your fault he chose to let his fear guide him after it became too strong to fight."

I stare at her for a moment, my mixed emotions coming in waves. Caleb Ford broke my damn heart and I'm not sure how to get past this. "If that's all true, then what comes next?"

"Just give yourself some time, babe. You're both hurting and instead of being honest with each other about how you're feeling, you're both fighting against it instead of fighting for one another."

"How do you know what he's doing or what he's feeling?"

She cocks her head, laughing softly. "Oh, Mia, are you really that blind?"

I stare at her, waiting for her to continue.

"You don't look at someone the way that man looked at you and not feel the pain of letting go." A ghost of a smile dances across her lips. "The way he feels for you was written across his face. He loves you . . . he loves you so much that he's pushing you away to protect himself."

"I understand *why* he's doing it, but I don't agree

with it. I don't think you can love someone, at least not fully, from a place of fear."

Willow purses her lips. "That's a tough one. I think it's natural to be afraid, but it comes down to whether or not you let that fear control you."

"Maybe . . ." I say softly, not sure how to dissect and decipher all the emotions I'm feeling. This has been nothing short of a mind fuck from Caleb and honestly, I don't know what I'm supposed to do. I'm torn between giving him space and letting him breathe but also wanting to fight for this. For us.

Pulling my attention from my best friend, I let my gaze drift back out to the lake. Back to the shimmering surface of the water and the quiet breeze that drifts from the trees. The two of us sit in silence for a few more minutes before Willow retreats back inside to get ready to head back home, leaving me alone with my thoughts.

My thoughts continue to circle back to the man I knew would have the power to break my heart someday . . . and that's exactly what he did.

CHAPTER THIRTY-THREE
CALEB

"Ford."

I slowly turn on the bench to look at the door of the dressing room. The room had cleared out at least twenty minutes ago, all the guys went home after our late afternoon practice. I came here right after my therapy appointment this morning.

Coach Landry walks deeper into the room, stopping as he comes over to the opposite bench and takes a seat. "You're here late."

Corkscrewing my lips, I chew on the inside of my cheek for a second. "I don't know what I'm doing, Coach."

His eyebrows tug together and he tilts his head to the side. "What's going on? Is it something I can help with?"

I drop my attention down to my hands as I hang them between my legs and steeple my fingers. Nothing in my life feels right at this moment in time. I pushed Mia away and haven't reached out to her because I'm afraid of the things I feel for her. I have my daughter bouncing between different houses while I'm playing hockey because I pushed Mia away. And I've been holding everything inside because I don't want to burden anyone with my fucking feelings right now.

I've walled everyone out and just haven't been able to bring myself to talk to anyone about any of this. Coach Landry, the man I look up to more than anyone else, wants to know what's going on. How the hell do I tell him that there's currently a war waging inside me because I'm in love with his daughter.

"I fucked up."

He's silent for a moment. "What did you fuck up?"

I suck in a deep breath, holding it for a moment before blowing it out. I slowly lift my gaze to his and swallow the lump in my throat. "Everything with Mia."

Coach Landry doesn't speak a single word. Instead, he keeps his eyes leveled on mine, the muscle in his jaw tightening for a fraction of a second before it loosens. He lifts his hand and scratches at the stubble along his jaw.

The silence is borderline deafening.

He carefully removes his glasses and inspects them, like he's looking for specs of dirt, to avoid looking at me. "I had an idea that you had something to do with her withdrawing."

My eyebrows cinch closer. "What do you mean?"

"She hasn't said anything to me, but she's also shut everyone out. Willow's staying with her right now and I texted her yesterday to check in. She said she's feeling better physically, but she still isn't herself." He pauses, sliding his glasses back up over the bridge of her nose. "Now it's evident that it has nothing to do with the accident and everything to do with you."

"Fuck."

"Yeah," he mumbles, pursing his lips and shaking his head at me. "You know she tried to prevent the accident from happening. Your daughter was her only concern when it happened."

Emotion lodges itself in my throat. "I know." I pause, inhaling deeply. "I'm not mad at her and I don't blame her for what happened. It's a relief that both of them are okay."

"Then what is the problem?"

I run my hand through my hair, tugging slightly on the ends. "The thought of something happening to either of them—it was something I couldn't handle at the time." I press my thumb and pointer finger to my eyebrows, smoothing them out. "The whole thing was triggering for me. I couldn't help but think back to Amelia's accident."

Coach Landry's expression softens and he slowly nods. "You know, I lost my wife too."

My eyes find his. "Mia mentioned something, but not the specifics."

"Of course she didn't," he says, shaking his head. "She never wants to burden anyone." He lets out a deep sigh. "My wife died giving birth to her. It was a traumatic experience that left me fucked up for years."

"I'm sorry," I say in a hushed tone. "I can't imagine what that was like for you."

"I'm sure eerily similar to your experience. Being a

single dad with a young daughter is so hard and so frightening."

I slowly nod in understanding. I know exactly what he's talking about. "It's why I'm just better at being single. I survived losing Amelia, but I'm not so certain I'd survive another loss."

"Do you know what fear actually does?"

I shake my head at him.

"It's like a chain that keeps you from living your life to the fullest. It makes you question everything that might bring you joy or happiness, all because your fear is too busy making you worry about what might happen if you lose it."

The words he speaks seep into my brain, lodging themselves in the crevices. He's right and I know it, I just don't know how to break the chains. I don't know how to fight the fear.

"You can't fully live while you're worrying about what you haven't lost already."

That sentence hits me like a ton of bricks in the center of my chest. My throat tightens, restricting my air flow. "How do you do it?"

"You have to just let go of it. It's a conscious choice and decision you have to make. Sometimes people are worth the risk of getting hurt." He tilts his head to the side. "If you knew you were going to lose your wife when you first met her, would you have chosen to not be with her? Would you have given up the opportunity to love her, even if it were for a short amount of time?"

Holy fuck.

Tears burn my eyes and I give a swift shake of my head. "No, I wouldn't have."

"So, are you going to throw this away with Mia because of what you're afraid might happen?"

I stare at him, my head moving again. "No."

Ever since losing Amelia, I've operated solely from a place of being scared to death of what might happen in the future. And by living that way, I've been sacrificing the chance to live in the present moment. I've pushed Mia away because I don't want to lose her, but by doing that, I'm only losing her sooner.

We both deserve the chance to be loved by one another, even if something bad happens one day. We can't predict what will happen and I need to stop pretending like I can control any of that.

"Then you need to go to her. You need to make it right . . . before you end up losing her forever." He pauses, his gaze trained on mine. "You still have a chance, Caleb," he says. "Make your shot and make it count."

I rise to my feet as his words sink into the fibers of my soul. He's right. I've been a goddamn idiot and being away from her has only been dragging me into the pits of misery. Mia is the good I need in my life and she makes it easy to forget about the bad. She's so good with Tella and it's clear to see that Tella loves her.

And so do I . . .

"My daughter deserves to be happy," Coach Landry says as he stands up and walks over to clasp his hand on my shoulder. He gives me a gentle squeeze, his eyes locked in on mine. "And so do you."

CHAPTER THIRTY-FOUR
CALEB

A cool breeze pushes strands of hair into my face as I stare down at the gravestone a few feet in front of me. The sun pokes through the clouds as it drifts closer to the horizon line. My shoulders lift as I take a deep breath and slowly exhale, emotion washing over me as I shake my head at Amelia's grave.

"I don't know what I'm doing anymore, Amelia." I let out a deep breath, raking a hand through my hair. "I wish you were here, I wish you could tell me what to do."

My forehead creases and I let out a harsh laugh. "Okay, that doesn't sound right. If you were here, I don't think I'd be in this position." My heart clenches as Mia's face flashes into my mind. "None of this makes sense," I say, my shoulders sagging in defeat.

"If you were here, I wouldn't have had the chance to fall in love with Mia. But the thought of not loving her feels equally wrong." I close my eyes, tilting my head back. "You're not here and you're not coming back and I've accepted that. Please don't hate me for moving forward with my life."

The soft breeze dances across my face again, except this time there's a subtle warmth to it. The faint smell of orange blossoms invades my senses. I slowly lift my eyelids and glance around.

I'm alone, except for the groundskeeper, who is nowhere to be seen.

"If roles would have been reversed, I would have wanted you to be happy. I wouldn't have wanted you to stop living your life and it kills me to not know how you would have felt."

A butterfly darts in front of me, fluttering in a circle before it comes to rest on her headstone. It flutters its wings once more as it turns to face me, the breeze blows a little harder. The memory of her voice enters my mind.

"Just remember to always find the joy in life. Laugh and love, always."

The corners of my eyes burn and I blink hard against the feeling. "I found the joy, Amelia," I whisper, my voice catching in my throat. "It's her. It's Mia."

The butterfly lifts from where it was resting and it flies toward me, fluttering in front of my face. My gaze is transfixed, my heart stuttering in my chest as it floats around my head lingering again in front of me before it drifts away.

I stare down at the gravesite, my throat constricting. "I'll always love you," I breathe, emotion washing over me. "And I will never forget you, but I have to let go of the guilt." The weight that's been sitting on my chest lifts and my heart stutters. "I have to let go of you so I can hold onto her."

The smell of orange blossoms drifts through the breeze again and something brushes against my hand. I glance down and there's nothing there. I can't see her, but I know she's here. I know she's telling me it's okay.

She's telling me to let go.

———

Slowly pressing my foot against the brake, I turn the wheel to the left, pulling my car onto the winding driveway. It's lined by four massive oak trees on either side and as I reach the clearing, I ease my car up to the front of the house. It's a beautiful home with a well manicured front lawn. Flower beds line the perimeter, grey siding for a modern appeal, and bright white trim around the massive windows.

Mia's car is parked in front of the garage and I park mine behind hers. I turn off the engine while simultaneously pushing my door open. I've already wasted too much time avoiding her. I've let her sit without an explanation or a viable response from me.

My chest still aches from the cemetery, but there's a renewed sense of hope. There's a weight that's been lifted, as if I can finally let my lungs expand fully. Like I can finally breathe again.

I need to fix this between Mia and me. I've let my fear get in my own way and unfortunately, I'm not the only one who suffers from it. I let her down. I did the one thing I never wanted to do to her.

I hurt her.

My strides are long and I break out into a jog in an effort to cover as much ground as possible. I reach the front porch and pause when I pull open the screen door. My left hand lifts and pushes the doorbell.

The faint sound of it ringing within the house touches my ears, but that's the only sound I hear. There's no hint of Mia moving inside. Lifting my hand above my brow, I duck to the side, peering through the glass pane along the side of the door. There's no sign of her from where I'm standing.

It doesn't seem like there are any lights on inside the house. Instead, it's just dimly lit from the fading natural light outside as the sun begins to fall beneath the horizon. I continue to look through the window, knocking on the door with my opposite hand as the screen door rests against my back.

Where are you, Mia?

My stomach knots with panic and my heart beats faster as I knock again. Her car is here, so she should be here, but I don't know where the hell she is. I don't want to walk in on her uninvited, but I can't stop myself from reaching for the door knob.

I expect it to be locked but it turns with ease. The door swings open as I give it a gentle push. I suck in a deep breath before stepping into the house. Silence greets me as I step into the foyer, the faint smell of lavender and vanilla permeates the air.

She's here somewhere.

She has to be.

Reaching behind me, I pull the door closed making sure to soften the contact with the frame to not make a sound, and kick off my shoes next to the door out of habit. I duck my head through the doorway to my left and find an empty living room. The pillows on the couch are ruffled with a book and blanket thrown next to them, as if she were sitting there earlier.

I look into the room across the hall—an empty office. My feet carry me through the foyer until I'm reaching the end of the hall and pause in the doorway that opens to the kitchen and dining area. The air leaves my lungs in the rush, relief encapsulating me. *Mia.*

She stands on the opposite side of the kitchen, her head bent over a book as she lightly taps a measuring cup to a steady beat beside a metal bowl. The faint sound of music drifts through the air and I find myself swallowing over the lump lodged in my throat as I stare at her from a safe distance. The invisible string that tethers us tugs on me.

Who am I kidding? There's nothing safe about this magnetic pull between us. There's nothing safe about Mia Landry and me and I'm tired of letting the fear control me. I'm tired of being afraid of letting myself feel these intense feelings toward her. I want to feel it all. The happiness, the joy, and the excitement. The fear, the sadness, and the pain.

And the love.

I move deeper into the room, stepping into her peripheral vision. Her head whips to the side, hand flying up to her ear to pluck out an earbud as she stares at me like a deer in headlights, frozen in place with her eyes wide.

"Caleb," she says in a rush. Her eyebrows cinch together and she removes the other earbud as her eyes bounce back and forth between mine. "What are you doing here?"

"I came here for you, pup."

She turns around to face me fully and stares at me for a moment, her jaw flexing on a clench as she gives a quick shake of her head. "Why? You were pretty clear when you pushed me out of your life earlier this week."

My heart cracks at the coldness in her tone. The muscles in my legs contract, wanting to go to her, but I stop myself from taking a step. "I fucked up."

Crossing her arms over her chest, she levels her gaze on mine. "Did your new babysitting plans fall through?"

"What? No," I tell her, shaking my head back and forth. This time I can't help myself as I take a step toward her. I immediately stop as she steps backward. My forehead creases, my heart cracking. "That's not all you are to me, Mia. Tella does miss you, but she's not the only one."

Her arms uncross and she sucks in a deep breath as she tucks her hair behind her ear. "Caleb, just don't," she says with a pained look in her eyes. "Please don't do this to me."

"I miss you, Mia," I press, my voice cracking around my words. "I was wrong. I shouldn't have pushed you away. I shouldn't have shut you out."

"Yeah, but you did," she says in a rush, shaking her

head at me. "You acted like everything between us was transactional. You were so dismissive, as if there was nothing else between us other than me being your nanny." She lets out a ragged breath, her eyes drifting away from mine. "I can't do this."

She spins on her heel, leaving me in the kitchen as she strides toward the back door. I'm frozen in place, staring after her like a goddamn idiot as she slides her feet into a pair of shoes and slips out onto the back deck.

I know I fucked up, I know the way I pushed her away was wrong, but I didn't expect to hear that from her. Nothing between us was transactional and that's exactly how I made it seem when I told her I didn't need her help anymore. I acted like a fucking coward and I need to make this right.

I head to the front door to grab my shoes, then run to the back of the house. She's already in the back yard, her feet moving quickly as she heads in the direction of the lake. In a haste, I shove my feet into my shoes, heading out through the back door and directly to the stairs.

"Mia, wait," I call out after her as I jog down the stairs after her. She doesn't bother to look back as she steps onto the dock, her gaze straight ahead, staring out at the water. The dark clouds are almost completely over us and in the distance, you can see the raindrops falling.

"Mia!" I practically yell her name as my feet hit the wooden dock. Her back is still toward me and my heart is falling to pieces.

"Goddammit, I'm in love with you!" My voice cracks, fracturing around the words as I watch her immediately come to a stop in the middle of the dock. She slowly turns around to face me, tears welling in her eyes. I step closer to her and tilt my head to the side as I take her in. "I love you."

"Caleb," she says, her eyes rounding as she stares up at me. Her expression is unreadable and her lips are parted, as if she's going to say something else, but she quickly closes them as I take another step closer.

"Pup," I say to her, emotion enveloping me as my voice shakes. "I'm so goddamn sorry. I'm sorry for hurting you. I'm sorry for making you think that there was nothing between us, because it's the furthest thing from that. This is everything. *You* are everything."

She closes the remaining distance between us, her hands reaching for me as something inside me finally breaks. My entire body sags and I collapse onto my knees in front of her. "Oh, love," she murmurs, closing the distance between us as she slips her hands through my hair.

Circling my arms around her waist, I pull her to me, burying my face in her stomach as she strokes my head. I surrender to my emotions, letting everything hit me at once. The pain, the fear, the joy, the love.

Everything.

"When you got in that accident, I was so scared and that fear paralyzed me," I admit, my tears staining the front of her shirt as I cling to her like my life depends on it. "It triggered me and all I could think about was losing Amelia." I pause, sucking in a deep breath, my shoulders shaking. "And how I couldn't bear the thought of losing you like I lost her."

"Shh," she whispers, her fingers smoothing my hair. "I know," she says, her voice soothing my soul. "It's okay. It's okay."

"I never imagined I'd be able to love someone after her and I have been afraid of losing the memory of her with that happening. Falling for you hasn't been easy. It's something I've fought the entire way because of feeling guilty for loving someone other than Amelia. But the love I feel for you is so different and I know I shouldn't feel guilty for any of it. The way I loved her was always safe and predictable. The way I love you is explosive and consuming."

I let out a ragged sigh, reveling in the way she feels in my arms. Knowing I never want to feel the absence of her again.

"I'm tired of fighting against my feelings for you. I'm tired of living in fear of things that haven't even happened yet. I just want to love you and whatever happens, happens. I know I can't control any of it, regardless of how badly I want to be able to."

"Caleb," Mia says, her hands sliding down to my arms as she tries to lift me upwards. I pull my head away from her, tilting my chin to look up at her. Tears streak down her cheeks. "Stand up."

Releasing my arms from her waist, I keep my eyes locked on hers as I rise to my full height. Mia's head is already tilted back, her eyes staring directly into my soul. She lifts her hands, moving to cup the sides of my face. I let out a sigh, pressing my cheek deeper against her palm.

"I'm sorry for pushing you away."

She tilts her head to the side. "I'm sorry for letting you. I won't make the same mistake again."

"I can't promise this will be easy and I can't promise I won't try to push you away again. I promise I will try not to or I will come to you when I start to feel scared."

"I promise I won't let you succeed." She pauses, her eyes growing damp. "I love you, Caleb," she says, her eyes shining back at mine through her tears. "I never have and I never will expect you to love me more than you loved Amelia. I don't want to replace her and I don't want you to ever forget about her. I just want you, broken, whole, however you are. I *just love* you."

"With you is the most whole I've felt in a really long time," I say as I slide my hands around the back of her neck. "I want to be the man who deserves to be loved by you."

"My love," she says softly, a smile dancing across her lips. "You are. You deserve all the good that the world has to offer."

"You are the good, pup." The corners of my mouth twitch. "You're the joy I've been missing in my life." My face dips down to hers. "I want you to be mine, Mia."

A soft laugh falls from her lips as she drags my face down to hers, her lips brushing against mine. "I already am, silly."

"I mean officially."

"Are you asking me to go steady, Ford?"

"If that's what you want to call it." My lips sweep

across hers, in a teasing, gentle kiss. "This is me giving you my heart, Mia. All I'm asking for in exchange is yours."

She stares up at me with nothing but unyielding love.

"It's already yours."

EPILOGUE
CALEB

My brother stares at Andi, spinning her away from him with her white dress drifting around her ankles before he tugs her back toward his body. She wraps her bare arm around the tops of his shoulders, her head tilting back as a string of laughter falls from her lips.

I slide my hand onto Mia's lap, her fingers immediately threading through mine as our eyes meet. The corners of her pink lips lift into the softest smile, her brown irises shimmering beneath the lights above.

"They look so happy," she says as her gaze drifts back out to the dance floor in the center of the barn. A soft breeze drifts through the massive wall of windows that were propped open to let in the cool night air.

Last summer, Andi and Carson came to Sugar Hill Hollow with us and when they saw Willow's family's farm, they fell in love with it and immediately booked it as the venue for their wedding. They decided on an early summer wedding this year, so they could have it just after the hockey season, but before it was too hot to have one where we could enjoy the cooler evening air.

My eyes trail over the side of Mia's face, pausing on her highlighted cheek bones. "They're not the only ones."

The song comes to an end, switching to something a little more upbeat as people from the reception begin to crowd onto the dance floor. Carson pulls Andi to his side, the two of them swaying together as Rowan and Hadley walk over to them.

I glance over to the table next to us where my mother and aunt sit, entertaining all the kids. Tella looks over at me, a bright smile on her face as she waves. Matteo says something to her and she cuts her eyes, her lips moving as she responds to him. Everything just feels exactly the way it's supposed to be.

"Dance with me?" I ask as I rise to my feet, holding onto her hand.

"I'd love to," she smiles, standing up with her. Her champagne colored dress falls just beneath her knees and it shifts around her legs as she walks on her heels, letting me lead her onto the dance floor.

Ignoring the beat of the music, I pull her flush against me and she presses her cheek to the side of my chest. "I love you, Mia," I murmur, grazing my lips up the side of her neck. "I can't wait until our wedding."

She laughs as she pulls away from me. She's still in my arms, leaning back against them, and shakes her head at me. "I think you're skipping a step."

The box I've been carrying around in my pocket for the last two weeks feels like it's burning a hole through my pants. Something has been holding me back from doing it, but it's not her. God, it could never be her.

It's me. It's me wanting to do it right. To have it be the perfect moment.

"Can I steal your date?" Andi asks as she slides her hand around my arm. Nova, Riley, and Hadley all linger around her, as if they're about to swarm Mia.

A chuckle rumbles in my throat and I press my mouth to Mia's, feeling her warmth beneath my lips. She kisses me back before Nova clears her throat and begins to drag Mia away from me. I release her, my heart swelling as they pull her into a circle and all start to dance together.

"Happiness looks good on you, Ford," Rowan says as he throws his arms over my shoulders, tugging me toward him.

"You and Mia are good together," Lincoln chimes in, a small smile on his lips. "I never thought I'd see the day, but I'm glad we've all gotten the chance to."

"If there's anyone who deserves to be happy, it's you, Caleb," Nash chimes in, holding his drink toward me as Carson steps up beside me. They all begin to close in, forming a circle. "To all of us."

We all clink our glasses together before taking a sip. My eyes survey the barn and I catch sight of Willow pausing by the door, her hand slipping into someone else's who stands just outside the door and she ducks out into the darkness. Forgetting about her, I look over at my brother. "I'm proud of you, little bro," I say to Carson. "You've done well for yourself. You've made a life with the woman you love and your son."

"I'm proud of you, Cale," he reciprocates, his arm replacing Rowan's around my shoulders. "After everything that has happened, look at where you are now." He smiles and hugs me closer. "Mia is the best thing that could have happened to you."

I look past the guys, over to Mia where she's dancing with Tella in the center of their little circle. All the girls and the kids are holding hands, circling around as Mia spins Tella around in the circle.

"She really is. I don't know what I did to deserve her, but I plan on making sure I do whatever I have to do to prove my worthiness for the rest of my life."

"Do you think you'll marry her?" Rowan asks.

The corners of my mouth twitch. "I do."

Lincoln raises an eyebrow. "Do you have a ring yet?"

I chew on the inside of my cheek. "I do."

"So what the hell are you waiting for?" Nash cuts in, his voice raised slightly. "Sorry," he laughs, shaking his head. "You're the last one left. What are you waiting for?"

"The perfect moment," I admit with a shrug.

Rowan laughs. "There is no perfect moment, bro. Just stop wasting time."

Time. What a fickle, fleeting thing.

He's right. What am I actually waiting for? There is no perfect moment other than the present, while we still have time.

"You're right," I tell him, nodding as I glance around at my teammates. My friends. My family. "I need to just do it."

"Fuck it. Do it tonight," Carson says, winking at me.

My eyes widen. "I can't do that. Today is your wedding."

"I'm telling you to do it tonight," he insists. "You don't want to wait any longer than you already have. You know how things can go . . . how quickly life can change."

A lump lodges in my throat and I chew on the inside of my cheek as I slowly bob my head. "I know."

"Okay, boys, he's mine now," Mia says, smiling brightly as she sashays her way into the circle, pulling me away from them. "You can have him tomorrow when you all go golfing."

Carson's eyebrows tug downward. "We're leaving for Paris in the morning. You guys are golfing without me?"

"Oops," Mia giggles as she drags me away from them. I let her lead me over to our table, but as we reach it, I slip my arm through hers, pulling her away from it. "Where are you taking me, Mr. Ford?"

"You'll see."

"Oh, wait," she says in a rush, stopping as we reach the door. "I need to find Willow. She wanted to get pictures together."

"I saw her leaving the barn a little bit ago," I tell Mia. Andi and Carson invited Willow and her brothers to the wedding, since they got to know them through Mia and due to wedding planning.

"Hm," she hums, her eyebrows cinching closer. "Well, I'll just have to try to find her later."

"I'm sure you will," I say, leading her through the

doorway and out into the grass. Mia falls silent and she tips her head up to the sky as thunder rumbles in the distance. I lead her past the barn, the clouds lighting up as heat lightning illuminates the night sky.

We walk together through the grass in the direction of the river that is just down past the farmhouse. Lightning streaks across the sky again, a cool breeze drifting past us. To the right is a weeping willow and I pause, releasing Mia's arm as I reach for her waist, pulling her flush against my body.

"I love you," I breathe. I slide my hand up the back of her neck and into her hair to tilt her head back. My lips find hers. "God, I love you so much it fucking hurts sometimes."

Mia pushes her hands into my chest, like she's trying to push away from me, her eyes slowly searching mine. "I don't want it to hurt you."

"No, pup, not in a bad way. In an 'I can't live without you' way."

A tender smile touches her lips. "I know that feeling," she says, her eyes staring directly into my soul. Mia Landry sees me, every single part, the good and the bad. Her love is unwavering and unconditional.

Her love is everything.

"I've been waiting for the perfect time to do this and I've realized it's been right in front of me this entire time. The perfect time is always the present, because it's all we know. It's all we have guaranteed. And I want every present moment with you, Mia."

I let go of her, taking a step back as I shove my hand into my pocket and fish out the black velvet box. Mia gasps, tears filling her eyes as her hands lift to cover her mouth. I drop to one knee in front of her, popping open the top. "Will you marry me?"

The tears begin to fall down her cheeks just as the sky above opens, a steady drizzle falling down upon us. "Yes, Caleb," she says in a rush, reaching for me, pulling me to my feet. "Yes, I'll marry you."

I pull the ring from the box, which falls into the grass as I slide the ring over her finger. Her gaze drops down to it for a moment, as does mine. The diamond looks perfect on her, exactly where it's supposed to be. I drop her hand, lifting mine to the sides of her neck as she tilts her head back.

My mouth finds her in a rush, our lips melting into one another, the rain drizzling down on us as heat lightning streaks across the sky once more. "I found you when I wasn't looking for anything," I say, murmuring against her lips, kissing her again. "I can't imagine a life without you."

Mia pulls back, her eyes searching mine as she lifts her arms and wraps them around the back of my neck. "My time is yours, my love. It was always meant for you."

Wrapping my arms around her in return, I pull her flush against me, my eyelids fluttering shut as I rest my head against the top of hers. I hold her close, breathing in her lavender and vanilla scent mixed with the petrichor as the drizzling rain fades. The willow tree rustles in the breeze and a faint smell of orange blossom drifts past.

I slowly lift my head and look over at the tree. Heat

lightning flashes, illuminating the sky and the meadow around us, revealing a small butterfly taking flight from the leaves of the willow tree.

I can't stop the smile that spreads across my face as it drifts past, flying up into the night as I hold Mia close to me. I press my lips against her forehead. "Come on, pup." I release her from the hug and slide my hand down to hers, threading our fingers together and brushing my thumb over her ring. "We should get back to the reception."

"I'll follow your lead," she says, smiling up at me as she squeezes my hand.

She thinks I'm the one who's been leading, but it's been her leading me all this time.

And I'll follow her to the ends of the earth, in this life and the ones to come.

Always.

WANT A LOOK AT WHAT'S COMING NEXT?

Scan the QR code for an exclusive sneak peek!

ACKNOWLEDGMENTS

I can't believe we've made it to the end of the Aston Archers series. This is such a bittersweet thing to write. This series has had my heart for the last two years and Caleb's story was the one I was the most excited to write. I knew it would be emotional, yet so rewarding after he finally lets himself love again. Thank you so much for all your support and for reading and loving the Aston Daddies!

So much goes into writing and producing a book and I owe a huge thank you to everyone who has been there through various phases of this series: Maddy, Amy, Emma, Jamie, my content team, @Glavreads, @Boundtoread (Sierra), my author friends for sprinting and hand holding, and the artists who have created amazing character art!

Always to my husband and kids for listening to me ramble about book ideas and for helping me to brainstorm, while also being okay with cereal for dinner when I wait until the last minute for my deadline. I love you three endlessly.

And of course, thank you to my dear readers. If it weren't for you, none of this would be possible <3

Thank you for being on this journey with me!

ABOUT THE AUTHOR

Cali Melle is a USA Today Bestselling Author who writes love stories that will pull at your heartstrings. In her free time, Cali can usually be found living in a magical, fantasy world with the newest book or fanfic she's reading or freezing at the ice rink with her husband while they watch their kids play hockey.

ALSO BY CALI MELLE

<u>ASTON ARCHERS SERIES</u>

Make Your Move

Make Your Play

Make Your Save

Make Your Change

Make Your Shot

<u>ORCHID CITY SERIES</u>

Meet Me in the Penalty Box

The Tides Between Us

Written In Ice

Dirty Pucking Play

The Lie of Us

<u>WYNCOTE WOLVES SERIES</u>

Cross Checked Hearts

Deflected Hearts

Playing Offsides

The Faceoff

The Goalie Who Stole Christmas

Splintered Ice

Coast to Coast

Off-Ice Collision